A thought wa

Meg would hate it.

He couldn't wait to share it with her.

His face turned angelic. "I have an idea."

Recognizing the look on his face, Meg instantly turned cautious. She grabbed her fork and stabbed a piece of pasty. "About what?"

"What if you and I dated?" he suggested just as she took a bite of her food. She immediately began to choke, hitting her chest hard. "Are you okay? Do you need the Heimlich?"

She waved her hand in the air as she took a deep breath before grabbing her soda pop. She took several large gulps and started coughing again until her eyes watered.

"Are you sure you don't need the Heimlich?" he asked, getting ready to jump to his feet.

"Wh—" She coughed again. "What the hell are you talking about, we should date?"

"You said it yourself, something else needs to happen to distract people from what went down between you and Lucas."

Meg dabbed at her eyes, which had started running from coughing so hard. "And your solution is for us to *date*?"

"We don't actually have to date. Just, sort of, fake date."

Dear Reader,

When life gives you lemons, you either make lemonade...or develop severe anxiety. Meg has always called Holiday Bay her hometown, but after a very public breakup with her longtime fiancé and some unexpected family issues, Meg starts to suffer from anxiety attacks. It doesn't help that her childhood neighbor and eternal nemesis returns to town, now a world-famous singer-songwriter. She expects Tyler to gloat at her downfall. He shocks her by daring her to fake date him instead. She'll get to save her reputation, and he'll get a much-needed distraction from the career rut he's in. Meg was never one to resist Tyler's dares. But could this dare lead to her biggest heartache of all?

Years ago, I had some personal things pile up in my life. Deciding I needed to focus on myself and my health, I tried a dieting app. The result was a three-day anxiety attack. While it was terrifying at the time, it gave me the inspiration to write Meg's story. It was both cathartic and healing, and my wish is that *The Fake Dating Dare* helps someone as much as it's helped me.

I hope you enjoy reading Meg and Tyler's story. For more, you can visit my website, kellistorm.com, where you can also subscribe to my newsletter.

Kelli

THE FAKE
DATING DARE

KELLI STORM

Harlequin

SPECIAL EDITION

Harlequin®
SPECIAL EDITION™

Recycling programs for this product may not exist in your area.

ISBN-13: 978-1-335-18007-0

The Fake Dating Dare

Copyright © 2025 by Kelli Du Lude

For questions and comments about the quality of this book, please contact us at CustomerService@Harlequin.com.

TM and ® are trademarks of Harlequin Enterprises ULC.

 Harlequin Enterprises ULC
22 Adelaide St. West, 41st Floor
Toronto, Ontario M5H 4E3, Canada
www.Harlequin.com

Printed in Lithuania

MIX
Paper | Supporting responsible forestry
FSC® C021394

Kelli Storm's debut novel, *His Small-Town Challenge*, was inspired by her love of boy bands. She graduated with a BA in public relations from Grand Valley State University. In a former job, she did publicity for a dog rescue and had press releases used by *People*, I Heart Dogs, MSN and Yahoo. Kelli resides in the Great Lake State with her three rescue dogs and a fourteen-year-old fish named Henry O'Malley.

Books by Kelli Storm

Harlequin Special Edition

Challenge Accepted

His Small-Town Challenge
The Fake Dating Dare

Visit the Author Profile page at Harlequin.com.

For my mom, who used to buy me Harlequin novels
when I was a teen.

Chapter One

Meg Archer hated endings.

Endings made her feel like she was suffocating. Like that time when she was a kid and her parents went away to plan her grandfather's funeral, leaving her and her brother with a babysitter. She'd acted up during bath time, and the babysitter shoved her under the water, not letting her up for air. Whenever Meg faced endings these days, it was like that time in the tub all over again—in over her head, unable to breathe.

And Meg was currently dealing with one of the biggest endings of her life.

Lucas Beaumont, the mayor's son—the hometown golden boy—had dumped Meg six months before their wedding. It was supposed to be the event of the century for their small Northern Michigan community, but the news that Lucas had ended their engagement spread like wildfire and rumors soon swirled. Horrible gossip saying that Lucas found another woman who was better than her. That Meg had embarrassed the upstanding Beaumont family one too many times. That she was simply too wild for his uptight family.

Well, that last one was a fair accusation. People had given Meg a wide berth since she was a kid. She was the classmate who spent more time in the principal's office than in class. It hadn't helped Meg's reputation that after she and Lucas broke up, she'd stumbled around town like a zombie for a year afterward, her hair a mess, wearing the same outfit for days straight.

She figured she had that right. She and Lucas had been together off and on since she was sixteen. They had broken up for brief time while they were in college, having attended separate schools. They ran into each other a few years later and fell back into their relationship. It had been easy. Uncomplicated. They'd talked about marriage on more than one occasion, but neither had been in a rush. They'd both wanted to accomplish other dreams first, to see what life had to offer before they settled into marriage and raising a family. Perhaps in the back of her mind, Meg had still been waiting for her *real* life to begin. One that included working at her family's business and…well, lots of things.

So Meg had been a little stunned when Lucas finally proposed. It felt off, like he'd asked more out of expectation than any real desire to marry her. She should have listened to her instincts.

But, per her usual style, she jumped feet first, all the way into their engagement. Because she realized that Lucas *was* her life. Her one constant. They'd get married and have a couple of kids. Who cared if their relationship was more of a soft sigh than a sizzling zing. The life Lucas would offer her was what was meant to be, she'd figured. She became obsessively focused on becoming Mrs. Lucas Beaumont. Until her world went to crap and he ended their engagement.

Lucas, the traitor, had left her to deal with it all on her own. He'd taken off for a job opportunity somewhere in Grand Rapids shortly after their breakup. He'd never had to deal with the garbage she did. Lucas didn't know what it was like to walk into a room and have people stop talking. He'd missed the gloating faces of former classmates who'd always hated that Meg landed the Prince of Holiday Bay.

She loved her hometown. But lately, home felt more like prison.

Even now, as she headed down the sidewalk of Main Street, she could hear people talking across the road, her name whispered on their lips. It had been one year and three months since Lucas dumped her. When would people move on?

When would she?

"Meg!"

Meg inwardly sighed before plastering on a fake smile to greet the older woman standing in front of her. "Hello, Mrs. Humphrey. How are you today?"

"Good, good," her former fifth-grade teacher said. She glanced from the top of Meg's light brown hair to her feet. Meg's already fuller-than-average curves had gained even more weight recently due to her lack of motivation to do anything but binge on Snickers Ice Cream Bars while watching true crime shows on Netflix.

"You look…better," Mrs. Humphrey said politely. "It looks like you washed your hair. Great job!"

Meg's lips pursed, but she answered in an equally polite tone. "Thanks."

"You know, I always thought you were too good for that Lucas Beaumont. He's too straight-laced. You need someone with a little more…fire," she said, wiggling her eyebrows as though that helped take away the sting of Meg's public humiliation.

"Right," Meg replied, her tone strained. "Well, I need to get going. It was good seeing you."

She didn't wait for a response, just increased her speed as

she headed toward her best friend Julie's store. She pulled at the collar of her fall jacket. It felt constricting around her throat, making it hard to breathe.

Meg took a deep breath and then another. She couldn't seem to get enough air into her lungs these days. Meg swallowed another large intake of air, shoving it toward her diaphragm, tightening the muscles in that area until they began to hurt.

The sight of Julie's store, Pieces of Home, came into view, giving her a welcome distraction. A large group of tourists exited the shop as she approached, their bags full of merchandise. It warmed Meg's heart to see.

Not too long ago, Holiday Bay's outlook looked bleak. Many of the shops in town had closed when a large corporation tried to do a takeover. They'd come close to succeeding too. Main Street would have looked much different today if they had. The corporation had planned to rip down the town's historical buildings and replace them with a modern monstrosity of a warehouse, the town's crisp air and clean bay possibly polluted by industry.

Julie had been a big reason why the town not only stayed the same but also became a tourist destination. If Meg was being honest, she'd had a small part in the town's recovery as well. She'd convinced her best friend to make a video pleading for Jake Reynolds to visit their town and give it a publicity boost. Jake was their former classmate and, more importantly, an ex-member of the Holiday Boys, one of the biggest boy bands of all time. Much to both Julie and Meg's surprise, their video went viral. Jake came to town, reunited with Holiday Boys and threw a charity concert for the town. The band not only raised enough money to save the struggling businesses from the takeover, but they officially put Holiday Bay back on the map. The town's economy had been going strong ever since.

Meg entered the store and automatically looked to her right, as she always did. Her lips curved when she saw the large poster of Jake Reynolds on the wall, a string of leaf-shaped lights circling his head like a crown. She had put the poster on the wall as a joke when Julie first opened her store, her friend's longtime crush on Jake well known.

What surprised a lot of people was that when Jake returned home, he fell head over heels for Julie. Despite the fact that Julie was asexual and experienced little to no sexual desire, the two made their relationship work. They were still going strong almost a year and a half later.

Meg's eyes drifted to the section of the store underneath Jake's poster. There was an entire collection of homemade Holiday Boys merchandise for sale. She zoned in on a mug that had a shirtless Tyler Evans on it. Her expression soured. If Lucas Beaumont was her greatest heartache, Tyler was her biggest adversary. Her former neighbor had held that title since she'd been old enough to walk.

A memory flashed unwanted across her mind…a warm spring evening. A heated embrace. An unforgettable kiss… no matter how hard she tried.

"Hello, *Liebchen*."

Meg's flustered attention flew to the counter at the sound of her mom's pet name for her. She stood behind the register, arranging a display of large crocheted pumpkins.

"Mom, hey." She frowned. "What are you doing here?"

Greta picked at a piece of lint on one of the gourds. "Julie's been so busy lately, I asked if I could work here part-time."

Meg walked over to the counter, her senses tingling with the knowledge that she was missing something to this story.

"Why aren't you at the campground helping Dad?" Her parents had built Archer Campground together from the ground up. It was hunting season in Michigan, one of the campground's busiest times.

"Oh...you know." Her mom smiled, but it didn't meet her eyes. "With Stephen getting Kimmy more involved, I'm not as needed as I used to be," she said, mentioning Meg's brother and his wife. "Besides this makes a nice change after working at the campground for so many years."

"I'm surprised Dad didn't have a hissy fit once Stephen got Kimmy involved." Meg's bitterness was evident. Her dad certainly never wanted *Meg* to be involved with the family business.

As she'd once overheard her dad say to her mom, *Meg will get married someday and change her last name to her husband's. I want Archer Campground to stay in the family, to be inherited by someone who will always bear the Archer name.*

It was a stupid and antiquated idea, but that was her dad in a nutshell. He'd become obsessed with family lineage and continuing his legacy after Meg's paternal grandpa died. As far as her dad was concerned, Meg was just the spare heir. Not needed for much of anything.

Greta frowned at her. "Your brother mentioned that he tried calling you a couple of times, but he hasn't been able to get ahold of you."

Meg's shoulders hunched. "I've been busy."

"So busy that you can't return Stephen's call?" Her mom gave her that look. The one she used on Meg all the time when she was little and in trouble for whatever reason— usually thanks to some stupid scheme Tyler had gotten her involved in. It was a look that said she was disappointed in Meg.

Meg *hated* that look.

She folded her arms across her chest defensively, feeling like she was ten years old again. "I'll call him when I can, okay?"

Her mom wisely changed the subject instead of rehashing the same conversation they always had when it came to either the campground or family. "Julie's in the back if you need her."

Meg gave a short nod before striding toward the storage room. As she moved through the store, she breathed in the scent of cinnamon incense mixed with lemon floor cleaner. It was a comforting smell. It symbolized Julie and friendship.

She entered the back room and saw Julie standing next to a teenage boy. They were both examining a small desk, its maple wood gleaming in the dim light of the storage space.

"It's beautiful, Dylan." Julie ran a finger delicately across the large Petoskey stone embedded in the corner of the desk. "You did a fantastic job as always."

"Thanks, Julie." He radiated with pride.

Dylan was Jake's son. It was crazy—the older he got, the more he looked like his handsome, famous father. He was tall like his dad and had his facial features and dark hair. But while Jake had deep blue eyes that made many teens swoon back in the day, Dylan had inherited his mom's hazel eyes.

Meg walked over to them, appreciating the craftsmanship of the desk. "Nice job, kid. It looks amazing."

Dylan blushed. "Thanks, Ms. A."

She gave him a light, affectionate punch on the arm. "How many times have I told you you can call me Meg. You make me sound like an old lady when you call me Ms. A."

"Right—sorry."

"Are you coming to your dad's for dinner tonight?" Julie asked him, her affection evident as she spoke to her boyfriend's son.

"Yeah, I'll be there." He gave Julie a hug before waving to both women and heading out the door.

"Hi," Julie said to Meg then, running her left hand through a lock of her flaming red hair.

"Hey...so you hired my mom?"

Julie let go of her hair and tapped her chin with her index finger. "Is that okay?"

"It's up to her." Meg shrugged. "It seems weird that she wants to work here instead of with Dad. I don't care what she says about Kimmy, and—am I boring you?" she asked when Julie let out an exaggerated yawn, covering her mouth with her left hand.

"Oh, for Pete's sake." Julie shoved her hand in Meg's face, wiggling her ring finger back and forth.

Meg went cross-eyed for a second before stepping back so she could focus on her friend. Her jaw dropped when she saw the huge emerald-cut gray diamond on Julie's ring finger.

"What is this?" she said, half in disbelief, half in excitement. "Julie Alleen, is this what I think it is?"

She beamed, her steel eyes sparkling. "Jake asked me to marry him last night, and I said yes."

Meg shrieked as she threw her arms around her. "I'm so freaking happy for you."

Julie pulled back, her eyes were swimming with tears. "Thanks. And you have to be my maid of honor."

"Absolutely, yes," Meg said. She took in her friend's beautiful expression and sighed. "You're going to be the most gorgeous bride. Jake better treat you right, or I'll cut off his dick."

Julie snorted. "I'll make sure to tell him that."

"Are you sure your sister will be okay with me being maid of honor instead of her?" Meg asked. Julie's sister, Veronica, lived on the other side of the country, and she rarely saw her. Her sister used the distance as an excuse to never help with their Alzheimer's-stricken mother.

"She actually did bring it up last night when I told her the news, but when I explained that the maid of honor had duties—time-consuming duties—she politely declined."

"Sounds about right," Meg said. She picked up Julie's hand so she could get a better look at the ring. "A gray diamond. That's different."

Julie's cheeks turned a delicate red. "Jake said they reminded him of my eyes."

"The sap." Meg grinned at how sickeningly sweet they were.

Julie grabbed her pricing gun off the nearby shelf and started fiddling with it. "Jake and I talked about the wedding last night. Since this is his second marriage and I'm busy with the store, we want to do something really low key. Simple and quiet. We're thinking of having a private ceremony at his house. Something that'll hopefully keep the paparazzi away."

Meg nodded. "Smart. That'll be perfect."

Despite how popular they were, Holiday Boys had only been together for five years. After the band broke up, Jake went on to a successful solo career. He was right up there with Beyoncé and Taylor Swift when it came to selling out arenas. But with his success came an unhealthy interest from the public in his personal life. Meg didn't know how Julie tolerated the invasiveness of it all. She could barely tolerate people butting their nose into her business after the whole Lucas thing went down. Not that she was thinking about Lucas. He was dead to her.

Meg tilted her head. "I'm sure he can give you the wedding of your dreams without any delay. Just make sure you *do* get the wedding of your dreams. I know you never thought you'd get married."

"That's what Jake promised me." Julie glowed. "But honestly, all I want is him. I'd marry him in a dungeon if I had to."

"Kinky," Meg joked.

"Oh, shush." Julie placed the pricing gun against Dylan's desk and ticketed it. "So…are you okay with all of this?"

She frowned. "Why wouldn't I be?"

"Well, you know…the whole Lucas thing."

Hands on her hips, Meg said, "Man, I would love to go a single day without someone bringing up his name."

Julie looked mortified, "I didn't mean—"

She gave her friend a tight hug. "Julie, you're the closest thing I have to a sister. I want you to have nothing but the best. This is a good thing. And selfishly, it gives me something to focus on besides my own situation."

Relief flashed across Julie's face. "I'm glad to hear it, because there's something else I want to ask you."

"Okay, shoot."

"Jake and I were talking about our bachelor/bachelorette parties. We'd love to do something the week before the wedding so we have time to recover. And at the end of the night, we want the two parties to get together so we can celebrate together."

"Because of course you do." Meg looked at her friend fondly. Jake and Julie were practically joined at the hip these days. She was surprised they even wanted to have separate parties to begin with.

"Well, the thing is," Julie continued, "we're both going to be so busy planning the wedding, we were hoping you and the best man could plan the pre-parties."

"Okay, that's fine." Meg's mind started spinning with ideas. "What do you think about bungee jumping off a hot-air balloon?"

Could you bungee jump off a hot-air balloon?

Julie laughed. "A hot-air balloon. In November?"

"Impractical maybe, but the pictures would be beautiful. Especially if it's snowing by then. The whole bridal party can do it."

"Can you imagine my sister bungee jumping?" Julie said drily, and Meg grimaced. Julie's sister was a yuppie prude. She'd be too worried about her hair for something fun like that.

"I'd really like us to do something that's not too crazy," Julie added, giving her a pointed look.

Meg's hand went to her heart, instantly offended. "When have I ever done anything *too* crazy?"

It was a familiar conversation between the two, and Julie didn't fail to respond with a prime example.

"What about the time you convinced me to do a beer-bong race at that frat house, forgetting to mention the loser had to go on a blind date with one of the guys?"

"I didn't know you were that bad at beer bong. That wasn't my fault. Besides, you got a free dinner out of it." Meg frowned. "Wait. Who's the best man going to be? James?"

Jake's cousin and former bandmate did make the most logical choice.

"James is currently filming his home-renovation show in Detroit. He's going to be too busy to help with the wedding."

Meg didn't miss that Julie was no longer meeting her eyes. She had a sinking feeling in her stomach, knowing instantly who the best man was.

"No."

"Come on," Julie implored. "He's been Jake's best friend since they were kids."

"He's also my mortal enemy."

"You haven't seen Tyler in years. You're not little kids anymore."

"You never grow out of being *that* horrible of a person. Do you remember that time he convinced me to toilet paper the principal's house and then took off running when we got caught, leaving me with a roll of toilet paper in my hand? I thought Principal Michaels was going to expel me."

"I'm pretty sure I remember you ran over his Game Boy with your bike."

"Because he buried my Furby on the beach. I never did find it."

Julie looked like she was about to laugh again. For the sake of their friendship, she managed to keep a straight face. "Please. Will you do this for me?" She gave Meg her most pleading expression.

"Ugh." Meg threw her hands into the air. "Fine. Stop with the puppy eyes. But if this ends in bloodshed, you have no one to blame but yourself."

Julie put an arm around her shoulder. "Thanks, bestie."

"Yeah, yeah," Meg said. "I promise, for your sake, I won't treat Tyler as he so rightfully deserves. We'll work together to make it a night no one forgets, so help me God."

"You are the *best*." Julie's face turned evilly angelic. "And who knows—Jake said Tyler's currently not dating anyone."

She held up a hand. "Ew, stop."

"You've seen him in recent pictures. Don't you think he's good looking?"

Meg glared at her. "Yeah, he's just dreamy. Did you also forget the part where I said he was my mortal enemy?"

Julie patted her arm, giving off *Sure, Jan* energy.

She switched the topic back to something much more important. "Why don't we get a late lunch and we can discuss all the ideas I have for your party?"

"That sounds good. Let me just wrap up pricing a couple more things."

"Sure. I need to run to the bathroom, and then I'll meet you up front."

But as Meg washed her hands a few moments later, the happy expression dropped off her face as she stared at her reflection. Her hands drifted to her stomach, and she pulled at the large roll of skin there. She glanced back up to her face. All she could see were the wrinkles around her eyes. The voice of Lucas's mom, Clarice, entered her head.

You should join our gym. You should look into Botox. We have an image to uphold as Beaumonts.

No wonder Lucas had dumped her. She was a hot mess. An anxious, suffocating feeling formed inside her. Meg's breathing became shallow. Forcing a sharp breath in, she pushed the air toward her stomach as she had gotten in the habit of doing lately, causing her midsection to hurt. Burying the memories of Lucas and Clarice deep inside, she turned off the bathroom light and hurried to the front of the store.

Chapter Two

Tyler Evans batted at his phone where it rang incessantly on the table next to his bed. Cracking an eye open, he picked up his cell and focused his blurry vision on the time it flashed. It was 5:49 a.m. Groaning, he hit Ignore before burrowing deeper into his comforter.

It started up a few seconds later.

Swearing, he yanked the phone toward him and answered with a grumpy "What?"

"Good morning to you too, sunshine," his best friend, Jake, said.

"For God's sake, it's not even six a.m."

"Whoops—forgot about the time difference. You in Wyoming?"

Tyler ran a weary hand over the bristles on his cheek. "Yeah."

"Sorry, man. But I needed to tell you my news."

Even in his exhaustion, he couldn't miss the excitement in Jake's voice. Sitting up, he plumped the pillow behind him so he could lean against it. "What's up?"

"Julie and I are engaged."

Tyler eased into a tired smile. "That's great, man. Congratulations."

"Thanks." Jake practically hummed with happiness. "We

want to get married in two months. We're thinking the weekend before Thanksgiving. Julie will be slammed at the store once the holidays hit, and the band has those commitments in Europe in January," he explained. "The wedding isn't going to be anything too elaborate. Just friends and family. We want to keep it as quiet as possible so the press doesn't get wind of it."

"Good idea," Tyler said. "If you need any help, let me know."

"Funny you should say that…"

He paused in the process of yawning. "What?"

"Well, I was hoping you'd be my best man."

"Of course I will," Tyler answered warmly. "Dylan didn't want to do it?"

"Julie asked him to walk her down the aisle." Tyler could hear the pride in his friend's voice. Dylan would have been touched that his future stepmom asked him for the honor since her own father passed away years ago. The gesture would have meant a lot to Jake as well—seeing the two people he loved most in the world have that kind of comfortable relationship.

"That's awesome!" Tyler responded. He chuckled as he thought about another person who'd make a great best man. "James won't get jealous?"

"Nah, he's too busy with his show. Besides…"

Tyler frowned at the sudden seriousness in Jake's voice. "Besides?"

"I don't know. You know how tight-lipped my cousin can be with me when it comes to Mason."

Tyler nodded though Jake couldn't see him. James and his husband, Mason, had been together for years. Jake had never come out and said anything, but Tyler knew that he'd always felt Mason wasn't as in love with James as he was with him. Since James was more of a brother to him than a cousin, Jake tended to be protective of him. Because of that, there was an unspoken agreement between the two men that they didn't discuss Mason.

"You think there's trouble in paradise?" Tyler asked.

"I'm not sure. When I called to tell him about the engagement, I asked how Mason was. James gave me a pretty clipped response. But I'm not going to butt in if he doesn't want me in his business." Jake changed the subject. "So Julie and I were talking about the bachelor and bachelorette party. We thought we could have two separate parties before we have one big celebration at the end of the night with both groups meeting up."

Tyler snorted.

"What?" Jake asked.

"Nothing. You two are becoming one of those couples—that's all. You know, the ones who have to do *everything* together."

"What can I say? I love her." The adoration in his voice was clear.

The sound of it caused something to ache inside Tyler. He was beyond ecstatic for his best friend, but a part of him was a little envious of the contentedness he heard in his voice.

"Do you think you can handle planning the bachelor party?" Jake continued. "I know you're busy."

Tyler looked around his bedroom, at the crumpled sheets of paper surrounding his bed. "I'm not too busy."

Jake picked up on his tone. "Rough night?"

"Just having a little trouble with a song right now. I was up until one a.m. trying to get something on paper."

"Oh hell, now I feel even worse for waking you up," Jake said before offering, "If you need any help, let me know."

There was a reason that Jake and Tyler were considered the Lennon/McCartney of boy bands. Their songs tended to become instant classics, putting the Holiday Boys at the top of the charts.

"Don't worry about me," Tyler said. "You have a wedding to plan."

"Yeah." That sugary happiness returned to his friend's voice. "Anyway, you're going to need to coordinate the after-party with Julie's maid of honor."

"Anyone I know?" Tyler asked as he threw back the bedsheets.

"Meg Archer."

He froze in the middle of swinging his legs off the bed. "You're kidding."

"You know Meg has been Julie's best friend since forever."

"Meg Archer," he repeated. "The same girl who broke my nose."

He could almost hear Jake roll his eyes. "It's not like she did it deliberately."

"Didn't she?" Tyler argued, running his finger over his straight nose. Thankfully, the doctor was able to set it back in place, but he'd sported two black eyes for weeks.

"You should have caught the ball when she threw it at you," Jake said. Tyler did not appreciate the humor he could hear.

"I would have if she'd given me a heads-up that she was throwing it." Tyler stood and stretched. His back gave a satisfying crack. "We'll end up killing each other. You know that, right?"

"I very much doubt it." Jake's tone was dry. "You should see her these days. She's just your type—short and cute."

"It's Meg. She'll always be the annoying neighbor my

parents forced me to hang out with when we were younger."
Though she hadn't always been, his treasonous mind reminded him.

"Look," Jake replied, "can you get in contact with Meg
soon and see what you two can come up with for party
ideas?"

"Yeah, yeah. I'll take care of it. I'll talk to you soon."

"Sounds good."

After he and Jake ended their conversation, Tyler lum-
bered over to his window and threw open the black curtains.
The stars above twinkled brightly in the inky Wyoming
sky. In the distance, he could see the mountains highlighted
by the thin light of the crescent moon.

His ranch had always been his happy place, the place
where he wrote most of his hit songs. After Holiday Boys
disbanded, Jake had gone on to become a solo megastar, but
Tyler had preferred to stay out of the spotlight, becoming
one of the music industry's most successful songwriters.
He had so many Grammies at this point, he'd lost track of
how many he'd actually won.

Ever since the band reunited though, Tyler had felt pressure to write another hit song for them. Songwriting was
usually an easy process for him. But lately, Tyler felt…
stuck.

He leaned against the window frame, staring at the gorgeous landscape through heavy eyes until the sun peeked
over the horizon. Maybe what he needed was to go to his
Malibu home and find a woman to spend the night with. He
couldn't remember the last time he'd gotten laid.

He wasn't like his bandmate, Paul, who'd slept his way
through groupie after groupie, but he wasn't like Jake either. Jake had married his first wife when they were both
young, after getting her pregnant, and he'd stayed loyal to

her throughout their marriage, even after she cheated on him. He'd never been one to sleep around other than the rare hookup, which was why Tyler wasn't worried that he'd fool around on Julie, who was asexual. He was as loyal as a bloodhound.

But Tyler needed the physical release of a woman. It had been months since he'd had that pleasure. Maybe that was why'd he'd been feeling so off lately.

He had everything he could ever want. A successful career. More money than he knew how spend in one lifetime. But he was restless. And with the restlessness, writer's block had formed, stopping him from creating songs that usually came as natural as breathing to him.

His mind drifted to what Jake said about Meg. She'd always been tiny compared to him, but he wondered what she looked like now. Against his will, he thought back to his graduation night. That was the last time he saw Meg Archer, despite going home multiple times over the past twenty years.

He'd gotten drunk that night, celebrating not only graduating from high school but his recently signed contract for the Holiday Boys. His bags had already been packed, ready to head to California to record their first album.

He'd run into Meg at a party. She'd made a snide comment about how drunk he was. He'd called her a prissy prude. The next thing he knew, he'd had her up against the side of the house, his tongue tasting the sweetness of her mouth. Even now, he could still feel the fullness of her lips, the way her leg wrapped around his thigh. It had been the hottest moment of his life up until that point. But when she'd let out a quiet moan of pleasure, it had been like a bucket of water thrown over his head. Meg was a girl about to enter her sophomore year, and he'd been on the cusp of manhood, about to start his life far away from Holiday Bay. So he'd pulled away from her, muttering something about being drunk, ignoring the flash of pain on her face before she stomped away.

Tyler hadn't seen her since. Sometimes he wondered if she avoided him whenever he did go home. Holiday Bay was a small town. He should have seen her at some point.

He'd thought about her more times than he wanted to admit over the years. Considering how they used to needle each other, it surprised him how much he missed her presence in his life once it was gone. It didn't help that his mom made sure to give him updates on his former neighbor whenever they spoke, sighing about what a cute couple they would have made. When Tyler heard that Meg had gotten engaged, something had thumped painfully in his chest. It felt as though he'd missed out on something, though not necessarily anything to do with Meg.

You sure about that? a dark voice whispered from the deep recesses of his mind.

He ignored that voice as he always did when it came to Meg. She was, after all, his fondest pain.

Tyler rubbed at his face again, annoyed with himself. He was just being sentimental because his best friend was getting married.

He turned around and stared at the sheet music all over the floor. Maybe what he needed was a change of scene. Clearly, coming to the ranch hadn't helped with his writer's block. It might be nice to go home for a little while and regroup.

Besides, he had a bachelor party to plan. It could be just what he needed to give his mind a reset. And if he had to work with Meg, so be it. They'd just have to find a way to plan a party together with minimal bodily harm.

A slow smile formed on his lips. If there was one thing that sparked joy in him when he was a kid, it was to find a way to get under Meg Archer's skin.

Meg might have been able to avoid him over the past couple decades, but those efforts were about to come to an end.

Tyler's skin buzzed with anticipation.

He suddenly couldn't wait to return to Holiday Bay.

Chapter Three

Meg sat her desk, staring blankly out the window of her office. It was raining outside. Now that it was officially fall, the season was trying to make its presence known. Then again, it was Michigan. As the old saying went, if you didn't like the weather, wait five minutes. The day could begin at thirty degrees and end at seventy.

Meg let out a quiet sigh. She was so bored. She'd never expected to work as a recruiter for the town's employment agency. Meg had gone to school for business administration and had fully expected her father to relent and let her work at the family business. She'd grown up in the campground's office, trailing her parents around, taking care of the campsites, welcoming new customers in.

After Meg graduated college, she'd approached her father, asking how she could get more involved in the business. He'd smiled that smile he always gave when he thought Meg was being funny and then told her they were all set on office needs, but if she wanted to help keep the campground clean, he'd be happy to hire her.

Apparently, all she was good for in her father's eyes was cleaning the latrine.

Meg told him to forget it. Instead, she found a job at Wendy's Staffing Agency. Wendy Wayland had been in the same class as Tyler. Much to Meg's dismay, she was obsessed with Holiday Boys and still played their music over the office speakers on rotation, even though the band hadn't had a hit in fifteen years. It was embarrassing when you were trying to fire someone and you had Tyler's voice crooning in the background, *Every time I see you, baby, my heart skips a beat.*

Her personal phone started ringing where she'd left it on her desk. Turning it over so she could see who was calling, she went rigid when Lucas's name flashed across the screen. She couldn't look away from it.

She and Lucas hadn't spoken to each other since he left town. Her emotions twisted in a million different directions. Sorrow combated with anger, along with a betraying sense of longing.

Her mind flashed to a memory she longed to forget. The day he'd broken their engagement.

The night before, she had gotten into a fight with his horror of a mother. Clarice had been harping on her like she always did, making sure to remind Meg with her not-so-subtle jabs that she wasn't good enough to be a Beaumount. And Lucas stood there, letting it happen, his face a mix of frustration and vacantness.

Now, Meg had the patience of a saint when it came to Clarice. She had taken her abuse for *years*. After putting up with her own dad acting like Meg was never enough, she was naive enough to think she could handle Clarice. But that night, something shifted in Meg. Maybe it was getting a front-row seat to seeing Julie fall in love with Jake, risking everything for true happiness. Maybe it was the stress of the overall situation. As Clarice continued to needle her, Meg had turned to Lucas with pleading eyes, silently imploring him to defend her from his hideous mom. He'd turned away, leaving her to defend herself.

Which she finally did. Colorfully, she might add.

When she was finished, Lucas stared at her like he'd never seen her before, while his mom looked…satisfied. As long as Meg lived, she'd never forget the cruel happiness on Clarice's face before she smoothed it out, facing her son with crocodile tears in her eyes, whimpering how she only wanted the best for her only son, her baby boy.

The next day, Lucas broke off the engagement, telling her he couldn't take the constant bickering between Clarice and Meg anymore. When he turned away from her, his shoulders stiff, he said something that continued to bother her to this day.

I'm tired, Meg. I'm so tired of this life. Of living like this.

If you'd just defend me once in a while, she'd pleaded. *Why can't you see your mom is toxic?*

And then he'd said, his entire body set in defeat, *Don't you see she's not the problem? It's* us. *No, it's* me. *I can't do this anymore. I've tried and tried, and I can't…*

He'd ended their relationship right then and there and soon after disappeared out of her life.

The phone went silent. Meg brushed away a stray tear that drifted down her cheek. She should have blocked his number that night. When it rang again with Lucas's name blasting across her screen, she hit Ignore before blocking the number and powering her phone off.

Her breathing became shallow as she sat there feeling numb. She took a breath in but went panicky when she couldn't get the oxygen deep enough into her lungs. She closed her eyes, trying to distract herself from her punishing thoughts. Pressure built inside her, and she added to it, pushing air toward her diaphragm, her stomach muscles tensing until they hurt.

Stop doing that!

The pressure increased.

Her work phone rang and she grabbed it. "Wendy's Talent Agency, this is Meg."

"Meg?"

The familiarity in the voice made her instantly picture Lucas. Rage made her tone thick as she practically screamed, "Stop calling me, tool!"

She slammed the phone down just as Wendy walked by her office, looking at Meg in concern.

"Everything okay?"

"Yeah, I'm fine," Meg replied, her shaking hands clasped tightly in her lap, away from her boss's view. "Sorry for the noise."

Wendy nodded and continued to her office.

The phone rang persistently again.

Through gritted teeth, she spit out, "Wendy's Staffing Agency, this is Meg."

"Meg, it's Tyler."

Not wanting to do her job in that moment, but knowing she had to, she hit a key on her computer to wake it up from sleep mode. Pulling up the Applicant Tracking System that stored all her clients' information, she said, "What's your last name, Tyler, so I can pull up your application?"

The man's voice sounded amused as he said, "Evans. Tyler Evans."

Anger returned like a vice. "Sure, and I'm the *Mona Lisa*."

She hung up the phone and went back to staring out the window. Thanks to Holiday Boys reuniting, people had been ruthless in digging up whatever dirt they could find on the Boys. Social media hadn't been big when the band first got together, and now that it was, reporters and vloggers made it their mission to blast out whatever facts they could find on them. Including making sure people knew that she was Tyler Evans's former neighbor. She usually got a prank call two or three times a week from people who thought it was hilarious to call her, pretending to be Tyler.

The phone rang again and Meg picked it up with a snap. "Wendy's Talent Age—"

"Meg, look—"

"You again?" she interrupted impatiently.

"Do you remember that time when you were in kindergarten and you punched Billy Hudson in the face because he pushed Julie Alleen to the ground to steal her lunch?"

Meg froze. She did remember that rather embarrassing event. Billy had always been a jerk and he deserved the punch, but the incident had kickstarted her reputation as a wild child. It was also the moment that her lifelong friendship with Julie began. Tyler had gotten a front-row seat to the whole thing on the playground. When Meg had cocked her arm to punch Billy again, Tyler had dragged her away, laughter in his voice as he told her to calm down before she embarrassed Billy any further. It was funny how all these years later, she could still remember the slight pride she'd heard in his voice.

"T-Tyler?" She was stunned. "How did you get this number?"

"Your mom told me where you worked."

Meg frowned. "When did you talk to my mom?"

"I stopped by your parents' house earlier."

The jitteriness Meg had been feeling since Lucas called, stilled. "You're in town?"

"Yeah."

"Why?"

Silence filled the line before Tyler said awkwardly, "Um, look, maybe you should talk to Julie. I don't want to spoil her news."

"I know about the engagement, if that's what you're alluding to," Meg said.

"Great," he replied. "Then I'm sure you're also aware that Julie and Jake want us to plan a party for them."

"The wedding isn't for two months. I'm sure we can come up with something closer to that date."

"I figure we should meet sooner rather than later. There's going to be a lot of planning we're going to need to do, especially if we want to keep this out of the press."

Meg tapped her index finger anxiously against the surface of her desk. She wasn't mentally prepared to see Tyler just yet. Her hand fluttered to the extra roll of skin on her stomach, and she pinched the area, hard.

"Meg, you still there?"

She pulled her hand away. "Yeah, I'm here."

"I was thinking we could meet for dinner tonight and brainstorm some ideas. What do you say to meeting at Florentina's?"

"We don't have to meet," Meg said hurriedly. "Why don't you email me your ideas and—"

"I'm already in town, so what's the big deal?" Tyler argued. "It'll give us a chance to catch up. I haven't seen you since…"

Her mouth tightened. "Since your graduation night."

Another awkward silence filled the space between them.

Tyler finally said, "Come on, Meg. Let's have dinner." Amusement filled the timbre of his voice as he added, "I dare you."

If there was one thing people knew about Meg and Tyler

back when they were kids, it was that if they got in trouble, it was usually because one of them dared the other to do something stupid. For the most part, it was Tyler coming up with the dumb ideas, even if he never would admit they were bad.

And Meg, always needing to prove herself, would accept his dares.

Apparently, some things never changed.

Her eyes turned to slits as she leaned back in her chair. "What time do you want to meet?"

Chapter Four

Meg applied foundation under her eyes to hide the circles that lingered there. She glanced down at the loose, multicolored shift dress she wore, hoping that it did its job to hide her figure. With a final dab, she put down her blending sponge. Turning, she took in the imperfections that reflected back in the mirror.

Reaching up, she adjusted the loose bun of her honey-brown hair so that it wasn't off-kilter. She didn't know why she was so nervous about seeing Tyler. It was just Tyler. The bane of her existence. Tyler, who, according to the gossip magazines she saw in stores, dated supermodels and A-list actresses. She didn't need to go out of her way for him.

And it wasn't like she wanted him to find her attractive.

Shutting off the bathroom light with a frustrated flip of the switch, she walked toward her apartment door, grabbing a thick cable-knit cardigan to keep her warm, since it was supposed to be cool that night.

She slid into her old Chevy and made her way to Florentina's. When she entered the Italian restaurant, the mixed scent of garlic and tomato infiltrated her senses. A familiar figure stood behind the hostess stand.

"Hi, Meg. How are you?" Isabella asked.

"I'm good, Izzy. How about you?" Meg returned, affection in her voice. When she was a teenager, she used to babysit the younger girl on the rare occasions Izzy's many siblings couldn't.

"I'm good," Izzy said.

She looked pristine in her restaurant uniform, consisting of a white button-down top and black pants. Her jet-black hair was pulled into a high chignon. She was short like Meg and just as curvy, but she exuded confidence in a way that Meg envied. It was obvious that she was comfortable in her own skin. Izzy had been pure sunshine when she was a kid, and given her bright smile, not much seemed to have changed.

"Did you hear I finally graduated from Huron State?" she asked. "It took me long enough."

"That can happen when you attend part time, but congratulations." Meg observed the other girl. "Any plans now that you're done with school?"

Izzy shuffled some menus in her hands. "I'm not sure yet. Franki offered to take me on at the pasty shop," she said, mentioning her cousin. "But for the time being, I'm going to work here for my parents while I explore my options. I—"

She stopped talking abruptly. Her eyes widened as she stared at someone who walked into the restaurant. Meg had a feeling she knew who it was. She turned slowly.

"Well, well, well. If it isn't Mona Lisa," Tyler said, his voice deeper in person than over the phone.

Meg's face flushed, but she met his eyes head on. "Tyler."

His eyes ran over her, and she knew he was taking in the changes since he last saw her. She'd been a girl the last time they'd seen one another. She'd certainly wasn't one now. Instead of self-consciously fidgeting with her dress, Meg gave him the same once-over.

Much to her annoyance, Tyler was beautiful. She'd seen him through her parents' front-room window last year when he'd visited his parents. But that quick view hadn't done him justice. His body was lean. His biceps bulged against the arms of his black suit jacket. His short, dark hair was styled to perfection. Gray hair sprinkled through a two-day-old beard on his cheeks, reminding Meg that he wasn't too far off from turning forty. But his eyes were what truly captivated, a swirling mix of blue and green that had led many of his fans to debate their true color over the years. The hashtag #TylerEvansEyes trended on social media for days when the Holiday Boys had announced their reunion tour.

Tyler was still looking her over. She pulled her cardigan closer together, hiding her body in defense.

"You're looking…good," he said.

Meg swiveled around on her feet to face Izzy, her cheeks burning with humiliation. She knew what she freaking looked like these days. She didn't need Tyler to lie. He couldn't even say she looked good without stumbling over the words.

"Thanks," she said bitterly. Looking to Izzy, she asked, "Can we get a table for two?"

"Of course," Izzy said, her eyes still on Tyler. Seeming to remember that she was working, she grabbed some menus. "This way, please."

Meg walked after her, not bothering to see if Tyler followed.

Tyler was stunned. When Jake mentioned Meg was his type, he hadn't been joking. Meg was still tiny compared to him, but her body now had curves in all the right places. As he followed behind her to their table, he couldn't take his eyes off her, watching her feminine hips sway back and forth. The dress she wore made a swishing noise as she moved. Tyler wanted to reach out and bunch the fabric in his hands, if only to stop the temptation he felt to reach for the person underneath.

He'd told her she looked good. That wasn't the half of it. When she'd turned around to face him, he'd actually lost his breath. He'd tripped over his words, barely stopping himself from calling her beautiful.

This is Meg, he reminded himself. *Your childhood nemesis.*

The hostess led them to a lantern-lit table. Whispers started to fill the atmosphere as restaurant patrons recognized Tyler. But people remained in their seats, giving him his space. It was one thing he loved about Holiday Bay. For the most part, people left the Holiday Boys alone whenever they came to town. In Jake's case, people were used to his presence, since he lived there. The only times people freaked out anymore was if they were tourists.

Meg sat down and took a menu from the hostess with a relaxed smile. Tyler suddenly wondered what he could do to get that smile directed at him. And then he wondered why he wanted her to smile at him in the first place.

Meg looked over the food options as though he wasn't there. As they continued to sit in silence, Tyler began to feel uneasy. He wasn't a hundred percent sure, but he got the feeling she was upset with him about something.

After the hostess left, a waiter came over to take their drink orders. Meg ordered a glass of white wine. Tyler ordered a craft beer for himself.

Once the waiter was gone, Tyler opened his menu. "I haven't been here in so long."

"It's probably not up to your standards," Meg replied sharply.

"What do you mean?" Tyler asked. He tried not to feel triumphant when she finally looked up and met his eyes.

A delicate eyebrow shot up. "Don't you have a bunch of personal chefs cooking Michelin-star meals for you at your numerous mansions?"

He snorted. "I think you seriously overestimate my life."

The waiter returned to the table with their drinks and set them down. "Are you ready to order?"

"I'll take the house salad with your raspberry vinaigrette dressing, please," Meg said.

"Very good, ma'am," the waiter said. "Anything else?"

Meg handed the waiter her menu. "No, that's all. Thank you."

"And for you?" he asked Tyler in a rush. The man clearly recognized him, given the excited energy in the way he spoke, but Tyler gave him props for not freaking out.

"I'll take your chicken marsala."

"I'll be right back with your order," the waiter replied before leaving.

Tyler leaned back in his chair as he observed his former neighbor. "You still not eating meat?"

"You still eating a farm's worth of animals?" she retorted.

He smirked. "Speaking of, have you organized any more 'Meat is Murder' campaigns recently?"

Meg gave him a disgruntled look. "That was one time in ninth grade. I still maintain I saved the school from a possible lawsuit by pointing out how unclean the food was."

"You locked yourself to the kitchen freezer. They couldn't have seen the food if they tried."

She lifted a shoulder. "It was for a good cause."

Tyler shook his head fondly. "You and your causes. I remember that time you kidnapped chickens from Mr. Winkler's biology class after the students worked so hard to hatch them."

"It was barbaric. Once they reached a certain size, Mr. Winkler would sell them to slaughter farms."

"So you thought your only option was to hide them in my parents' shed?"

"It was better insulated than our shed." Tyler laughed at that. Meg's mouth twitched in response before her face turned serious. "I never understood why you told your parents you were the one to put them there instead of me."

"It was a genius idea. You think I wanted you to get all the credit?"

"I knew it!" Her eyes narrowed. "You never did like me to outdo you."

Tyler's lips twisted into a half smile. He missed this, he realized. He missed *Meg.*

Instead of answering her, he said, "So, Meg, what have you been up to? It's been decades since I saw you. Which is weird, considering I've come back to town multiple times. It's almost like you were avoiding me."

Her face scrunched, the perfect picture of adorable confusion. "Why would I avoid you?"

"You tell me," he said. Again, he thought about his graduation night. The feel of her against him. The hurt on her face when he sent her away.

"I had no reason to avoid you." She raised her head proudly. "You've simply been too busy living your fantastic life, dating celebrities and going to award shows. You most likely didn't notice me when you came home."

"I've known you your entire life. I would have noticed you," Tyler assured her. Aside from the fact that it was Meg and he'd been on the lookout for her whenever he came back to the Bay, he never failed to notice an attractive woman when one crossed his path. But he kept that to himself, unsure how she'd react if he confessed that he found her attractive. Clearing his throat, he said, "My mom said you got engaged."

"And then I got unengaged." A scowl appeared on her face before her features smoothed into complete blankness. It was a surprising look for someone he remembered as being constantly animated. "I don't really want to talk about that."

He nodded slowly, despite his curiosity. He wanted to know about her. He wanted to know what he'd missed in the years since he'd left. More than anything, he wanted to know how Meg had become a shell of herself and what needed to happen to spark some life back into her.

"Besides," she continued, "we're here to talk about Julie and Jake."

"Right." That was a safe topic. "Any ideas of what you want to do for their party?"

"I've got some ideas. Julie told me she didn't want to do anything too crazy."

"I wonder where she got the idea you'd do anything crazy."

Meg's eyes narrowed. "Yeah, I wonder who the bad influence was in my life who dared me to do crazy things, resulting in me becoming Holiday Bay's most notorious wild child, while he got away scot-free."

"No idea, but that person sounds like a lot of fun," Tyler replied innocently.

Her lips pointed upward. He took it as a win.

"Anyway," she continued, "I thought we could do something tastefully low-key. The girls and I could take Julie for dinner—maybe come here—and then both parties could meet up at Kyleigh's Knits. She sometimes hosts those Sip and Paint classes. We could drink wine and paint."

Tyler gave her a disgruntled look. "In what world do you think a bachelor party wants to sit around and paint pictures?"

Meg's shoulders stiffened. "I assumed Jake would want the guys from your band there. Aren't you a bunch of creatives?"

"First, even creatives want a day off from—you know—creating. Second, just because we're creative, doesn't mean we know how to paint."

A brief spark of fire ignited in her eyes. "Fine, so what's your big idea, then?"

Tyler had no idea, but he said the one thing he knew would turn that small fire in Meg's eyes into an inferno. "Strippers."

She became immediately indignant. "You're freaking kidding me, right? In what world do you think Julie would want—"

"Meg, hello."

The blaze in Meg instantly dampened as quickly as if someone had thrown a bucket of water on her. Her face went paper white as she faced the older couple that stood beside their table. The man wasn't paying any attention to them, too busy responding to something on his phone. The woman's eyes didn't stray from Meg.

"Clarice," Meg murmured.

"It is so good to see you out and about, dear. For a while, I was worried that you had forgotten how to shower." Clarice said it in a teasing tone, but Tyler's eyebrows shot up at the undercurrent of malice he heard in the woman's voice. She continued, "Have you heard from Lucas lately?"

Meg flinched. "He called today actually, but I missed him."

That seemed to catch Clarice off guard by the way her body went briefly rigid before she went on, "He was probably wondering where the engagement ring is that he gave you."

"He should hire a dive team, then," Meg muttered.

Clarice continued as though she hadn't spoken. "He's been traveling for his job. It sends him all over the world. He really is excelling at life right now. I wouldn't be surprised if he met a girl. Someone who's a better fit for our family. You know, you and Lucas were so unsuited. I tried to warn you. It's really best for both of you that your unfortunate engagement is over."

Holy crap was this woman serious? Tyler waited for Meg to yell at the woman, to throw her glass of wine in her face. That was what the Meg he knew would have done. But she just sat there, as though turned to stone. Fury licked at his insides. Who the hell was this woman to speak to her like that?

"Do you mind?" Tyler snapped just as Clarice opened her mouth to utter more of her vitriol. "We're in the middle of a conversation."

Clarice stared down at him as though he were a bug who'd crawled out from under a rock.

"And who is your little friend, Meg?" the older woman said.

The silent man next to Clarice looked up from his phone then. Greedy delight crossed his face. "Tyler Evans!"

He stuck his hand out for Tyler to shake. Tyler didn't return the gesture, and the man's hand fell limply to his side, embarrassment creeping over his face.

The older man cleared his voice. "It's been some time

since we've seen you in our neck of the woods. I'm sure you remember me."

"Not really," Tyler said, though as he stared at the man, he did recognize the mayor. The man had been in office for years.

A quiet snicker caught Tyler's attention. He looked at Meg, who was currently fighting a smile. The restlessness that was his constant companion these days seemed to disappear as something else took over. Something Tyler wasn't ready to label. But whatever the emotion was, it made him want to puff out his chest in pride while simultaneously wrapping Meg in a protective bubble.

"Mayor Beaumont," the man said, his neck red at having to introduce himself. "And this is my wife, Clarice."

"Charmed," Tyler said so sarcastically that it couldn't be missed, even by people as obtuse as the couple in front of them.

"Clarice," the mayor said gruffly, "this is Tyler Evans. He's one of our Holiday Boys."

Clarice looked like a fish gasping for water as she looked between Tyler and Meg. "It's…good to meet you. And how do you know our lovely Meg?"

Tyler didn't know why he did it, but he reached for Meg's hand and pulled it to him, placing a gentle kiss on the back of it. Meg's soft gasp drew his eyes to her face, and he was pleased to see there was color returning to her pallid cheeks.

"Oh, Meg and I go *way* back," he said, hinting at something that had never been there.

Except for graduation night.

But now wasn't the time to think about that.

"I…" Mayor Beaumont seemed to be at a loss for words before he said, "I'd love for you to stop by my office sometime. I can introduce you to our city council."

"Maybe," Tyler replied, having no intention of going near either horrible person again. He didn't pull his gaze away from Meg, whose soulful blue eyes were firmly on the table. He laced their fingers together.

It was perfect timing that their waiter returned with their food.

Tyler looked pointedly at the Beaumonts. "If you'll excuse us, Meg and I are having dinner."

"Of course," the mayor said. "I look forward to seeing you again soon." With that, he grabbed his wife's arm and pulled her away, leading them to the other side of the restaurant.

Meg tugged at her hand, and it was only then that Tyler realized he was still holding it. He let her go, and Meg drew her hands into her lap. Tyler's fingers felt a little colder as he slowly drew his palm back to his side of the table.

The waiter placed their food in front of them. "Is, uh, there anything else I can get you?"

Meg gave a short shake of her head.

"I think we're all set for now. Thank you," Tyler said, and the waiter left.

He picked up his silverware and began to cut into his chicken. When Meg continued to sit there like a statue, her only movement the rapid rise and fall of her chest, he asked quietly, "Are you okay?"

Her eyes shot to him, wide and unseeing. "I—I'm sorry. I need to go."

"What? You haven't touched your food."

"I know, I just… I'm sorry. I need to leave." She opened up her purse and started to pull out her wallet.

"I'll pay," Tyler interjected.

"I can't let you—"

"Please, I insist," he said. "But stay and eat something."

"I can't." She jumped up on legs that seemed to shake. "I—I'm so sorry."

She walked away from the table without a backward glance.

The waiter hurried over to him. "Is everything okay?"

"Sorry about the inconvenience," Tyler said, pulling out a hundred-dollar bill. "Will this cover the meal?"

"Yes, of course," the waiter said. "I'll bring you your change."

"We're all set."

"Th-Thank you, sir."

Tyler nodded and walked swiftly toward the exit. He was aware of people taking pictures of him as he left, and he wondered how much of the whole disastrous dinner would be trending on social media later.

He made it outside just in time to see Meg drive by in her car, looking like a ghost was chasing her.

Chapter Five

Meg woke up the next day feeling exhausted after tossing and turning all night. With a weary sigh, she swung her feet off the bed and stared listlessly at her toes. Despite her tiredness, she felt jittery. On edge.

Why, why, why did she still let Clarice get to her?

She and Lucas were done. *Finito*. Finished.

Why did Clarice still take aim at her whenever they ran into each other? Why did Meg let her?

Meg got up and used the bathroom. She stared at her red-rimmed eyes as she washed her hands. She looked terrible. More importantly, she felt embarrassed.

She was horrified that the exchange happened in front of Tyler Evans. It was bad enough that she had to have Clarice rub it in her face that Lucas was living his best life now that they weren't together, but to do that in front of Tyler, of all people, was beyond humiliating. She bet he enjoyed her misery.

Though…it didn't seem like he'd enjoyed himself. In fact, he'd been downright rude to the Beaumonts. For a family who put so much emphasis on their social standing, Meg had been very tempted to lean over and hug him when he said he didn't have a clue who Richard Beaumont was.

As she made her way to the kitchen for some much

needed coffee, her phone beeped from where she'd thrown it onto the couch the night before. She saw she had three texts.

The first one was from Julie, and she opened it. Her stomach twisted with dread when she saw a picture of her and Tyler speaking to Clarice and the mayor the night before. Meg looked upset in the picture. Interestingly enough, Tyler looked pissed as he glared at the couple.

Meg was only thankful that whoever took the picture hadn't caught the moment when Tyler kissed her hand. Her stomach fluttered as she remembered the warm press of his lips against her skin. It was unexpected and…not unwelcome.

She brushed that thought aside. She hadn't been touched by a man in so long. Her reaction to Tyler was instinct. Nothing to dwell on.

Despite telling herself that, her mind flashed to his graduation night. To being held in his strong arms. The feel of his body against hers as he pressed her against the house.

Nope, definitely not going there.

You've gone viral, Julie wrote, regarding the picture. I'm going to assume you two were meeting about the party. Why was Clarice there?

Meg sent her a text back, briefly explaining what happened the night before.

If you need to talk, let me know, Julie responded.

Meg's heart filled with love for her best friend. I'll call you later, she sent.

The muscles around Meg's diaphragm tightened as she pulled up a social media site. She grimaced when she saw that the picture was all over the place. Even though she told herself not to do it, she read some of the comments.

Who's that woman with Tyler???

He looks so mad. What do think is going on?

Who's the pig with Tyler?

Gross, her? He could do better.

Meg felt sick. Wasn't that the story of her life? Never good enough.

Not good enough for her dad. Not good enough for Lucas. And now Tyler.

Closing out the page, she looked at the next text from an unknown number.

Hey, it's Lucas. I'm guessing you blocked my main number, but I'm going to be back in town in a few weeks. Can we talk?

Meg stared at the message, her skin heating with anger. Who the hell did he think he was, contacting her after over a year of radio silence? Didn't his mom tell her he was living his best life? Why on earth would he reach out to her now? Unless it was to tell her what his mom already hinted at—that he'd found another woman and he wanted his engagement ring back so he could give it to his new fiancée.

If that was the case, good luck to him. She'd tossed it into the bay shortly after their breakup, mainly to piss off Clarice, who'd had the audacity to claim it was a family heirloom that Meg no longer had a right to. It wasn't. Lucas bought it for her on one of his trips to Grand Rapids. Clarice simply wanted to cause problems like she always did.

If Lucas was contacting her to tell her he'd finally met the woman he actually wanted to marry, Meg didn't want to hear it. The two of them had been together off and on since Meg was sixteen. She'd wasted years on Lucas. She'd given him enough of her energy.

She deleted his text before she looked at the next message.

This is Tyler. Hope you don't mind, but your mom gave me your number—Meg was really going to need to have a conversation with her mom about not giving her information out—I wanted to make sure you were okay.

Meg didn't respond to that text either, though she did add Tyler to her contacts. Pulling up her apps, she found a meditation one that she'd recently downloaded. She'd read that meditation was supposed to help with anxiety. Lord knew she had enough of it lately.

She thought about going to a therapist to get her emotions sorted out. She'd been so overwhelmed with everything since she and Lucas broke up, not to mention the inevitable downfall that happened afterward with people treating her like a pariah. Sometimes she felt like she was back in that bathtub again, being shoved underwater, slowly suffocating. It might help to speak to a professional about it so she could process everything in a healthier way. But the only therapist in town was Dr. Forester. Meg's mom took her to see him when she was a teenager after the chicken-kidnapping incident at school, thinking Meg was acting out for some reason. And maybe Meg had been trying to get her dad's attention on some subconscious level, as their relationship had started to deteriorate at that point. She'd told Dr. Forester about her concerns, and her dad didn't speak to her for a week after.

She never had any proof that the therapist had betrayed doctor/patient confidentiality, but Meg had forgotten that he was not only a frequent camper at the family campground but also one of her dad's favorite golfing buddies. She hadn't bothered with therapy after that.

Pressing Play on the meditation app, she listened as a woman began to speak.

"Hello. This is Tessa, and I'm going to guide you through today's meditation. First find a comfortable place to sit."

Meg planted herself in front of the slider that led out to her apartment's deck, adjusting until she got comfortable on the soft beige carpet.

"Make sure to sit straight or in a position that's relaxing for you. Next I want you to close your eyes."

Tessa had a slight whistle to her *s*'s that should have been annoying but somehow made Meg feel even more relaxed. She did as instructed and shut her eyes.

"Now I want you to take a deep breath in."

Meg stiffened. Lately, she had become somewhat obsessed with her breathing. If she concentrated on it too much, she stopped doing it naturally and then would force herself to breathe manually. After forcing air into her lungs one too many times, she eventually would start that weird diaphragm thing she'd been doing, putting pressure on her stomach until it hurt.

"Good. Now take another deep breath for four seconds. Hold it for four seconds, and then release it for eight. I'll help you. Breathe in, two, three, four..."

Meg did as she was told, ignoring how her heart began to race.

"Hold, two, three, four."

Panic started to set in. Meg. Couldn't. Breathe.

"Release, two, three, four, five, six, seven, eight."

Can't breathe, can't breathe, can't breathe.

With a shaking hand, Meg grabbed the phone and shut off the woman's voice. Standing up, she paced around the room, trying to focus on anything other than her breath. It didn't help. She wasn't breathing on her own, and she had to take several manual breaths in. The stomach muscles began to tighten around her midsection.

Meg needed a distraction. Fast. She grabbed her phone and called the campground.

"Archer Campground, Harry speaking."

"Hi, Dad," Meg said, continuing to move around her room at an erratic pace.

"Hey, Meggie. What are you up to today?"

"Not much." She ran into the corner of her living room table. Wincing, she rubbed at the spot. "Actually, I have some free time on my hands. I was wondering if you needed any help at the campground. I was looking at the website the other day, and I think if you upgraded it, it'd be easier for guests to book their reservations. I have some ideas of some webhosts that'll allow you to—"

"Thanks Meg, but Kimmy is handling all of that. She's doing an excellent job. Stephen thinks she'll be able to get our brand out there."

Resentment flourished inside Meg, but she kept her mouth shut. She loved Kimmy, but her sister-in-law didn't know webhosting from gameshow hosting.

"Fine," she said, trying to not sound bitter. "Can I talk to Mom?"

"She's not here." Her dad's tone was shorter. He muttered something under his breath. She may have misheard him, but she thought he said, "As usual."

"Oh, is she working at Julie's today?"

"No idea. I can't keep track of her anymore." Her dad's tone was definitely passive-aggressive, so she let it go.

Silence fell between them. They'd never been as close as Meg was to her mom, but some of her favorite memories involved helping her dad around the campground when she was little. It was as she grew older and started to offer her input that a wedge fell between them, the distance growing until they had nothing more to say to one another.

"Well, I should get going," Meg finally said awkwardly.

"Yeah, same," her father replied, already distracted as Meg could hear a customer enter the campground office, greeting her father. "Take care, Meg."

"Bye, D—"

He hung up before she could finish speaking. Meg's sense of unease grew as she put her phone down on the table. There was definitely something wrong with her parents, but she couldn't put her finger on what it was. She'd need to have a heart-to-heart with her mom soon. If she could track her down.

That thought only made the sense of franticness worsen. The pressure on her diaphragm made her stomach ache.

She should eat breakfast. That would offer a distraction. Meg went to the kitchen, opened up one of her cupboards and gathered her morning meal. She couldn't remember the last time she ate from her box of cereal, always in too much of a rush these days to get to work after oversleeping. She grimaced as she tasted the stale flakes, but she continued to eat methodically, crunching the food with her teeth until it was mush in her mouth before swallowing it down. After she finished, she grabbed a glass of water to help get the taste out of her mouth. But when she held the lifted glass up to her mouth, her jaw wouldn't unlock so she could take a sip. Just the idea of drinking water made her panic, feeling like she was about to drown.

Which was silly. She was being stupid.

She forced herself to take a tiny sip anyway. Her throat closed, unwilling to let her swallow it. Spitting the water out into the sink, she dumped the rest of it down the drain and put the glass on the counter.

Turning away from the kitchen, Meg strode back into the living room. She tried to sit on her comfortable beige couch, but her mind kept spinning and spinning with all the different things she didn't want to think about.

Clarice. Lucas. My parents. The viral comments. Tyler.
Clarice. Lucas. My parents. The viral comments. Tyl—

Grabbing the remote control, she turned on the TV and began to blast the volume until the noise was the only thing she could hear in her head.

The next day, Meg found herself staring out her office window, mentally counting the minutes until she could go home.

"Meg, are you okay?" the boy sitting across from her said.

She turned to look at Wyatt Erving and forced a smile to her lips. "Yes, sorry. What were you saying?"

"I said I didn't feel like the environment at the mill was the safest."

"Wyatt, you were at the job for less than a month and you had four safety incidents."

He was barely twenty and determined to spend his time goofing off rather than acting like an adult. If his parents hadn't threatened to cut him off, she suspected he'd be in their basement right now, playing video games.

"Like I said." His face turned insolent. "It wasn't a safe environment."

Meg did her best not to show her impatience. "You know this is a small town, right? If you continue to not take these jobs seriously, you're going to gain a reputation and people won't hire you."

"That's why I came to you. So you can find me a job that's worth my time." He looked down at his phone and sniggered at whatever video he was watching.

Meg didn't try to hide her sigh this time as she looked at her computer, searching for any new job openings that might have come in.

"It doesn't look like we have anything just now, but if I get something else, I'll let you know."

Wyatt jumped to his feet, obviously eager to return to his parents' basement to jerk off or whatever it was that he did all day besides play video games.

"Thanks, Meg," he replied. He bumped into someone as he was leaving her office.

"Wyatt, would you watch where you're going?" Wendy's annoyed voice said from the hallway. "We have an important guest here today."

"S-Sorry," he stuttered.

Meg looked up from her computer screen to see what was going on. Her heart stuttered when Tyler Evans came into view.

"Meg," Wendy said brightly from behind him. "Look who stopped by!"

"Hi, Meg," Tyler greeted. He stood with his hands shoved into the pockets of his barley-colored journeyman jacket, looking casual and carefree.

"H-Hi," Meg replied, her face flushing as she thought back to their embarrassing dinner.

He didn't bring it up though as he turned to Wendy. "It was great seeing you again."

"You too, Mr. Evans."

Tyler chuckled. "Wendy, we suffered through Mrs. Spencer's class together. You called me Tyler then. You can call me Tyler now."

Her eyes twinkled as she said, "In that case, it was good seeing you again, Tyler." She looked between him and Meg curiously before she added, "Don't be a stranger now, you hear?"

"I won't." But he'd already turned his attention to Meg, his eyes scanning her features.

After her boss went back to the front of the building, Meg asked professionally, "What can I do for you, Mr. Evans?"

Tyler rolled his eyes so hard, she was surprised they didn't get stuck.

"Well, *Ms. Archer*, I wanted to see if we could get lunch together."

She turned to her computer. "I'm pretty busy right now."

Tyler sat in the chair Wyatt just vacated, bridging his fingers together across his chest. "It's a good thing you have such an amazing boss. She said you could have the next two hours off."

Meg turned in her chair, instantly angry. "You had no right—"

"Our dinner got interrupted the other day, and we still need to decide what we're going to do for Jake and Julie's party. I need to run out to California tomorrow, and I'll be gone for a couple of weeks. Their wedding will be here before we know it. We need to start planning sooner rather than later, don't you think?"

She rubbed at her forehead, knowing he was right and hating him for it. "Fine, but I can't be gone for two hours— I don't care what Wendy says. I can't get behind on my workload."

"Perfect." A big smile broke onto to Tyler's face. Meg ignored how attractive it made him look.

After grabbing her coat where it hung on the back of her

door, they headed over to Franki's Pasty Shop. Meg walked in first, her stomach twisting with dread when she saw two people sitting inside the restaurant. They instantly started whispering as soon as they saw her. She didn't know them very well, but she recognized the two women, who'd been a year ahead of her in high school. Brynn and Heather were pretentious snobs back then, and not much had changed in the years since.

Brynn didn't bother to lower her voice as she said, "That's the one the mayor's son dumped. I heard she went crazy."

"Yep, that's me," Meg snapped. "You want to take a picture or something?"

Both women stopped talking, their mouths dropping open when Tyler walked in behind her.

He gave them a polite but cool smile before he said, "Is everything all right, Meg?"

He put a hand on the back of her shoulder. It felt weighted yet somehow anchoring. She didn't bother to shrug it off as she would have when they were younger.

"Everything is fine." Meg glared at the women until they both looked down at their meals.

She and Tyler walked up to the counter and rang the bell. Meg heard the shutter of a camera phone and knew the women were taking pictures of them, but when she turned around to flick them off, they were cleaning up the remnants of their meals and throwing their garbage into the trash. She hoped she wasn't about to have another picture go viral.

"Hey, Meg!" Franki, the shop's owner, came out from the back room. His eyes lit up when he saw Tyler. "Tyler, holy cow! It's been a minute."

He came around the counter and the two men did one of those bro hugs with loud pats on the back.

"Franki, how's it going?" Tyler asked.

"I didn't know you two knew each other," Meg said.

"James talked me into joining the track-and-field team my senior year," Tyler explained. "Franki and I ran long distance."

She frowned. "I don't remember you being on the track team."

He laughed. "That's because I only joined for a month to get Mitzy St. John's attention. When I realized she was more interested in baseball players, I quit the team."

Meg shook her head, trying to hold back a smile. "I should have known a woman was involved."

"This guy didn't need any help getting the ladies' attention." Franki tapped Tyler with his fist. "Especially when they found out he was in a band."

The humor left Meg. She turned to stare up at the menu behind the counter. She didn't know why something that happened decades ago bothered her so much. Tyler had always been swarmed by girls, from what she remembered in high school. But it made the moment that happened between them on his graduation night—a moment she'd thought about *way* too many times over the years—seem somehow cheap and unimportant. How many other women had he kissed that night with that level of heat?

Franki returned to the counter and took their orders. Meg asked for her usual vegetable pasty. She didn't say anything when Tyler ordered the same thing, but despite her earlier annoyance, his request sent a rush of warmth through her. When they were younger, anytime they had meals together, he'd go out of his way to order some meat dish, making some comment about how delicious it was because he knew she was a vegetarian.

They grabbed a table in the now empty restaurant. Franki's was more of a come-and-go establishment. There were only a few bright white tables set up, which stood out against the sharp red-tiled floor. Meg ran a finger nervously against the surface of the table as an uncomfortable silence settled between them.

Finally, she said, "About the other—"

"I wanted to—" Tyler said at the same time. His mouth tilted upward as he said, "You go first."

She took a deep breath and spewed out, "I'm sorry about the other night. I shouldn't have let Clarice get to me like that. It was incredibly rude to walk out on you like that, and I shouldn't have done it."

Tyler stared at Meg, taking in the pure misery on her face. Before he could respond, Franki delivered their food and drinks. Franki looked like he was going to say something else to Tyler, but he glanced between him and Meg, a grin appearing on his face. Shaking his head, he left them alone.

"Does that happen a lot?" Tyler asked.

"What?" she said, still not meeting his eyes as she cut into her pasty.

"The way this town treats you," Tyler said, his anger simmering.

He'd wanted to shout in the mayor's arrogant face for not stopping his wife's attack on Meg the other night. As it was, he'd barely resisted snapping at those two women just now to leave Meg alone.

It was ridiculous and unnerving to realize, but Tyler felt protective of Meg. It was an old, familiar feeling that he'd forgotten about. They might have fought when they were kids, but he was also always the first to cover for her when she needed it. He wondered if she remembered that.

Didn't people in this town understand they weren't good enough to breathe the same air as Meg? He might have always thought she was a pain in the ass, but he was the only one who got to decide that.

He continued to watch her as she ate a piece of pasty. It was strange. As he sat across from her, something flickered inside that he'd thought had abandoned him. He'd experienced the same feeling after their disastrous dinner. When she'd run out of the restaurant, he'd gone back to his parents', where he was staying while in town. And for the first time in weeks, he'd opened his journal and written lyrics. They weren't good lyrics, but it was still more than he'd been able to do in a long time.

It truly befuddled him. It didn't make any sense. But Meg seemed to be the key to unlocking his creativity.

He leaned across the table. "Meg..."

"Tyler..." she returned before her eyes drifted down. Her lips upturned into a sudden smirk.

"What?" he asked, wondering what brought on that expression. Not that he was objecting to it. He liked when Meg looked like that more than he wanted to acknowledge.

"Your shirt is dipping into your gravy."

He looked down and sure enough, his shirt was soaking up the warm sauce covering his flaky meal.

"Dammit." He grabbed a napkin and wiped at his shirt. It was going to leave a grease stain, but he had more pressing concerns.

He got back to the task at hand. "Do people in this town constantly harass you?"

Meg lifted a shoulder. "Lucas and I were the *it* couple

for years. People fawned over us because he was a legacy, the mayor's son. You know Mayor Beaumont has been in office since before we were born. People have fussed over Lucas his whole life—and then me by association. After we broke up, people came out of the woodwork, taking jabs at me because they didn't have to worry about any repercussions from the Beaumonts." Meg stared listlessly at the table. "As much as Clarice made insulting me a hobby, she wouldn't allow anyone else to publicly smear me when Lucas and I were together, because it didn't reflect well on her family. After we broke up, she no longer cared. She practically led the Meg Archer hate campaign. This town is small and full of busybodies who love to see the people they put on pedestals come crashing down. Others had no problem joining her."

"It's not right," Tyler argued.

A slight pang lanced his heart as her face turned to defeat. "It is what it is."

"Have you ever thought about leaving?"

Meg took another bite of her food, chewing it slowly before answering. "I think about it every day, but Holiday Bay is all I know. My best friend is here. My mom is here. My family—they're all here. I wouldn't know what to do with myself if I left. And I'm okay with that. The Bay is a part of who I am. Besides, something else will come along to take attention off me, and I'll be able to sink back into obscurity."

"Do you think so?" Tyler asked softly. "Not to put too fine a point on it, but your engagement ended a while ago. People still continue to talk about it."

"Believe it or not, it's not as bad as it used to be. Especially since the Holiday Boys reunited and did their charity concert last year."

She smiled and it brightened her face. Tyler was momentarily distracted by how beautiful she looked. It was brief, but her eyes sparkled in that second, and he felt himself unwillingly drawn to her. He wanted to lean toward her again, but he didn't want to risk dipping his shirt back into his food. Not when a thought was forming in his head.

Meg would hate it.

He couldn't wait to share it with her.

His face turned angelic. "I have an idea."

Recognizing the look on his face, Meg instantly turned cautious. She grabbed her fork and stabbed a piece of pasty. "About what?"

"What if you and I dated?" he suggested just as she took a bite of her food. She immediately began to choke, hitting her chest hard. "Are you okay? Do you need the Heimlich?"

She waved her hand in the air as she took a deep breath of air before grabbing her soda pop. She took several large gulps and started coughing again until her eyes watered.

"Are you sure you don't need the Heimlich?" he asked, getting ready to jump to his feet.

"Wh—" She coughed again. "What the hell are you talking about?"

"You said it yourself—something else needs to happen to distract people from what went down between you and Lucas."

Meg dabbed at her eyes, which had started running from coughing so hard. "And your solution is for us to *date*?"

"We don't actually have to date. Just…sort of…fake date." When she continued to stare at him like he'd lost his mind, he said, "Think about it, Meg. Narrow-minded jerks like Clarice Beaumont think they have the right to treat you like crap just because Lucas broke up with you.

They treat you like you don't matter or have feelings. Don't you think that's bull?"

"Of course I do!"

"Then what could be better than showing everyone that their opinions don't matter because you've not only moved on but you've moved up—by dating a Holiday Boy."

Meg's nose scrunched. He hated that he found it endearing.

"You think awfully highly of yourself," she said.

"It's not conceit or ego. It's simply a fact. I'm rich and famous, and as you just said, Holiday Boys saved our hometown. In the minds of the residents here, I've got to outrank Lucas Beaumont—don't you think?"

Meg's eyes narrowed. "So what exactly are you suggesting?"

"We date—or I should say—*fake date* until after Jake and Julie's wedding. And then you and I can have a very public breakup. In fact, you should dump me. Can you picture Clarice Beaumont's face if it gets around that you dumped a Holiday Boy? Maybe it'll make people think twice about who broke up with whom between you and Lucas."

Meg looked out the window, her expression thoughtful. He could tell she liked that idea very much.

She frowned as she looked back at him. "What's in it for you?"

Tyler grabbed his own silverware and speared a piece of his food. He didn't want to tell her the truth—that Meg might just be the answer to his writer's block. Even as they sat there, his fingers itched for his journal, wanting to put the moment into lyrics. Sitting across the table from this beautiful woman in a tiny shop in a small town, watching the way the light from above danced across her luminescent eyes.

But that wasn't the only reason he wanted to do it. The fact was he hadn't been able to stop thinking about Meg since their dinner.

No.

The real truth was he hadn't stopped thinking about her since Jake mentioned she was going to be Julie's maid of honor.

Hell, if he was completely honest with himself, he hadn't been able to stop thinking about her since they kissed all those years ago. It was a memory that haunted him for years.

He settled for a half-truth. "Let's just say this town's not the only one who needs a distraction."

"Explain," Meg insisted.

Tyler chewed his food, swallowing it before answering. "I've been in a creative rut lately. I can't seem to write anymore. I can't focus. I need a change—a distraction. Something to concentrate on other than my own life."

"You have writer's block."

"That's one way to put it," he grumbled. "So what do you say? Do you want to be my fake girlfriend?" A mischievous smile popped on his lips. "Come on, Meg—I dare you."

Meg bit her lip to keep from smiling back, but he still felt satisfaction when he saw the movement.

"Are you forgetting that you're suggesting dating me?" she said. "It's *me*, Tyler. You and I have never gotten along on a good day. How are we supposed to fake date each other?"

"We had our differences when we were kids—"

"Differences? Anytime we were around each other, it

was nuclear. We ended up in detention more than we did in class. You were my greatest enemy."

"People do grow up, Meg," Tyler reminded her gently. Her gaze wandered over his face, as though realizing he wasn't the little boy who used to chase her around with a Super Soaker anymore.

She slowly nodded but didn't quite cave in. "Let me think about it, okay?"

Tyler tried to hide his disappointment, but he tactfully changed the subject. "Fine. Let's talk about Jake and Julie's party. What do you think of naked acrobats?"

Meg threw her hands in the air. "Oh, for Pete's sake. How about I give you a long list of why that's a stupid idea. Reason number one…"

As she went off on a tangent, Tyler kept his expression carefully blank, while he silently basked in the glow of getting under her skin. He felt confident Meg would cave. He'd dared her. She'd never been able to resist his dares. They were her kryptonite.

Tyler already looked forward to their impending battle of wills. He just hoped that he would end up the winner of their little game.

But what the prize was, he still wasn't sure.

Chapter Six

Meg's mind wouldn't stay quiet as she pulled into her parents' driveway. She hadn't been able to stop thinking of Tyler, the cursed man, since he proposed his stupid idea.

And it *was* stupid. It was ludicrous. It was… Tyler.

It was hard for Meg to wrap her mind around the fact that Tyler, her childhood tormenter, might just end up being her knight in shining armor. As much as she hated to acknowledge it, Tyler had spoken the truth. Dating him would certainly get everyone talking about something other than pathetic Meg who got dumped by Lucas Beaumont.

Could her nemesis end up being her savior?

Ugh, she couldn't even picture it.

She got out of her car and strolled toward her childhood home.

Unlocking the front door, she called out, "Hello? Anyone here?"

"I'm in the kitchen," her mom responded.

Meg walked to the back of the house to find her mom assembling lasagna. The sight made her nostalgic. How many times had she come home after school to find her mom behind the kitchen island, putting together a delicious meal? She glanced around, taking in the white cupboards, sage-green subway-tile backsplash and white granite countertops. This place would always be home to her.

"Hey, Mom," Meg said, sitting on the bar stool opposite of where her mom stood.

"Hi, sweetie." Her mom finished layering the lasagna noodles before she grabbed the towel next to her to wipe her hands. She frowned when she glanced at Meg. "I mean this with all the kindness in my heart, but you look terrible."

Meg laughed. The sound turned into a sob as everything rushed over her. Clarice. Lucas. Tyler. The whole wretched town and their attitude toward Meg.

Her mom ran around the corner and wrapped her in her arms. "*Liebchen*, what's wrong?"

"Everything…" Meg sniffled. "Everything has been complete and utter garbage lately. Every time I step outside, someone in this stupid town makes a comment about Lucas. And then when Tyler and I met to discuss Jake and Julie's party, we ran into Clarice, who humiliated me. And it happened in front of Tyler freaking Evans of all people."

Her mom ran her fingers comfortingly through her hair. "Clarice Beaumont is a stuck-up snob. She always has been. Don't pay her any attention. Or anyone else for that matter."

"That's easier said than done. Especially when people *constantly* throw my breakup with Lucas in my face."

Her mom was quiet for a moment before she asked, "What did Tyler do?"

Meg opened her mouth to confess Tyler's ridiculous dare, but she held back. Instead she said, "He pretended he didn't know who the Beaumonts were—the mayor was there too—and then he asked them to leave."

Her mom chuckled as she pulled away from Meg so she could grab her dish. "I've always liked that about him. He's had a good head on his shoulders since he was little."

Meg let out a watery laugh. "Really? Because I remember you used to refer to him as a troublemaker or *that boy* when we were kids."

"Well, he *was* a troublemaker." Her mom put the lasagna into the oven and set the timer. "That didn't mean he wasn't a good kid."

"He was diabolical," Meg argued.

"Pfft." Her mom waved a hand through the air. "I always thought it was interesting how he used to go out of his way to involve you in his schemes."

"Yeah. 'Cause he was a prick."

"Language," her mom admonished despite Meg being thirty-six. "Was it him trying to get you in trouble? Or was it the proverbial pulling on pigtails to get your attention?"

Meg scoffed. "It wasn't pulling anything other than your leg if you thought he had any intentions other than being a big pain in my a—butt."

Her mom reached for a head of lettuce on the island. "Don't think I didn't notice how you'd go out of your way to get him in trouble too. Do you remember the time you put butter on his skateboard? You're lucky he didn't break his arm."

"I only did that because he threw my Barbies into the creek out back to see if they could swim. I ended up losing several, including my favorite one."

"Whatever you say, dear." Her mom pulled a knife from its wood block. "Do you want to stay for dinner?"

Meg glanced over at the oven. She hadn't missed that her mom had used her smaller baking dish to cook the lasagna.

"Are you sure there's going to be enough for you, me and Dad?"

"Oh, it's fine," her mom said, slicing through the lettuce with a loud whack.

That familiar sense of unease Meg always got these days when talking to her parents tingled down her spine. "Mom, what's going on?"

"What do you mean?"

"I feel like there's something wrong."

"What could be wrong?" Her mother's tone was innocent. A little *too* innocent.

"Is there something going on between you and Dad?"

The chopping increased. "Why would you ask that?"

"When I called Dad the other day, he said you were never at the campground anymore. And you got that job at Julie's. I don't care if Stephen has been getting Kimmy more involved with the campground lately—"

"Speaking of Stephen, did you ever call him?"

"Stop deflecting," Meg said. "Running the office has always been your baby."

"So that's a no, then."

"I'll call him," Meg insisted, unwilling to be distracted by guilt. She didn't miss the strain on her mom's face. "Mother!"

"What?"

"Tell me what's going on."

With a deep sigh that seemed to come from the depths of her soul, her mom put her knife down and gripped the side of the counter until her knuckles turned white. "We... we didn't want to tell you when you had so much else going on, what with Lucas and everything."

Meg went as still as a statue. "Tell me what?"

"Your father and I have decided to divorce."

Her head started to spin. "What are you talking about?"

Her mom grabbed a large bowl and threw the chopped lettuce into it. "Your father and I have been growing apart for some time. To be honest, I've never been happy with how he kept dismissing your efforts to be involved with the campground, simply because you were born female."

Meg felt sick to her stomach. "This is my fault?"

"Of course not—don't be ridiculous," her mom said firmly. "The campground is just one of many things we haven't been agreeing on. The truth is he's always put too many expectations on both you and your brother. I don't even know if Stephen would have wanted the business if your dad hadn't put so much pressure on him—"

"It wasn't like he ever said anything," Meg said bitterly. "He never once intervened on my behalf with Dad."

"Do you think your dad would have listened to him even if he did say something?" Her mom gave her a straight look. Meg hated to acknowledge that she was right. Stephen could have talked to their dad until he was blue in the face when they were younger. It most likely wouldn't have changed anything.

"Have you ever talked to your brother about any of this?" her mom continued. "Gone to him directly and asked where you could help with the business?"

Meg remained silent.

Her mother looked grim. "*Liebchen*, you and your brother really need to talk. I'm sure he'd be happy to get you more involved, especially as he's taking over more from your father."

"I have a life outside of the campground now," Meg replied. "A career."

Her mother huffed. "You hate that job."

When Meg opened her mouth to protest, her mom said, "You can be just as stubborn as your father—do you know that? He didn't give either you or your brother a choice in what you wanted to do with your lives. But that's also on me, and I have to live with that. I should have fought harder for you."

Her mom rubbed at her eyes tiredly. "And now with Stephen and Kimmy taking over, your dad has essentially put me out to pasture. He let me know that he thinks Kimmy should run the office…make it her own. He insisted on it, as a matter of fact. That's when things started to really fall apart between us. That campground is as much mine as it is his. I put my blood, sweat and tears into it. I sacrificed our family for it. And that's when I realized I was done. With all of it."

"I'm so sorry, Mom," Meg whispered. "Are you and Dad going to try counseling?"

"We've been in counseling for the past year and a half. We mutually agreed that this was the best course of action for both of us."

Meg felt like she didn't even recognize her own life anymore. Everything she thought was real was a facade. Her relationship with Lucas. Her parents' marriage.

Lies, lies, lies.

She took a deep breath and realized she couldn't get enough air in. Panic crept in.

Meg jumped to her feet. "I need to go."

"Stay and have dinner. We can talk some more."

"No." Meg immediately shook her head. "No, I need to go."

"Honey, I don't want you driving when you're so upset."

"I'm not upset," she lied. She walked quickly over to her mom and kissed her on the cheek. "I'm fine, really. I just need a second to process everything. I'll call you later, okay?"

"Meg…"

She didn't stick around. Hurrying out of the house and

into her car, she drove over the speed limit to get home. Her breathing grew increasingly shallower as she drove. Meg haphazardly parked her car in her spot and raced up the sidewalk leading to her apartment on legs that felt like jelly.

She couldn't believe it. Her parents were *divorcing*. She wondered if Stephen knew and guessed that he did. Her dad probably told him as soon as her parents agreed to separate.

Meg entered her apartment and shut the door firmly behind her. She leaned against it, closing her eyes. She tried taking several shallow breaths, but that didn't help to get her breathing back on track. Pulling her shirt off, she threw it onto the floor, followed by her bra. She kicked her shoes in the direction of her couch before she undid her jeans and pushed them down along with her underwear and socks. Stumbling her way into the bathroom, she turned on the shower, letting the hot water run until the air grew thick and foggy.

Meg wiped at the moisture gathered on the mirror so she could stare at her reflection. Her skin was ashen. Her cheeks seemed hollower than normal. The dark circles under her eyes were even more pronounced.

Looking away, she stepped into the shower, tilting her head to let the water hit her skin, hoping the heat would return some of her coloring. As she got her hair wet, she took a deep breath in.

Steam greeted her lungs. The air felt suffocating. She tried to breathe again but couldn't seem to get enough cool, clean air inside her body.

Meg ripped the shower curtain back so that fresh air could hit her face. She desperately sucked in a breath that wasn't as stifling, but her anxiety made it difficult to fill her lungs. Turning back to the shower handles, she turned off the water with hands that shook.

Meg took a couple steps backward until her back hit the wall. She slid down to the floor of the tub. Pulling her trembling legs toward her, Meg rested her forehead against her knees. It was only then that she broke. A soft sob escaped her mouth followed by another.

She cried out her pain over Lucas, her fury with Clarice and her confusion over her parents.

Her mind drifted to Tyler.

Her whole life was a lie.

So what was one more to add to the list? Stumbling out of the tub, she hurried into the hallway, water dripping onto the carpet. Grabbing her phone, Meg sent Tyler a two-worded message.

I'm in.

Chapter Seven

Tyler caught glimpses of Lake Michigan as he drove his rental car to the studio in Charlevoix where the Holiday Boys were practicing for their upcoming tour in Europe. They wouldn't leave until the beginning of the year, but aside from the charity concert they'd done for Holiday Bay, they hadn't actually toured together in over fifteen years.

It was one of the most anticipated events of the year. They'd already sold out every venue. All the Boys were in agreement that they needed to practice to ensure this was their best tour ever. It was what their fans deserved after waiting so long for them to reunite. Tyler couldn't afford to be distracted right now.

But he was.

He'd been in meetings over the last two weeks in California. It had taken all his willpower during his last meeting not to pull out his phone to see if Meg had responded to his suggestion yet. He had already checked his cell enough while he was away.

Tyler hadn't seen or spoken to Meg in the time he'd been gone. He was trying to respect her, give her time to think over his proposal. But the anticipation had been killing him. He didn't fully understand why he wanted her to say yes so badly. Sure, he wanted to help her, and she was inspiring him to write again, but…there was more to it than that. He wanted to see *his* Meg again. The one willing to fight the world with so much spirit that no one could break her.

So it had been a relief when he'd finally received a text from her on his flight back to Michigan, agreeing to their plan. In fact, it was surprising how relieved he'd felt. He hadn't realized how stressed it was making him, waiting for her answer.

After parking his car, Tyler walked into the dance studio. He paused as he took in his friends, who'd arrived before him. James was talking to their choreographer, practicing some of the moves the woman showed him in front of a set of large mirrors that ran the length of one side of the room. He stumbled as he turned, causing Tyler's lips to tilt upward.

James had always been the weakest dancer of the group, but at least he tried. Paul was on his phone, pacing in front of the large curtained windows on the opposite side of the studio. Knowing Paul, he was talking to the director of his hit reality show, *First Comes Marriage*. Their other bandmate, Zan, sat in a folding chair, a frown on his face as he read something on his phone. Jake hadn't arrived yet, but that wasn't surprising. Jake was always notoriously late for everything.

Tyler strode over to Zan. "Hey, man. You just get in?"

Zan lived in Maine. After the band broke up, he'd turned to writing, becoming an international best-selling author.

"Hmm? Oh, yeah. Just flew in." He typed something into his phone before looking up at Tyler. "How about you?"

"Same."

Tyler frowned as he looked at his friend. Zan had tight lines around his mouth. His short black hair was sticking up at different angles, as though he'd run his fingers through it several times recently.

"Everything okay?" he asked.

"Yeah, it's…" Zan rubbed at his face. "It's Mary."

He and Mary had been married for years and had two beautiful children.

"Is she all right?"

"I hope so…" His worry was evident. "I mean, I think she is. She's just been feeling off lately. She's getting some tests done soon."

"What do you mean by 'off'?"

Zan frowned. "She went to her ophthalmologist a couple of weeks ago, and they saw something of concern on her eye exam. They suggested she go see her primary doctor. She'd already scheduled an appointment to meet with her anyway. She keeps getting bruises and she can't figure out how they happened, and she's exhausted all the time. Like *barely able to get out of bed* exhausted. Her mom's staying with us to help with the kids while I'm here."

"Hey. If you can't do this right now"—Tyler nodded around the room—"say the word, and we can reschedule. Family comes first."

"It's fine." He put on a brave smile. "Mary insisted I come. You know what a huge fan she is of Holiday Boys."

Tyler chuckled. Zan and Mary's love story had started when the model showed up to one of Zan's book signings and asked him to sign her Holiday Boys' CD. It had been pretty much love at first sight for the both of them.

"When does she see her doctor?" Tyler asked.

"Next week."

He squeezed Zan's shoulder. "Keep me updated, okay? And if either of you need anything, you let me know."

He gave a strained grimace. "I will. Thanks, Ty."

Tyler left him and walked over to Paul, who had finished his call. He was staring out the window, his hands clasped behind his back.

"What's up, man?" Tyler said.

Paul smiled, though he too seemed a bit distracted. "Hey. How was your flight?"

"Good. Uneventful, thankfully."

Other than Meg's text. That was definitely something of note.

"What about you?" Tyler asked. "Where'd you fly in from this time?"

Paul gave his signature smirk. "Just came in from New York. We finished filming."

"And how's *First Comes Marriage* this season?" Tyler grinned. "You finally succeed in marrying two strangers who actually want to *stay* married?"

"Guess you'll have to watch the show and find out," Paul said before a familiar, determined expression popped on his face. "You know, anytime you want to be on the show, just let me know."

Tyler groaned. Paul had been trying to get Tyler and Jake on his show for years, since they were the only two single members. Now that Jake was officially off the market, it looked like their bandmate was going to focus his efforts entirely on Tyler.

"No, thanks," he grumbled.

"But think of the ratings," Paul implored.

Tyler crossed his arms over his chest. "As I've asked you every time you bring this up, why don't you do the show?"

"I can't—I'm the host," Paul repeated as he always did. "Besides, I'd rather tie weights to my ankles and go swimming in Lake Michigan in December than get married."

"And you think I want to get married?"

"Please. You *scream* desperate for married life."

"Umm, thanks?"

"Don't mention it," Paul replied dismissively. "I actually just got off the phone with my director. The network wants to do an upcoming season in Holiday Bay."

Tyler's eyebrows shot up. "Why?"

"They think it'll give the show a new twist. Finding love in a small town. Plus, thanks to all the recent publicity the Bay has received over the past year, Shawnee—she's the show's director—said, and I quote, 'the town is absolutely the perfect idyllic setting' and 'made for the camera.'"

"That'll give the town more publicity. You'll have to tell Julie. It'll do wonders for her store."

"Yeah, and with Jake living there now and you going back to visit your family all the time, we're pretty much guaranteed to get a lot of contestants to choose from. Women will apply just in the hopes of getting a glimpse of you two. They'll probably hope you'll be a contestant—"

"I'm not doing your show," Tyler said firmly.

"Bah, fine." Paul threw his hands into the air just as his phone started ringing again. He answered the call with a professional, "Paul Rodriguez. Hi, Dorian…"

Tyler shook his head as he walked away. As much as Paul had been a jokester and the fan-labeled "bad boy" of the group when they were younger, he'd surprisingly turned into a very astute businessman who took his position in the entertainment world seriously.

As Tyler strolled over to James, Jake burst into the room. "I'm so sorry I'm late."

James laughed. "It would have been more surprising if you'd been on time."

Jake walked over to his cousin and hugged him with a one-hand slap on the back before doing the same to Tyler.

"How was it traveling?" Jake asked them both. "No issues, I hope."

"I drove in," James said.

"You need a place to stay while you're here?" Jake asked him.

"No, I'm good—thanks. I'm staying with my parents."

"Aunt Terri is always in my ear about how she doesn't see her baby boy enough these days," Jake teased.

"Yeah, yeah," James replied good-naturedly. "She's been giving me the same guilt trip."

"Mason come with you?" Tyler asked about James's husband.

Neither Tyler nor Jake missed how James's face tautened. "No, he wanted to stay in Detroit. He had a bunch of meetings with the director of our renovation show."

"You'd think he was the star instead of you," Jake muttered.

"Don't start," James said shortly.

"How are the wedding plans going?" Tyler asked Jake in order to steer the conversation out of dangerous territory.

He instantly brightened, a happy smile appearing on his face. "Good—that's why I'm late, actually. Julie and I went to a food tasting this morning. I think we have our caterer."

"That's great," Tyler said. "But how did you explain it so they don't go running to the press? Did you tell them it was for your wedding?"

"No, we told them we were hosting a surprise party and left it at that."

"Good," Tyler replied. "That's one less thing to worry about."

"Yeah, it's been a little hectic lately, but I want to make sure everything is perfect for Julie, especially since this is her first marriage." Tyler and James exchanged amused smiles. Jake looked like a lovesick puppy whenever he spoke about his fiancée.

Jake turned to Tyler. "Speaking of the wedding, how are things going with you and Meg? Have you come up with the perfect idea for pre-wedding party?"

He snorted. "Well, we haven't killed each other yet, if that's what you're asking. But no, we haven't come up with something we can agree on."

"She hasn't suggested leaping out of an airplane or something wild?" James asked with a grin.

"Actually"—Tyler frowned a little—"her ideas have been really...tame. I almost wish she'd suggested something crazy. It'd be more in line with the Meg I knew."

"I do think she mentioned something about bungee jumping off a hot-air balloon, but Julie nixed the idea," Jake remarked.

Tyler couldn't stop the warmth from spreading in his chest. "Yeah. That sounds more like Meg."

When he looked at his two closest friends, they were wearing the same pleased expressions.

"What?" he asked cautiously.

"Nothing," Jake said. "You sound almost—dare I say it—affectionate when you mention Meg."

"I do not," Tyler argued. "Meg tells everyone that I'm her mortal enemy. Just ask her."

"And now he sounds disgruntled," James added.

He sent them both a scathing look. "Shut up."

"But you have to agree, she's your type, right?" Jake said. "You've always gravitated toward women like her. Shorter, full figured. Full of sass."

"Hmm." James tapped his chin with his index finger. "You know, I never really thought about it, but he does have a type similar to Meg. He has for years."

"I have not," Tyler said weakly before glaring at James. "Besides, how would you know what Meg looks like these days? You haven't seen her in years."

James gave him a dirty look. "Unlike you two heathens, I've actually snuck back to Holiday Bay multiple times over the years to visit my family—"

"I had no reason to come ba—" Jake said.

"I've been back—" Tyler defended himself.

"And believe it or not," James continued, talking over them, "I haven't gone out of my way to live like a hermit when I do come back to visit. I've seen Meg more than once over the past twenty years."

"You never said anything about her," he grumbled.

James frowned at the ground. "I never talked to her. I saw her from a distance a few times. She was always with her fiancé."

Jake looked confused. "I thought you said you were on the track team with Lucas. I assumed you two were friends. You never said hi to him?"

"No," James said shortly. "Anyway, I agree with Jake. Meg's totally your type."

Tyler scowled. "It doesn't matter if she is."

"So you agree that she's your type," Jake replied.

He walked over to the dance bar next to the mirror and gripped it. "Meg's life is in Holiday Bay—mine's not. Besides, did you not hear me when I said she still thinks I'm the devil?"

Both of his friends were quiet for a minute before Jake said gently, "Do you want her to think of you as something else?"

Tyler swallowed. Did he? He hadn't stopped thinking about her since he saw her last. He'd felt like the world lifted off his shoulders when she'd agreed to fake date him, an idea he'd been obsessively thinking about ever since he proposed it. He was really looking forward to it—to spending time with Meg and getting to know her all over again. But did he want more?

"It doesn't matter what I want," Tyler repeated, turning around to face the other two. "Do I like spending time with her? Yes. The few interactions I've had with her recently, I really enjoyed. But like I said, she still sees me as her childhood nemesis."

"So change her mind," James said simply.

"Why would I want to do that?" Tyler replied stubbornly.

The family resemblance between Jake and James was remarkable as they both gave him matching annoyed looks.

"Because you like her," Jake said.

"I never said I liked her."

James crossed his arms over his chest. "You don't have to say anything. We know you better than anyone. We know you're interested in her."

Tyler's eyes narrowed. "Is that so?"

"That's so," Jake said. "If you weren't interested, you wouldn't keep insisting she hates your guts while simultaneously looking like you swallowed a lemon."

He instantly smoothed out his face. "So what do you want me to do about it?"

"Stop being a stubborn ass, for one thing," James remarked.

Tyler leaned against the dance bar behind him. "She's still heartbroken over her engagement ending."

"It's been a year and a half," Jake replied. "Besides, Julie told me Lucas and Meg weren't exactly the happiest couple, even when they were together. Show Meg you won't make her miserable like Lucas did."

Tyler glanced up to the ceiling before finally caving. "How?"

Jake gave him a level look. "Woo the woman, idiot."

"You're Tyler Evans," James added. "You were in *People* magazine's *Sexist Man Alive* issue."

Tyler rolled his eyes. "We all were. Sexiest boy band of the year."

"All we're saying is you've dated A-list celebrities," Jake reminded him. "Some of those women are not known for having the easiest personalities, yet you were still able to get them to fall for you. Use your skills and woo Meg Archer."

Tyler's lip curled. "Please stop saying the word *woo*."

Jake ignored him. "Flirt with the woman. Find excuses to touch her."

"Look lovingly into her eyes," James said just as Paul walked over to them.

"What's this?" he asked. "James, did you tell them your news? A network is interested in picking up his home-renovation show."

"That's great!" Tyler responded. "Congratulations!"

"It's all thanks to Paul," James said, rubbing the back of his neck sheepishly. "I'm just a renovator. He's the producer."

Paul grinned. "The show will be the perfect vehicle to launch my production company."

"Congrats, man," Jake said. "You've been talking about doing that for years."

"Yeah," he acknowledged. "I have the connections now, but I was waiting for the right show to come along. It finally feels like the right timing." He nodded at James. "But we can talk more about that later. What were you talking about before I came over? It sounded good."

James snorted. "Tyler's love life."

Paul's eyes sparked with interest. "Are we giving Tyler dating advice? Why are you listening to either of these two knuckleheads? Always come to me on matters of the heart. I have a whole show related to this very subject, after all."

"Pretty sure that show doesn't make you an expert on jack crap," James muttered, but Paul waved him off.

"Let me pull up a chair and give you my long list of dos and don'ts," he told Tyler. "First off—"

"Yeah, no. Not from you," Tyler said. "I don't want to end up with a restraining order against me."

Paul gripped his chest. "You wound me."

"Gentlemen," the choreographer interrupted. "Are we ready?"

Zan walked over to them, worry still evident on his face. "Let's get going."

He met Tyler's eyes. Tyler silently asked him again if he wanted to do this, and Zan gave a tight nod in response.

As they got into their places, Jake turned to him and said, "This weekend is Harvest Festival."

Harvest Festival was always a big deal in Holiday Bay. Shops would get decked out in fall decor. The local orchards offered pumpkin picking and fresh cider and doughnuts. The town also hosted their annual band contest. That was where the Holiday Boys first performed.

"Harvest Festival?" Paul asked, clearly eavesdropping. "We should do a surprise appearance."

"I can't," Zan replied. "I need to run back to Maine and check on the family."

"No worries," Tyler said quickly in case any of the guys tried to talk Zan into staying. He wasn't sure if the rest of the band knew what was going on with Mary. It was really up to him to share that news.

As the guys worked through the dance steps the choreographer showed them, Tyler's attention kept going back to Meg. Did he want to really date her, or was he just doing this to help with his writer's block? He couldn't deny that he found her incredibly attractive.

But date her?

His thoughts were conflicted, but he knew one thing for sure. Meg had absolutely zero interest in dating him. Maybe he could use this fake dating as an opportunity to test the waters.

When they got a break, he grabbed his phone and sent her a text. I think we should make our debut at Harvest Festival this weekend.

He had to wait until they were wrapped up for the day before he could check his messages again. There were plenty from his agent and various other business people, but there was only one text he read.

Meg's response.

It's a "date."

Chapter Eight

Meg's stomach hurt as she paced around her apartment.

What the hell had she been thinking, agreeing to this stupid fake dating idea?

She'd agreed in a moment of weakness. And sure, there was a lot of appeal to Tyler's plan. A part of her really couldn't wait to see Clarice Beaumont and everyone else's face when she showed up hanging off the arm of one of the most famous men in the world. They'd looked down on her for years, never thinking she was good enough for Lucas.

Never good enough for the campground. Never good enough for the mayor's son.

She was about to show them all that maybe—just maybe—she was enough in the eyes of someone. Someone whose name everyone knew. She'd caught herself a bigger, better fish—at least, that was what some of the people in town would think.

But…it was Tyler. Tyler, who'd either teased her mercilessly when they were kids or ignored her when she was a teenager. At least, until the night he'd kissed so long ago.

She didn't know how she was going to fake having feelings for him. She'd always been so stupidly impulsive. It would be her greatest downfall one day, she just knew it.

Her phone buzzed indicating she had a text. She opened the screen to see a message from her brother.

Hey, sis! I was hoping to catch you. It's been a minute. Do you have time to talk?

I'm headed out, but I'll call you soon.

He responded with a thumbs-up emoji. She tried not to feel too guilty about that, but she wasn't in the mood for family drama tonight. Not when she was about to go on her first fake date with Tyler Evans.

A knock on the door interrupted her internal berating. She glanced at the hallway mirror. She'd dressed for a fall evening in October, wearing a long flowing skirt paired with knee-high brown faux-leather boots and a thick, cream-colored cable-knit sweater.

She'd pulled her golden-brown hair into a loose bun on top of her head, but a few strands had come loose, fluttering down around her rose-colored cheeks. She examined her face briefly, only seeing the imperfections. How the loose hair did nothing to hide the wrinkles on her face, or how the sweater seemed to emphasize her round stomach instead of hiding it as she'd hoped.

Sighing, she opened the door and immediately wanted slam it shut again. Tyler stood in front of her looking like a slice of heaven on legs. He wore a red-and-black flannel shirt under a green cargo jacket. His beard wasn't as scruffy as the last time she saw him but trimmed neatly against his cheeks. His jeans looked as though they'd been painted on him. He wore them with a pair of brown work boots. Everything about him screamed rich and stylish. Meg felt like a slug in comparison.

No one would believe they were actually dating.

"Wow," Tyler said, his eyes running over her. "You look great." She gave him a narrowed glare. He tilted his head. "What? I can't say you look great?"

"We're not really dating. Save it for when other people are actually listening."

She turned to grab her purse where she left it on the back of the couch. Tyler followed her inside, stopping just inside the living room. His eyes scanned the area, and she tried to see it through his eyes. Her apartment wasn't anything fancy. She had mismatched furniture that she'd found on discount, an ugly beige couch that was the most comfortable piece of furniture to ever exist, which she paired with a floral blue recliner chair and a midcentury green one. Behind the two chairs was a fireplace, the bricks whitewashed. The dark wood mantle had different knickknacks on it that she'd collected over the years. A large crystal ball she bought when she'd visited Salem, Massachusetts, and a 1930s composition doll she found in an antique shop, its face and eyes cracked. Through Tyler's eyes, the place must have looked like a dump. She was about to launch into a speech regarding social differences when a slight smile appeared on his mouth.

"What?" she asked defensively.

"No need to get your hackles up," he said. She opened her mouth to tell him off, but before she could speak, he continued, "This place is just so you—cool and eclectic."

Meg paused in the process of picking up her purse. "You think I'm cool?"

"And eclectic."

And then Tyler honest-to-god winked at her.

What in the...?

She ignored the fluttering feeling that suddenly inhabited her stomach as he walked over to her small hallway table. He picked up a medium-sized statue of a fertility goddess.

When he lifted his eyebrow, she started fumbling with her purse strap. "I bought it as a joke, okay?"

"You hoping to have a ton of kids?"

Meg stared him down. "It amazes me that you even know what that is."

Tyler gave a one-shouldered shrug. "I've traveled all over the world. In between concerts, I'd take in as much local culture as I could. I learned about this particular fertility goddess on one of my trips." He gave her devilish smile that made her heart pick up its pace. "I was spotted at an Aztec ruin years ago when the Holiday Boys were in our prime. The amount of fans that showed up at our concert that night with signs regarding the love goddess, Xōchiquetzal, should have broken records."

Meg grinned, despite her mood. "I bet that was a sight to see."

"It was horrifying, considering that most of our fans back then were tweens."

Meg laughed. As they exited the apartment, she felt herself relaxing for the first time in weeks.

"So what was the joke?" Tyler asked.

"Hmm?"

"You said you bought the statue as a joke. What was the joke?"

"Oh," Meg replied as they stepped outside. The cold evening air smacked her in the face, and she pulled her coat closed. "I gave it to Lucas as an April fool's joke. I told him I wanted us to have at least two dozen kids, and I bought the statue for good luck. He looked horrified. He said I could keep the statue at my place."

Meg frowned as she thought back to his odd reaction. He'd played it off like he was joking, but there'd been something in his reaction that she hadn't picked up on at the time. Panic, perhaps?

She blinked away the memory. No need to look back and overanalyze her relationship with Lucas for the millionth time.

"Do you want kids?" Tyler asked, his tone serious.

"It was just a joke," Meg replied.

Even if she did want kids, she was already thirty-six. Her biological clock had been ticking. She'd thought more than once what it'd be like to have a baby. Lucas never brought up the subject. He'd certainly been in no hurry to become a father, since not only did Meg take birth control but he'd also wore condoms whenever they'd been intimate.

She really needed to stop thinking about Lucas. He was, after all, dead to her.

When Tyler put his hand her on her waist to guide her to the passenger door, she stopped abruptly at his touch. His hand accidently brushed her bottom due to the sudden jolt. Meg's cheeks flushed in response.

Tyler stepped back, looking mortified. He held his hands up in front of him. "Sorry—I didn't mean to touch you inappropriately."

"Does that include putting your hand on my waist?"

"Meg," he said in a slow tone as though speaking to a child, "if people are going to believe we're dating, we're going to need to touch once in a while. No one is going to believe this if you act like a skittish animal anytime I get close to you."

Meg crossed her arms over her chest. "What exactly do you mean by touching?"

Tyler's eyebrow lifted. "You want to break down the rules right here and now?"

"It seems like we're going to need to."

He let out an exasperated breath. "Okay, but let's get in the car before we hash out our relationship."

Before she could stop him, he opened the car door for her. When she just stood there, he said, "Are you getting in, or are we standing here all night?"

"Fine," Meg said waspishly. Once she was inside, Tyler shut the door before getting into the driver's side. He started the engine and adjusted the heat so that the car could warm up.

"All right," he said. "You want ground rules, let's talk ground rules."

Meg stared out the front window. "How physical are you planning on taking this?"

When he didn't answer, she glanced over at him. Despite the beard and evening darkness, she could still pick up the slight blush in his cheeks.

She opened her mouth to mention it, but he spoke before she could say anything. "We should definitely hold hands."

Meg nodded. "That seems fair."

"And when we're not holding hands, we should find another way to keep touching. You put your arm around my waist, I hug you. Things like that."

Meg gulped, tensing the muscles around her diaphragm until it hurt. "O-Okay."

He frowned at her. "Are you all right?"

"Yep. Yes. Totally fine over here."

"Meg…" Tyler turned in his seat. "I'm not going to put you in a position you don't want to be in. I'd never want to do something you're not comfortable with. If you're not good with any of this, we won't do it."

"Just like that?" she said, not sure if she was feeling relieved or mad that he wanted to stop fake dating her before they'd even started.

"Just like that," he repeated back to her.

She stared at the lights on the dashboard. She could easily open the door and go back into her apartment. She had a carton of almond-milk ice cream sitting in her freezer, and there was a new true crime show debuting on TV tonight. It was her typical Saturday night. Hiding from the world, burying her head in misery.

Clarice's smug face flashed in her mind, and she raised her chin. Looking over at Tyler, she said, "No, I want to do this."

"Okay, then here." He held out his hand to her, palm up. She looked at him in confusion and he said, "We need to practice so we can really sell this."

Meg gave a short nod before placing her hand in his. Tyler laced his fingers with hers. His huge hand engulfed hers, and she could do nothing but stare at it. Her treasonous mind wondered what else those hands could engulf on her body.

"Are you sure you're okay?" Tyler's voice sounded different… Was that humor? When she gave him a questioning look, he looked pointedly down at where her wrist was resting against his. "Your heart is racing."

She yanked her hand away and didn't miss his low laugh. It did something to her. She shifted in her seat, ignoring the sudden tingling sensation dancing across her insides. "I'm nervous. I'm not used to lying."

"I know that," he said. "You were always a terrible liar. That's why we got busted all the time when you came up with a scheme."

"My schemes were brilliant," she argued. "You could

never execute them in a timely manner, so we always got caught, thus leading me to confess."

"Sure, Meg," he replied. If she didn't know any better, she would swear she heard affection in his tone.

As he pulled away from the apartment, he said, "Have you given any more thought to Jake and Julie's party?"

"Yes, I did come up with a brilliant idea. One that even *you* won't be able to disagree with." When he gave her an expectant look, she said proudly, "Axe throwing."

"Axe throwing…"

"Yes, it's got a party vibe and not even the bachelor party could say it was dumb."

"No, of course we won't say it's dumb. Because chances are we'll be so blitzed at that point we won't even know where we are. And you want us to throw pointy weapons?"

Well…she hadn't thought about that.

Meg threw her hands into the air. "I give up. You and I are never going to agree on anything. Everything I want to do is too boring for you, and everything you come up with will make Julie pass out in horror. This is hopeless. I'm going to tell Julie we can't agree on anything and be done with this whole affair."

"Calm down," Tyler said. "We still have time before they're going to get married. We'll be able to figure something out."

"Then tell me what your next brilliant idea is," she ranted.

Tyler's smile turned evil, and Meg knew she was already going to hate it.

"We can do a circus theme. Invite some clowns…"

Meg glared. She'd been pretty fearless when she was a child, with the exception of a few minor phobias. One major fear was creepy, freaky clowns—something that Tyler was well aware of.

"You *know* I think clowns were invented in hell. Absolutely not."

They continued to banter about the party until they reached the festival. As they got out of the car, Tyler held his hand out to her. Taking a deep breath, Meg put hers in his, and they made their way to the center of town. People stopped in the middle of conversations as they passed. Some openly stared. Whispers began to explode through the crowded Main Street as they walked. She saw Brynn and Heather in the distance, staring at them open-mouthed, and she stood a little taller as she remembered their hateful words at Franki's.

As Meg and Tyler continued to traverse the crowd, they neared the fairground. She could see the large stage set up in the distance where the band contest was taking place. On the opposite side of the fairground, a line of junky cars was getting prepared for the demolition derby that'd take place after the contest wrapped. A band on stage began performing Journey's "Don't Stop Believin'," which made the crowd go wild, especially when they got to the line *Born and raised in South Detroit*. Tyler stopped walking so he could listen to the band, a warm smile appearing on his face.

Meg tested the waters and leaned against his arm, their clasped hands trapped between their hips. Tyler looked her way briefly. The approval she saw in his eyes made her glow.

"I didn't know you were a Journey fan," she said.

"First of all, everyone is a Journey fan. But I was thinking more about how everything started for us on that stage," he said, nodding toward where the band was. "Jake, James and I performed together on that stage. It's where we met Zan and Paul for the first time. Where Holiday Boys were born."

Meg looked at it and then took in their surroundings. For the most part, the crowd didn't notice Tyler was there. They were too busy watching the show in front of them. But there were people who recognized him.

Townsfolk were being respectful and giving him his space. That was just the way Holiday Bay was. Tyler was a part of this town. He always would be, so people left him alone. He was just another member of the community enjoying Harvest Festival. That didn't mean they had forgotten how far he'd gone either. More than one person was whispering about them or taking his picture.

Meg shook her head before she turned her attention toward the band. "Sometimes I forget that outside of our town, you're actually a ridiculously famous person. That anywhere other than Holiday Bay, you wouldn't be able to stand in a crowd like this without getting swarmed. You've always been just Tyler to me."

She felt his eyes on her face, and when she looked at him, she saw that he stared at her with a soft expression.

"What?" she asked.

"Nothing." He glanced down at the ground somewhat bashfully. "It's nice to hear that. Most people think of me as Tyler Evans, famous singer and songwriter first. It's good to be just Tyler with you. You know what I mean?"

She didn't. She really had no clue what his life had been like after he left Holiday Bay. It made her a little sad when she thought about it. He'd always been such a huge part of her life. Now he was virtually a stranger. That was probably more her fault than his. After they'd kissed on his graduation night and he'd taken off without a word, she'd done her best to block him out of her head, like she always did when the going got tough. Instead, she'd accepted a date from Lucas Beaumont and spent years wasting all her energy on him. The couple of times she'd seen Tyler in the distance when he had come home over the years, she'd hidden from him.

She could only guess what his life was like now. Julie had told her about how crazy fans could get over Jake, though Jake had stayed in the spotlight after leaving Holiday Boys, whereas Tyler had gone more behind the scenes. But she had seen him on enough award shows over the years to know that he was a beloved figure with tons of adoring fans—tons of adoring women.

"Hey," he said, interrupting the internal downward spiral that she was about to go on. "Let's find some food. I really hope they still have those caramel apples. God, I've dreamt of those so many times over the years."

"That sounds good," Meg replied. "They should be off of East and Main if they put the food vendors in their normal spot."

They continued to walk to the center of town and made their way over to the food truck area. As they stood in line, a group of teenage girls approached them, bursting out with nervous giggles as they moved. Teenagers were the one rare group that never minded *not* giving the Holiday Boys their space when they were in town. Meg almost envied their tenacity. Once upon a time, she'd had the same carefree, can-do attitude.

"Mr. Evans, could we get a picture with you?" one asked.

Tyler gave Meg an apologetic side-eye before saying, "Sure."

The girls started arguing over who would take the picture and who would stand next to Tyler.

"Here, I'll take it," Meg offered, and the girls screeched their thanks so loud she was confident she lost some of her hearing.

After the girls left, Meg and Tyler were able to order their food. He got fresh corn on the cob, a veggie sub and his beloved caramel apple. Meg got a cup of mac-and-cheese bites. She nibbled on one as Tyler scarfed his food down.

"Sorry about the picture," he said between bites.

"It's fine. Comes with the territory, right?"

"Yeah, but I'm still sorry," Tyler said before eyeing her food. "Not hungry?"

Meg shrugged. "I guess I'm feeling a bit nervous by all this." She nodded toward the gawkers before popping a piece of mac in her mouth and chewing it methodically. "You didn't have to pay for the food. I don't want you to waste your money on me."

He gave her a look. It made her feel like he was dissecting her to see what was going on inside.

"It's not a big deal. If it bothers you so much though, you can pay the next time we go out."

"Fine," she agreed.

Tyler bit into his apple, a happy sound escaping him.

"God, these are just as good as I remember," he said, wolfing it down. Caramel collected at the corner of his mouth.

Meg's lips ticked up. "You have a little something…"

She reached over and wiped at the caramel. He stilled as she pulled her thumb away and licked it on instinct, her tongue darting out to savor the flavor. Tyler made a noise that he quickly turned into a cough.

Meg blushed brightly. What the hell was she thinking? This wasn't a real date. She shouldn't be flirting with him.

Jumping to her feet, she said in a high-pitched voice. "You ready to go?"

Tyler cleared his throat as he stood slowly. "Sure."

Once they finished throwing away their trash, he grabbed her hand again. She ignored how natural it felt to have his fingers laced with hers.

They entered town square, which had been set up for dancing. Four large posts connected together by a long string of Edison bulbs created a dance space cast in warm light. Another makeshift stage was set up in front of Julie's shop. A female-led band performed for the crowd, playing guitars and banjos. A banner hung up behind the musicians, their name—Mums and Daughters—printed across it. Meg smiled, recognizing their local Mumford & Sons tribute band.

Meg and Tyler continued through the crowd. Due to Tyler's close proximity distracting her, it took Meg a minute to realize people were losing their ever-loving minds. Even though everyone was still being respectful of Tyler's space, excitement sizzled through the air. People waved frantically at him like he was their best friend or took selfies as he and Meg passed, making sure to get Tyler in their shot. Considering that so far the evening had been pretty tame, the change in atmosphere seemed sudden and extreme. Then things made sense when someone called her name.

"Meg!"

Meg looked over the shoulder of a man wearing a cowboy hat to see Julie waving at her from the side of the stage. Standing next to her was Jake. No wonder the crowd was slowly losing their minds. With two Holiday Boys at the festival, Meg was surprised people hadn't spontaneously combusted.

"Hey," Tyler said when they walked up to Jake and Julie.

Jake didn't look remotely surprised to see them together. "Hi, glad you were able to make it."

Julie, however, looked like a fish hanging from a fishing line, her mouth opening and closing as she stared at Meg, then Tyler, then at their hands clasped together.

"What—" she started to say, but they were interrupted by a large man hurrying over to them. Meg's stomach twisted when she saw it was Mayor Beaumont, followed closely by Clarice.

"Well, as I live and breathe," the mayor said loudly, drawing the attention of the few remaining people who weren't staring at them. "Two of our hometown heroes returning to our little festival."

He completely ignored Julie and Meg, but that wasn't unusual. The mayor never bothered with the little people unless it was an election year.

"Mayor Beaumont," Jake said stiffly. Tyler didn't say anything at all.

"Meg, what a surprise to see you here, dear." Clarice's eyes missed nothing as she stared down at their hands. "You certainly seemed to have moved on quickly."

Meg lifted her chin. "I thought it was time to get back into the dating pool."

Clarice looked like she recently drank poison. "And how convenient, especially after our recent conversation that Lucas had also moved on."

Witch.

The woman never missed anything.

To Meg's embarrassment, Tyler dropped her hand, but an instant later, he wrapped his arm around her waist, pulling her completely against his side.

"Meg, have I ever told you how much I love this song?" he said, continuing to act as though Clarice didn't exist.

Meg looked at him, and her breath stumbled in her chest. He was staring at her like she was the only person that existed in the world. Maybe he should have gone into acting.

"You want to dance?" He brushed his finger along her cheek to tuck a loose strand of hair behind her ear. Her skin felt electrified where he'd touched her.

"I'd love to," she said. She turned back to Clarice. "If you'll excuse us."

"Oh," the mayor said, "but I wanted to get a pic—"

Tyler pulled Meg onto the dance floor as the band played Mumford & Sons's *I Will Wait*. Tyler grabbed both of Meg's hands and pulled her toward him, one of his palms dropping to her waist so that they could slowly sway back and forth, even though the song's tempo was building to its quick refrain. All around them, Meg could see phones coming out to record them.

"Don't pay attention to them," Tyler murmured. "Keep your focus on me."

As the song picked up, he twirled her away from him. Meg's skirt swirled around her legs and barely had time to settle before Tyler pulled her to him again, so fast and hard that she hit his chest, the breath knocking out of her. She laughed at the sheer ridiculousness of the situation, and he grinned at her.

As he continued to twirl her around the dance floor, she forgot that this was supposed to be awkward. She forgot it was supposed to be an act. She forgot about everyone and everything around her and simply enjoyed being in Tyler's arms.

The song changed to something slower, and Tyler pulled her to him once more. She ran her hands up the muscular length of his arms so that she could wrap them around the back of his neck. Meg leaned in closer and took a deep breath in of his cedar scent that she'd never really paid attention to before but always recognized as something associated with him. Contentment drifted over her. She placed her cheek against his chest and closed her eyes, letting Tyler's warmth envelope her.

"You doing okay?" Tyler said, his lips so close to her ear that she could feel the heat of his breath against her skin.

Her eyelids snapped open. "Yes, I think—um—they're really buying this."

"Yeah…right, I'm sure they are," Tyler said, his voice sounding a little weird.

Meg could see Clarice in the distance, the woman's eyes boring down on her. She looked away.

This wasn't real. Tyler was helping her out. It was for show.

And to think otherwise was not only stupid but dangerous to her heart.

Chapter Nine

Meg walked toward Julie's store the next day, knowing she had to rip off this Band-Aid sooner rather than later. The town's cleanup crew was busy taking down the string lights and stage from the night before, returning Main Street back to its normal self.

"Hi, Denny," she said to one of the guys on the crew she'd gone to high school with.

"Hey, Meg," Denny replied as he put part of the stage's flooring on a trailer. "Did you have fun last night?"

She stopped so that she could converse with him. "I did. Were you there?"

"I was. Had to keep an eye on the stage."

"You should have said hello."

Denny snickered. "You looked a little preoccupied. I didn't want to interrupt you."

"Oh," she said, tugging at her coat nervously. Even if Tyler was a nobody, the fact that Meg was dancing with someone other than Lucas Beaumont would have been news. But add to the fact that she'd spent the evening dancing exclusively in the arms of a Holiday Boy, she should have been prepared for the town's gossip mill to be in overdrive.

"I never would have thought you and Tyler would end up

together," he said as he grabbed another piece of the stage. "You two used to be at each other's throats."

"I wouldn't, um, say we're together," Meg interjected. "It's still pretty new."

"Well, I'm happy for you. Especially after that crap Lucas pulled."

"Right," she replied. And that was her cue to leave. "It was good seeing you, Denny. Tell Anne I said hello."

"Will do," he said, continuing with his task.

Taking a deep breath, Meg walked into Pieces of Home. Julie stood next to the counter, surrounded by a group of tourists.

"Jake was always my favorite," a woman in her seventies told her, patting her dyed pink hair before taking a selfie with Julie.

"Mine too," Julie said with a playful smile that made the woman laugh.

Another tourist noticed Meg standing there and ran over to her. "Meg, can I get my picture with you?"

"W-What?"

"Linda has terrible taste—no offense, Julie," the fan said to Julie and the pink-haired woman, who huffed. She then turned back to Meg and explained shyly, "Tyler was always my favorite."

"Oh," Meg said blankly.

The woman took a picture with her before she knew what was happening. "What's he like? Is he as perfect as he seems?"

"He's…he's something," Meg stumbled.

"We need to get going," a third woman in their group said, holding what appeared to be bags of all three women's purchases as the other two continued to fawn over Meg and Julie.

As they started to leave, Meg heard the third woman say, "I can't believe Tyler is dating *her*. Wasn't he dating a supermodel not too long ago?"

Meg's face flamed. She turned to face Julie, who was staring at her friend through narrowed eyes, her arms crossed over her chest, having clearly not heard what the woman said.

"Hi there," Meg said after the women left. She tried pushing thoughts of Tyler and some model out of her head so she could focus on the impending conversation with her best friend.

"Hi there?" Julie repeated. "That's what we're starting with?"

"Um, should I start with something else?"

"How about *Guess what, I'm dating Tyler. You know, the guy I once wished had a thousand warts break out on his skin after he got me in trouble for one of his various schemes.*"

"Oh...that," Meg muttered.

"Yes, that," Julie said. "Look, I know I've been a little preoccupied with the wedding and I know I've been spending a lot of time with Jake lately, but I don't want you to think that I'm ever too busy for you. You could have come to me about this. I—"

"It's not real," she interrupted.

Julie paused as she was about to launch into another speech. "What?"

She shifted from one foot to another. "Tyler and me. It's not real."

"What are you talking about?"

Meg glanced around to make sure they were alone in the store. Even after confirming that they were, she still lowered her voice as she whispered, "We're fake dating."

Julie stared at her. "Okay, start at the beginning."

So Meg did. She explained everything from running into Clarice at Florentina's to Tyler offer to fake date her so that she could get a one-up on her bullies while he got a distraction for his writer's block.

When she was done, Julie walked around the counter of her store and started fiddling with a doll-sized papier-mâché scarecrow.

Meg eyed it suspiciously. It had huge painted blue eyes and a leering red grin. "That thing is creepy as hell. Are you selling it for Halloween?"

"Are you sure it's just an act?" Julie asked, ignoring her question.

She pulled her gaze away from the scarecrow. "Yeah, of course. Tyler's just helping out an old neighbor."

"He didn't look like he was doing you a favor last night. He seemed to really enjoy dancing with you."

"Funny—I actually thought he should have gone into acting instead of songwriting."

Her friend gave her a very deliberate look. "Then you should get an Academy Award."

Meg picked nervously at a loose thread on the sleeve of her purple sweater. "What's that supposed to mean?"

Julie placed the scarecrow on the shelf behind her before facing her again. "I've known you since we were in kindergarten. I *know* you. And what I saw on that dance floor last night made me hopeful for the first time in a very long time."

"Hopeful about what?" Meg said, avoiding her eyes.

"You've been so upset since everything went down with Lucas, but last night I saw *you* again. You were happy and laughing. And it wasn't some act. You seemed like you really enjoyed being in Tyler's arms."

"I..." Meg's breathing started to get shallower as she tried to think of a response. Tears sprang to her eyes. Julie immediately ran over to her, hugging her tight.

"Oh, Meg," she murmured. "Why won't you let yourself be happy?"

"I'm happy," she muttered. Her diaphragm started to hurt from the pressure she kept sending its way.

Julie sighed before she pulled back and wiped at an errant tear running down Meg's face. She mercifully let the subject of Tyler go as she said, "Let's talk about something else, okay? How are the pre-wedding plans going?"

Meg let out a watery snort. "Tyler suggested we have a circus-themed party with clowns."

Julie shook her head in amused disbelief. "The sadist."

"Exactly."

Later that day, Meg went to her mom's house. They hadn't really spoken since her mom told her about the divorce, except for a few text exchanges about nothing important. Her mom said they could talk whenever she was ready. Meg didn't know if she'd ever be ready, but she missed her mother.

When she walked into the home, she found her mom sitting on the couch, playing *Bejeweled* on her phone while the Detroit Lions game blared on TV.

"Who's winning?" she asked as she sat next to her.

Her mom glowered at the screen. "Not the Lions."

They sat in silence for several minutes before Meg finally spoke. "I'm sorry for walking out on you the other week. I should have stayed."

"You needed time to process. I understood that. I'm sorry it came as such a shock to you."

She glanced around her family home. "So what happens now?" she asked. "Are you going to sell the house?"

"No, it's paid for. Your dad and I agreed that he could have the campground and I could keep the house."

Meg frowned. "That doesn't seem fair. The campground will continue to make money."

"I do still get a percentage of the profit," her mom assured her, "but I'm giving up any controlling interest I have."

Meg looked at her. She didn't seem upset by that. In fact, she seemed at peace with the idea.

"Are you sure that's what you want?" she asked anyway.

Her mom nodded. "I'm too old to butt heads with people. Stephen and Kimmy are talking about expanding to another location. They have a good idea of how to turn Archer Campgrounds into a chain. I'm fine with stepping down and letting them do their thing. Frankly, I'm excited to try something different after all these years. I'm really enjoying working for Julie and taking things at a slower pace."

"I get that," Meg said. She wouldn't mind quitting her job and doing something else with her life, but she had bills to pay, and she honestly didn't know what she'd do anyway.

"I wish you would talk to Stephen," her mom said with a sigh.

"What for?" Meg realized she'd stopped breathing. She forced a breath in. "He's just like Dad—wanting to leave running the business to the menfolk."

"You're just assuming that because it's what your father made you believe all these years. Stephen said he tried reaching out to you again the other day but you still haven't followed up with him."

Meg shrugged and didn't say anything.

Her mom grabbed the remote control and turned off

the TV. "I think Stephen is a lot more open to having you help than you think." She reached over and patted Meg's cheek. "Talk to your brother. He might be glad for your help, especially if they expand the business like they're talking about."

A knock on the door interrupted their conservation.

"That's probably Marie," her mom said, mentioning Tyler's mother. "We're going to Traverse City for the day to do some retail therapy. Do you want to come?"

"No, that's okay," Meg said, getting up and stretching. "I should go home and do my laundry."

As her mom walked by her, she grasped Meg's shoulder. "Let's go out for dinner soon, okay?"

"Okay," she replied. Her mom grabbed her purse from the hall tree before answering the door.

Marie Evans stood on the other side. At sixty-three, she was still one of the most beautiful women Meg had ever met. Her blond hair had streaks of gray in it, but it was stylish on her. While Tyler was a miniature of his dad, he'd inherited his mom's swirly eyes, which always shone brightly on Meg, even when she'd gotten her son in trouble for something.

"Meg!" Marie called out excitedly when she saw her. She hurried over and gave her a hug. "How are you, honey?"

"I'm good." She hugged her back. Marie had always been like a second mother to her, despite the numerous fights Meg got into with her son.

"And what's this I hear about you dating my boy?" Marie asked, her eyes sparkling.

"What?" her mom said. "You and Tyler are finally dating?"

"It's about time, right?"

"I'm surprised that it took as long as it did," her mom

told Marie. "I guess I owe you money. I thought it would have happened much sooner."

"Oh, that's right. You owe me twenty bucks," Marie said before sighing. "We're going to have the most beautiful grandchildren."

"Oh my God, will you both please stop," Meg groaned. "We literally just went on our first date yesterday. Don't send out the wedding invitations yet."

Meg shook her head as she watched the two women leave, disregarding what Meg said and letting their imaginations go wild as they discussed a wedding venue. After they left, Meg went out on the front porch and sat on the porch swing, not quite ready to go home, despite what she'd told her mom.

She grabbed her phone and nervously turned it back and forth in her hand.

Opening her text messages, she saw another one from Lucas, which she deleted without reading. Pulling up her contacts, she found her brother's name and typed out a short text. She sent it before she could second-guess herself.

Hey Stephen, Mom told me you were opening a second location. Congrats.

She pushed the swing back and forth with her sneaker. It only took a few minutes before he replied.

Yep, Kimmy and I are going over some options. I actually wanted to talk to you about it when you get a sec. Let me know a good time.

Was her mom right and Stephen wanted to get her involved in the campground? Meg tried not to get too excited.

Sounds good. We can meet at Franki's.

Why don't you come over for dinner? Kimmy and I would both love to see you. We don't see you enough these days, Trouble.

Meg smiled at her brother's nickname for her. When she was younger, she thought it was a coded name, perhaps how her brother and her dad actually thought of her. Through grown-up eyes though, she could see it for what it was—an affectionate term of endearment.

I'll let you know a good time.

Sounds good. I really want to talk soon.

Since Meg made it a rule to never have anything work related on her phone, she wrote, As soon as I get home and grab my laptop, I'll look at my work schedule and let you know.

"Meg?"

Her head shot up in surprise. Tyler stood next to her. Her heartbeat skyrocketed at the sight of him. He wore a dark blue Henley that made the mixed color of his eyes pop. The shirt only emphasized his rugged arms, which reminded her of the night before…how they'd felt embracing her as they danced.

They'd felt good. Strong and safe.

"Hi," she said and cursed how breathless she sounded.

He sat next to her on the swing, swaying it into motion. "I didn't expect to see you today."

"I wanted to spend some time with my mom, but she and Marie made plans to go shopping."

Tyler chuckled. "I don't know why my mom bothers. There's no more space in that house. I keep offering to buy my parents something bigger, but they're happy here."

"I can't imagine your parents not living next door." She let out a sad sigh. "But I guess things change, no matter how much you don't want them to."

Tyler nudged her lightly with his elbow. "You okay over there?"

Meg ran a finger over the smooth edge of the wood seat.

"My parents are getting divorced," she admitted. She pulled her finger away when something sharp jabbed her. "Ouch."

Tyler picked up her hand and examined it. "Splinter. I think I can get it out without tweezers."

He managed to pull it out with his blunt nails. "There. All better."

To Meg's surprise, he kissed the tip of her finger.

She tugged her hand away, her face coloring. "You don't have to do that. No one's watching us."

"You never know when someone's watching. Trust me." They fell into silence as they both pushed the swing into movement with their feet.

Tyler finally said, "I'm sorry about your parents."

"I guess I should have seen it coming. I don't think either one of them has been happy for a while, but I thought it was just the stress of the campground."

He lifted his arm and then motioned with his head for her to move closer to him. Meg should have found it strange how quickly she followed his instructions, settling into his side. He wrapped his arm around her, giving her a soft hug. He didn't loosen his grip, so she didn't bother to move back.

"I think people are buying this," she said. "You and me.

I ran into Denny Rowen earlier today. He commented about us dating. And a fan of yours wanted my picture."

"The fans aren't bothering you, are they?"

"No," she said, trying not to remember the person comparing her to his supermodel ex-girlfriend. She wanted to ask about the other woman, but it was none of her business who'd possibly owned Tyler's heart at some point. Besides, *she* was the one currently in Tyler's arms.

Not that this actually means anything, she reminded herself.

They continued to sit in silence, the swing creaking as they rocked back and forth.

"I had an idea for the pre-party," Tyler said after a few more minutes of comfortable silence.

Meg turned her head so she could glare at him. "Let me guess—stripper clowns?"

Tyler burst out laughing. "Damn, I wish I would have come up with something that cool."

She slapped his stomach lightly. He grabbed her wrist, holding her palm against his shirt. She could feel the ridges of his abs through the thin layer of material, and she was tempted to explore them more with her fingers.

She tried to focus on their conversation. "So…uh, what's your big plan?"

"How about I show you? We can make it one of our dates. It's in a public place in town, so we can kill two birds with one stone."

Meg couldn't think of any reason to say no. "Sounds good. When do you want to go?"

"I'll pick you up Saturday. Wear something comfortable. Flexible."

Meg peered at him questioningly. "Are you taking me hiking? Because I don't think a drunk wedding party should go strolling through the woods at night. It's not a good idea."

"Oh, ye of little faith," Tyler teased. "Trust me."

"Famous last words," she muttered and felt the rumbling of his laughter against her hand which he still held against his chest.

They continued to sit in companionable silence for several more minutes. The rocking was making her sleepy, and she looked at the large expanse of Tyler's chest longingly.

Slowly, hesitantly, she put her cheek against it. She waited for his rejection, but instead he wrapped his arm around her even tighter.

"Tell me something," Meg said.

"About what?" Tyler asked.

"Anything," she replied. "Tell me about your life since you left Holiday Bay. Something no one else knows. A fact that you can't find by doing a Google search."

Tyler rested his cheek on top of her head. Her pulse pounded at the intimacy of it all. If anyone walked by them in that moment, they wouldn't see anything that people would consider salacious or controversial—words that were synonymous with Meg's name as of late. They'd merely see a couple enjoying one another's company.

"Hmm, something no one else knows," Tyler repeated. Meg could feel the vibration of his voice on her scalp. It sent goose bumps down her spine. "I hate going to award shows."

"Really? You always seem like you love them."

His grip on her waist tightened as he teased, "Oh, you've been watching me on TV, huh?"

She pinched his abs softly. He grabbed the offending hand and threaded their fingers together.

"Holiday Bay has watch parties anytime you're nominated for some award, which is every freaking year," Meg explained haughtily. "You literally can't avoid them no matter how hard one tries—which, trust me, I have."

"Sure, Meg," Tyler replied. It might have been her imagination, but she thought he may have nuzzled her head with his chin, but he probably was just shifting his hold on her.

"Why do you hate them?" she asked. "They always look so glitzy and fantastic. Rubbing elbows with all those stars."

"Um, are you forgetting I'm one of those stars?"

"Every day of my life."

She could feel his laughter against her cheek.

"I like staying out of the spotlight," he said. "Having cameras thrown in your face and reporters shouting your name so they can get a soundbite out of you…it gets exhausting. You always have to be on, because if you have one moment where you show your annoyance over the whole superficial thing, you suddenly become a meme. I'd rather be on my ranch, enjoying the peace and quiet."

She thought that over. "That actually does sound pretty nice."

"I can take you there sometime. Anytime you want."

"I'll keep that in mind," she said drily, knowing he didn't mean it.

"I'm serious," he insisted. "I think you'd really love it. It's in the middle of nowhere, so you can relax and be yourself without any busybodies trying to see what you're up to. You're surrounded by meadows and mountains, and there's nothing but nature to disturb you."

"That…sounds really perfect actually." She could picture it so clearly in her head.

"It is." Tyler's smartwatch chimed, and he looked at it with a grimace. "I need to get back to work. I'm trying to get this song finished."

Reluctantly, Meg pulled away from him, immediately missing his warmth once it was gone.

He got up from the chair and walked over to the porch steps. He looked over his shoulder at her. "I'll see you Saturday, then."

"See you Saturday."

Meg watched him go, her head and her heart both screaming at her to acknowledge emotions she'd prefer to ignore.

Chapter Ten

Tyler knew he messed up when he saw Meg's pale face.

"Are you kidding me with this?" she said, clutching the rope that made up the railing of the wood bridge. The bridge wasn't really a bridge at all, more a glorified balance beam.

The adventure park seemed like a good idea in theory, though he had no idea when he read the description that the bridges would be so far up from the ground.

"You've got this, Meg!" a voice shouted from far—*far*—below.

"Kenny Wheeler, if I survive this, I'm going to kill you!" she screamed at the park's owner.

"Meg, I swear," Tyler started, "I had no idea you were afraid of heights."

"I'm not afraid of heights," she snapped as she took another cautious step toward the platform he was currently standing on. The bridge rocked under her feet. "I'm afraid of swinging bridges that are thirty feet off the ground." She took another step, causing the bridge to sway even more. "How the hell is this any safer than axe throwing? You drunk idiots will fall and break your necks if you try this. In fact, I hope you do!"

Tyler bit back a grin in the middle of her rant, not bothering to remind her that she wore a safety harness. Even if she slipped, she wouldn't fall. He took a slow step toward her. The bridge let out a loud moan of protest as it bore some of his weight.

"Stop!" Meg shouted. "Only one adult is supposed to be on this death trap at a time. It'll break between both of us. Didn't you read the rules when we signed those disclaimers—which, FYI, was probably a sign that this place isn't safe!"

"It won't break. That's just a precaution," he assured her. He glanced down at Kenny for confirmation, but the man shrugged his shoulders. "Oh, for God's sake," he muttered under his breath, but he didn't take another step.

Reaching out his hand, Tyler encouraged, "Meg, focus on me, okay? Don't look down. Look straight at me."

When she didn't move, he deliberately gave her a cocky smirk and said, "Come on, Meg. I dare you."

Her eyes jerked to his, taking in his deliberately insolent expression, and she straightened her shoulders. She didn't look down again as she slowly made her way over the rest of the bridge, her hand so tight on the rope railing, Tyler was sure she'd end up with blisters.

Once she got close enough, he offered his hand again. She looked at it before releasing one of her hands from the death grip she had on the railing. Her shaking fingers lifted toward his outstretched palm, and he grabbed her, pulling her into his embrace. She shuddered as she wrapped her arms tightly around his waist.

"I've got you," he murmured against her hair. "You're safe."

"I hate you so much right now," she said, her voice muffled against his flannel.

He was careful to hide his smile against her silky hair.

"Excuse me, are you planning on moving?" a ferocious-looking Girl Scout said from the other side of the bridge. The rest of her troop stood behind her, looking at them impatiently. They were clearly waiting for them to get out of the way so they could get on with the adventure park.

"Wait," one of them said. "Are you... Tyler Evans?"

"We'd better go," Tyler whispered.

"No freaking way am I going across another bridge," Meg said, her grip on his shirt tightening. "Leave me here to die."

This time he didn't try to hold back the laugh that escaped him. "Come on—there's a ladder on the other side of the platform."

He guided her toward it. "I'll go down first. That way I can catch you if you fall."

"Funny," she grumbled.

He started down the ladder, Meg soon following. He tried not to act like a pervert as her luscious bottom came within his eyesight.

Once they reached the safety of the ground, Meg took several deep breaths. It seemed like she couldn't get enough air into her lungs.

"You okay?" Tyler said. "You're safe now."

She nodded but didn't answer. He grabbed her hand. "Come on—let's go to the canteen."

He led her to a small building where they were selling drinks and food. "You hungry?"

"I'm trying hard not to throw up right now from, you know, almost dying," Meg snapped.

"Oh good," Tyler responded lightly. "And here I was thinking it was my presence ruining your appetite"

"Oh, it's that too. Every waking moment. Whenever I picture you in my head, I think, *Ugh, Tyler Evans exists somewhere in the world. I can't eat knowing that troll is out there.* In fact—"

"Yeah, yeah," Tyler interrupted her, his lips quirking at her sarcasm. God, he missed this side of her. He was also relieved to see that her attitude brought some color to her cheeks and she didn't seem to be breathing as erratically as she'd been a few minutes before.

"How about this?" he offered. "I'll get a large fry, and you and I can split it."

"Fine, but if I throw up, that's on you."

Tyler snorted. "Got it. Do you want anything to drink? Water?"

"No!" she said immediately.

"You have something against water?" he joked, but then he remembered Meg never drank water if she could help it, preferring soda pop instead.

"I don't like the taste of it," she said, her manner nonchalant. She didn't meet his eyes as she added, "But I will drink soda water, if they have it."

Tyler nodded. "I'll see what they have. Can you find us a table while I get our stuff?"

"Sure."

Meg headed for the seating area as Tyler went to get the fries and a couple of drinks. The teenager at the window flipped out when she saw him, and he graciously posed for a picture with her before she gave him his food. As he carried the tray over to the table where Meg waited, he stumbled to a stop, almost spilling their drinks.

Like the adventure park, the food court and seating area was in the middle of the woods. Meg sat at a picnic table with her head tilted to the sky, her eyes closed. Her oversized green sweater did nothing to hide the delectable curves of her body. Surrounded by the large trees, Meg reminded him of a renaissance painting.

As he stared, his body began to fill with desire.

He wanted her.

He wanted to lay her on that table and damn whoever was watching. He wanted to feel and taste every bit of skin that her sweater tried to hide from him. It surprised Tyler how much he had to fight not to give into temptation. Then again, it really shouldn't have.

He'd been craving Meg Archer since his graduation night.

Sitting down quickly before anyone could notice his reaction, he cleared his voice and said, "Here."

He handed Meg a soda water, while he took a sip of his Pepsi. He'd gotten the largest basket of fries they had and pushed it toward Meg.

"Have some," he insisted. "Grease and salt will put some color back into your face."

She took a few fries and popped them into her mouth. She let out a pleased murmur, as though she'd never tasted anything so exquisite. The sound made him ache—made him wonder what other noises she made when she enjoyed something.

And he really needed to get his mind out of the gutter.

Tyler ate a few fries himself, enjoying the salty flavor combining with the sweetness of his drink. "These are really good." He pushed the basket closer to her. "Have some more."

Her eyes narrowed. "So I don't look like a corpse?"

He instantly held up his hands. "When did I say that? I never said that. I said you needed to get some color back in your face after you, and I quote, 'almost died.' Even if you looked like death, you'd still be beautiful."

"Yeah, okay."

"I mean it," he insisted.

"Says the guy who's dated supermodels."

"Meg." Her eyebrows flew up at Tyler's determined tone. "I'm serious. You have gorgeous skin and eyes that draw anyone in. Your body is perfect and—"

"Stop." Meg glanced around before lowering her voice into a vicious whisper, "Stop acting like you're attracted to me. That wasn't part of the deal."

"I think acting attracted to you should be a very *important* part of the deal. Besides, I'm not acting."

"Please stop," she pleaded, and the only reason he didn't persist was because he caught a glimpse of tears in her eyes before she blinked them back.

He bit back his frustration but changed the subject. "How about this? Next weekend, we'll do one of your choices for the pre-party. Maybe I'll reconsider them."

Meg's face brightened. "Even though you're going to think it's lame?"

Tyler grinned. "Especially if I think it's lame."

"Okay, you're on."

Chapter Eleven

"**W**hat do you think?" Meg asked as they sat in her car.

Tyler stared at the building as though it physically pained him. "Wine & Stuff?"

Meg tried to view the winery through Tyler's eyes. Wine & Stuff was on the outskirts of Holiday Bay. One of Meg's classmates, Sarah, and her husband, Ted, bought the vineyard a few years ago from an elderly couple who'd let it go to seed. They'd tried to make it into something special, but Wine & Stuff was more gimmicky than classy. The appeal to the place was that it was conveniently located fifteen minutes from Main Street.

A gigantic wood pirate the size of the building stood outside the main entrance, a word balloon attached to its mouth that said *Ahoy, Matey*. In his beefy wooden hands was a large wine bottle, the words *Wine & Stuff* scrawled across it. Florescent orange paint covered the brick surface of the building. On the other side of the main entrance was a human-sized steel parrot, which glared at them from its perch.

"What's wrong with the place?" Meg asked, pretending not to notice how tacky it was.

Tyler gave her a look of disbelief. "You've got to be kidding."

"It's close to town, so it'll be easy for both parties to get to." She grabbed the handle of the car door. "Don't be so stuck up. Or do you think the lofty Holiday Boys are too good for a place like this?"

"Paul will," Tyler muttered.

"It's not that bad," she said, though truth be told, she'd never been here before. Lucas wouldn't have been caught dead in a place like this, and Meg hadn't felt like going out to socialize after they broke up. Trying to be optimistic, she nodded toward the crowded parking lot. "See, look at all the people who are here."

"Sure," Tyler replied skeptically. As they walked toward the entrance, he eyed the ginormous pirate as though he was afraid it'd fall on them. "Why pirates?"

"I'm guessing it has something to do with the town being named after the bay."

"It's not like there were ever pirates in the area."

"You obviously never had Mrs. Yuhas in second grade." Meg stopped at the door to get a closer look at the parrot. The amount of detail carved into the steel feathers was impressive. "The woman was obsessed with some pirate named Calico Jack. She used to tell us about how he'd terrorize fisherman and steal ships around the Great Lakes in the 1700s. I was afraid to go in the bay when I was a kid because I was scared I'd get kidnapped by pirates. Did you know that?"

Tyler's eyes crinkled in amusement. "I don't think so."

Meg gave him some serious side eye. "No, you probably didn't. I would have done my best to keep that little gem out of your head. You would have shown up on my front porch in a full pirate suit had you'd known."

"No, I wouldn't have," Tyler protested, though they both knew that was absolutely something he would have done.

And she would have retaliated in some way. It was how they operated back then.

Meg ignored him. "It took my mom a lot of convincing for me to believe pirates were no longer in the area."

Tyler ran a hand over the parrot's metallic nose. "And to think, I had boring Mr. Delaney in second grade."

"You missed out. I swear I saw Mrs. Yuhas wearing a patch over her eye one day when I was supposed to be at recess. I'm pretty sure she had some kind of pirate fetish."

Tyler let out a surprised laugh as they walked into the winery. Meg couldn't help but feel pleased. He looked happy, and she had caused that to happen. His eyes reflected his amusement. A grin captured his wide, firm lips. She barely resisted the sudden temptation to lean up and explore that mouth with her own.

He looked so handsome, it actually caught her off guard. Even when she'd hated him years ago, she'd always recognized he was a good-looking guy. When had she started to feel this attraction though? Sure, something sparked between them years ago. But…her eyes drifted to his mouth again.

She yanked them away to look around the building. Row upon row of wood kiosks greeted them. Each shelf contained a variety of wine glasses and knickknacks that had cheesy sayings on them like, *It's Wine O'Clock Somewhere.*

Meg went over to a shelf of wine stoppers and let out a wheezy laugh. "Tyler, do you want me to buy you this one as a present?"

She picked up a stopper that had a picture attached to it of a shirtless Tyler Evans. He must have been around nineteen or twenty at the time of the photo. As she skimmed over the rest of the box, she saw an equal amount of shirtless Holiday Boys.

Tyler looked at the stopper in horror. "No! Put that away. Actually, let's pretend none of those exist at all."

"Why is it that you're always shirtless in every piece of Holiday Boys merchandise I come across?"

"Because I have killer abs, obviously."

"Obviously," Meg repeated sardonically.

The two stared at each other, humor and what almost felt like affection, drifting between them. That desire to do something stupid again—like kiss him—sizzled over Meg.

A loud roar of noise came from the back of the building, giving her a welcome distraction. Exchanging cautious looks, Tyler and Meg walked toward the commotion. They entered a large banquet hall where two dozen elderly people were doing the foxtrot on a large dance floor. A disco ball hung from the ceiling above, sending sparkly light around the space. Tables and chairs were stacked on one side of the room. A teenage boy stood on the other side behind a DJ booth, looking bored as he spun records from the 1960s.

"Meg!"

She looked over and saw Sarah hurrying toward her. Sarah had a hippy-chic vibe about her that Meg had always envied. Her long, dark hair was piled on top of her head in a messy bun, and she wore one of the loose-fitting skirts she always preferred, no matter the weather.

"Sarah, hey," Meg replied, giving the taller woman a hug.

"What are you doing here?" she asked.

Before Meg could respond, a couple in their eighties waltzed by. The man's hands cupped his partner's butt.

"Jerry and Gertrude, keep it PG, please," Sarah yelled over the music. "My teenaged son is present."

"Sorry, Sarah," they both shouted in unison. Jerry put

his hands on the woman's waist before whispering something into her ear that made her giggle.

"Those two," she grumbled with a shake of her head. "I swear, they're worse than teenagers. Now"—she turned back to Meg—"what brings you into my humble abode?"

"We're looking for a place to host a party." Meg pointed over her shoulder at Tyler. "Someplace that'll be discreet."

Sarah's eyes widened as she became aware for the first time that she had an incredibly famous person standing in her winery.

"As I live and breathe," she murmured. "A Holiday Boy in my place."

"Stop it, Sarah, or you'll scare him off." A man about the same height as Sarah walked over to them. He had wavy blond hair streaked with gray that hung to his shoulders.

"Ted! It's good to see you again," Tyler said, sticking out his hand.

"Tyler, long time, no see," Ted replied, shaking his proffered hand.

"You two know each other?" Meg asked.

Tyler gave her a fond shake of his head. "Believe it or not, I actually did live in this town once upon a time. Ted and I had Biology together. You know, the class you kidnapped the chickens from."

"Are you ever going to let that go?" she complained.

"Never." He teased a smile that was contagious.

"Don't worry, Meg. Tyler and I got busted on more than one occasion for goofing off," Ted added before he waved his hands around. "We appreciate you coming to our winery. We're short on men, and my feet are killing me from Dolores stepping on them. Maybe someone who used to do fancy dance moves in a boy band is just what these ladies need."

"Wait, what?" Tyler said as Ted grabbed his arm and pulled him to the center of the room.

"Ladies and gents," Ted announced loudly. "This is Tyler, and he loves to dance."

A loud cheer went through the crowd. Tyler was soon being whirled around the dance floor by an old woman who clearly preferred leading, pulling Tyler this way and that.

Meg laughed so hard her sides hurt. She pulled out her phone and recorded him for blackmail purposes.

"So when is this party you want to do?" Sarah asked as they watched Tyler go around the floor for the second time, looking slightly panicked.

"It's the second Saturday of November," Meg answered as she put her phone away.

"Hmm, I feel like we might already have something going on."

Sarah walked to the front room with Meg following. She went behind the winery's counter where they served drinks. Activating her computer from sleep mode, Sarah looked at her calendar before giving Meg an apologetic smile. "It looks like the Holiday Boys Holiday Bay Fan Club is meeting here that night. The irony, right? They shouldn't take up too much room, but if Tyler and any of the other guys are planning on being in attendance…"

Considering all the Boys were planning on being in attendance, Meg knew that Wine & Stuff would be out of the question for them, unless they wanted a bunch of drunk fans hanging all over the men all night.

"No," Meg replied, "unfortunately, that won't work."

Sarah looked disappointed. She kept herself professional though, as she pointed to the back room. "I'm sure the ladies are going to claim Tyler's attention for a while. They don't usually have men show up who can still move without a walker. Do you want a glass of our latest specialty before you go? On the house."

"Sure, thanks." Meg sat at a stool at the bar and watched as Sarah poured red wine into a glass that read *Liquid Therapy* across it.

"We're pretty proud of this one," she said as she pushed the wine toward Meg. "We're calling it Heaveninely, because it tastes like heaven in a wine cup."

Meg picked up her glass and took a large sip. She instantly regretted it. It tasted as ridiculous as its name, like juice that had gone bad three years ago, but they'd tried to cover the sour taste by adding thirty pounds of sugar to it. She wanted desperately to spit it out, but Sarah was eyeing her closely, waiting on her reaction.

Forcing the tortuous concoction down, Meg smiled painfully. "It's delicious."

"Good." Sarah topped off her glass and went back to her register. She kept glancing at Meg like a parent making sure their kid ate their Brussels sprouts.

Because she didn't want to hurt Sarah's feelings, she kept taking sips. She prayed to any deity out there that the old women who'd kidnapped Tyler would release him soon so they could get the hell out of dodge. He finally appeared, sweaty and disheveled, as Meg was on her second glass, feeling queasy and lightheaded.

"You're out here drinking while I can barely walk from having my feet stepped on?" Tyler grumbled.

"Here—this should make you feel better." She pushed the glass of her half-drunk wine toward Tyler.

He drank it down in one gulp and stilled. His eyes began to water and his skin turned green.

"Good, right?" Meg smirked.

"Archer, retribution is coming your way," Tyler whispered. "And I'm going to make it painful."

She giggled as she slid off the bar stool, wobbling when she hit the ground.

"How much did you have to drink?" Tyler asked as he steadied her with his hands.

"Just two glasses."

"It's a wonder you're still alive."

He didn't let her go, and she didn't move away. She liked how his palms felt on her hips. Big and strong.

"Are you leaving?" Sarah asked, coming over to them from where she'd been working on some paperwork at the winery's register. Tyler took a step back so Meg could face their host.

"Yeah, but thank you," Meg said politely. "It's been a lot of fun."

"Tyler..." Sarah said, looking unsure. "Would you be willing to take a picture with Ted and me before you go? It'd be a great boost for us if people could see that a Holiday Boy stopped by our winery."

Tyler looked like he wanted to do anything else given that the wine was still likely torturing his taste buds, but he relented. Meg tried to get out of the picture, but he grabbed her waist and hauled her up against him.

"I suffer, you suffer," Tyler murmured against her ear. Despite herself, she shivered at the sensation of his breath against her skin. She needed to get herself under control.

Dolores came out and took a picture of Tyler, Meg, Sarah and Ted. Sarah giddily posted it on the winery's Facebook page.

"Don't you be a stranger now," Dolores said to Tyler with a wink. "In fact, you should come back next week. I have a granddaughter about your age that I'll drag along. You two would make such a cute pair."

Maybe it was the wine not settling right. Maybe it was the idea of Tyler meeting Dolores's granddaughter—Isabella, who worked at Florentina's and whom Meg used to babysit—but something took over Meg.

"Honey, we should get going," she said, maneuvering so that she was in front of him. And before she could stop herself, she gave into the desire she'd been fighting all afternoon. Meg leaned up onto her tiptoes and kissed Tyler in front of Dolores and Sarah and god knew who else.

It was supposed to be just the brush of her lips against his. Nothing more, nothing less.

She felt Tyler stiffen under her hands, where she'd settled them on his chest. She went to take a step back, mortified at what she'd done, when Tyler grabbed the back of her neck, keeping her firmly in place. His mouth deepened their kiss, meshing their lips together.

Heat ignited inside Meg. She wanted to press herself against him. To wrap her arms around him so that they'd never stop doing this.

When someone catcalled, they broke apart. Tyler's chest rose rapidly in front of Meg's eyes before she averted her gaze. Muttering her goodbyes to Sarah, she almost ran out the front entrance, eager to escape the whole scene. She went to open the driver's side door of her car, when Tyler took the keys abruptly from her hand.

"No way are you driving," he said. Putting his hand on her waist, he guided her around to the passenger side. She got in without protest, still horrified at what she'd done.

When Tyler got behind the wheel, he adjusted the seat before starting the car. He didn't put it in Reverse, despite

Meg silently pleading for him to do just that so she could go home and wallow in her embarrassment.

"I'm sorry," she finally whispered when the silence stretched on for too long. Her breathing grew ragged. She took several small gulps of air and pushed them toward her stomach. Her diaphragm tightened in response. The pain that caused, mixed with whatever Sarah had served her, made her nauseous.

Tyler frowned at her. "What are you sorry for?"

"I kissed you."

"I know," he said drily. "I was there."

Meg stared miserably down at her hands, trying to not reveal any signs of her anxiety. "I assaulted you."

"Meg, stop. You did no such thing."

"Yes, I did," she insisted.

"I kissed you back. Or did you forget that part?"

"I—"

"I didn't mind our kiss," Tyler said softly. "I actually really enjoyed it."

"But, I—"

He grabbed her chin and kissed her again. Meg froze in surprise, forgetting her budding panic. The feel of his mouth caressing hers soon had her melting.

"You can kiss me anytime," he said, his lips bare inches from hers.

"To convince people we're dating?" Meg asked. She wanted him to deny it, to say it didn't feel so fake anymore. She hoped he would prove it wasn't her imagination thinking that maybe—just maybe—there was something building between them.

Instead, he pulled away, letting her go to grip the steering wheel. "Right...exactly."

As Tyler left the parking lot, Meg grabbed her phone out

of her pocket for something to do other than scream. She felt skittish, like she was about to lose control. She tried not to dwell on her breathing, which was increasingly ragged. She didn't want to have a panic attack in front of Tyler. She pulled up her social media for a distraction and went to the winery's main page.

"That picture is already going viral," she said, watching the number of views on the picture steadily climb. Her eyes drifted to the comments about her, and her chest tightened.

Who is this freaking troll with Tyler? He's not dating her, is he?

Does he need a restraining order? Look how she's clinging to him.

Ew, she's disgusting.

"Meg, don't read that garbage. Trust me. Nothing good ever comes from it," Tyler stated, pulling the phone from her grasp and turning it over.

Too late.

"So…" he said as they started down the road. "Did you get a chance to talk to Sarah about the party? Are we going to have it there?"

Meg shifted her mind from her shallow breathing to focus on Tyler. "You're actually willing to have the party there?"

"It's not ideal, but like you said, it's convenient. We'd just need to bring our own wine, because, dear God, we'll end up poisoned before the wedding if we drink that stuff."

Meg allowed a short smile despite how unhappy she was. "If it's any consolation, we won't be able to have the party at Wine & Stuff. Sarah said they were booked that day with a Holiday Boys Fan Club meetup. She said we could still have our party there, but I didn't think it'd be ideal with all of the guys in attendance."

"No, definitely not." Tyler grinned at her, and her heart lurched. She had to fight from kissing him again. His face turned serious. "So what are we going to do about the party?"

Meg rubbed at her forehead. "I don't know but we're running out of options. Where can we hold a party for ten to twelve people, where five of the people are internationally famous? It needs to be somewhere where cameras won't follow your every move."

Tyler made a sudden sharp turn with the car, causing the tires to squeal.

"What the hell!" Meg shouted as he pulled into the town park that overlooked the bay.

"Come with me," he said as he hopped out of the car.

"Where are we going?" Meg asked as she stumbled after him.

They made their way to the rocky shoreline, going through an archway of trees before coming to a large log close to the water. Tyler sat down and Meg followed. She pulled her plaid coat tighter around her as the cold October weather pummeled her.

"You asked where we can go where we won't be disturbed," he said before pointing at the water. "There's your answer."

Meg stared at the bay in confusion. "Come again?"

"We rent a boat."

She shook her head. "You're not serious."

"Why not?" Tyler asked.

"For one thing, it'll be almost the middle of November

when we have the party. Take a look around. Do you see any boats on the water? Everyone will already have theirs stored away for the winter. Not to mention that we'll probably have snow by then. Are you hoping we'll freeze to death before the wedding?"

"I'm not talking about a fishing boat, Meg," Tyler said, his lips turning upward. "I'm talking about a large enough yacht where we can hang out indoors if it's too cold outside. One that has enough bedrooms where we can sleep peacefully if things get out of hand. Besides, you know how Michigan is. We could very well have seventy-degree weather by then."

"We could also have a blizzard." Meg sniffed, but she could see there were benefits to Tyler's plan. "Let's say we do this. I can't have you pay for all of it."

Tyler gave her an incredulous look. "I can cover the cost."

She lifted her chin. "No. We do this together or not at all."

He looked thoughtful before he snapped his fingers. "I think I can get it for free."

"You're just saying tha—"

"No, I'm serious. I have a producer friend who lives in Charlevoix. He has a yacht that rivals the royal family's. I'm sure he'll let us borrow it at little to no cost. He loves Jake. I have to head out of town for the next few weeks—"

"You're leaving again?" Meg didn't know why that made her sad, but it did.

"I have some obligations in New York that I can't get out of, but I'll get everything organized with the yacht while I'm away and keep you updated."

Meg stared at the water as the cold air soaked through

her coat, and she shivered again. They'd be stupid to go out on the bay in November.

"Come on, Meg," Tyler teased. "I dare you."

She glared at him. "Fine, but if I die from hypothermia, I'm going to haunt you for the rest of your existence."

He wrapped his arm around her, bringing her into the warmth of his body. "That's the spirit."

Chapter Twelve

As Meg walked into Bridal Barn, she felt a slight ache in her heart. The last time she was there, it was to return her wedding dress. Luckily, the shop's owner, Jessica, had been kind and accepted the return without issue. She'd been there the day Meg tried to find her wedding dress, Clarice tearing Meg down until she'd agreed to wear a heinous gown that did nothing for her figure.

Meg had been grateful Jessica was willing to take the dress back. She didn't think anyone with a sense of taste would buy it. The shop owner had probably been secretly relieved when Meg had given her money for it in the first place. Jessica had probably cut her losses, chopped the dress into pieces and used it to clean toilets or something.

"Meg!" Julie ran over to her and hugged her tight. "I can't believe I'm here picking out a wedding dress. It's so crazy."

Meg pulled away from her grip. "What's not to believe? Jake would've been an idiot not to snatch you up as soon as he could."

"That's what I told her." A woman with blond hair and bright blue eyes walked over to them.

"Hey, Kyleigh," Meg greeted, giving her a brief hug.

Kyleigh owned the shop across the street from Julie's

store. She and Julie had grown close over the years, especially after a large corporation tried to buy them out. They were one of only a few holdouts, and thanks to them, they saved the town square. Kyleigh was officially going to be in the wedding party, along with Meg and Julie's sister, Veronica.

Jessica came out from the back of the shop. "Meg, it's good to see you again. Kyleigh, I meant to ask earlier, are you planning on bringing your world-famous pumpkin pie to our next Small Business Association meeting?"

"If I have time to bake, I will." Kyleigh laughed. "The shop's so busy right now with craft classes, and I'm trying to get things ready for the holiday season. Plus, Holly has a dance recital coming up, not to mention her school assembly," she explained, mentioning her daughter, pride written all over her face. "If I can survive the next few weeks, I'll see what I can do about the pie."

"Good," Jessica said before turning to Julie. "I have a few dresses picked out that meet the style you requested."

"What about that dress you tried on last time we were here? Is it still available? You looked beautiful in it," Meg said. She'd seen a stunning dress the day of her disastrous appointment. It was just Julie's style. Even though Jake and Julie weren't together at that point, Julie still tried on the dress and looked like an angel in it.

"Oh, that was a beautiful dress," she replied, "but I'm going for something a little more...simple. Something fitting for a backyard wedding."

"And while I agree it was absolutely gorgeous on you," Jessica added, "I sold that particular one months ago."

With that, Jessica led Julie away to the dressing room. Meg took a seat on one of the yellow-and-white striped chairs. She peeked around the room, taking in the gorgeous dresses that hung from the different hangers and displays. A lump grew in her throat as she thought back to how awful her own appointment was, but she instantly brushed it aside. Today was about Julie, not her own misery. Julie's mom had Alzheimer's, and her sister lived halfway across the country. Julie needed her best friend to be there for her.

"What do you think she'll go for?" Kyleigh asked as she settled into the opposite chair.

Meg cracked a smile. "No idea, but it'll look fantastic on her. She could wear a burlap sack and still look like she stepped off a runway."

Kyleigh nodded. "That's true. Some people have all the luck."

She refrained from saying anything. Like Julie, Kyleigh was tall, thin and perfect. She was a few years older than Meg, but she somehow managed to look younger.

Julie and Jessica came out of the dressing room. Meg's eyes grew misty as she watched Julie step onto the pedestal next to the trifold mirror. She wore an A-line teacup dress with a high neckline. Lace covered the entire dress, which fell just below her knees.

"Julie, that's gorgeous," Kyleigh murmured.

"Jake won't know what to do with himself if he sees you in that," Meg added. "But what do you think?"

Their friend glowed. "It's crazy to choose the first dress you try on, but I think this might be it."

Jessica gave an approving nod. "Why don't we try on a few more dresses before you make any final decisions?"

Julie turned this way and that in the mirror before agreeing with her. As they headed back to the dressing room, Meg's cell chirped. She pulled it from her purse and unlocked it.

She stared at it for a moment as she read and reread

the text from her brother. Are we still on for dinner next Sunday?

Her fingers hovered over the letters on her phone before she sent a quick response. Yes, I'll be there.

Julie came out in another dress, but it didn't do her justice like the first one did. She tried on several more before ultimately deciding on the first one. Thanks to Jake working his magic, Jessica assured her she'd have the dress ready to go in plenty of time for the wedding.

Kyleigh soon left to return to her store, since she'd already tried on her bridesmaid dress before Meg got there. Jessica went to gather several maid-of-honor dresses for Meg to try on that would match Kyleigh's. Julie sat across from her, texting something on her phone with a happy expression on her face. She had to be messaging Jake. He was the only one that made her best friend look like that.

"So," Julie finally said, putting away her phone. "What's the latest with you and Tyler?"

"I think we finally agreed on a destination for your party. I personally think it's a stupid idea, but our other ideas were either too dangerous for a possibly drunk wedding party or they were already booked."

"I don't know if I should be worried or not." Julie laughed. "What did you come up with?"

"He's borrowing his friend's yacht, and he wants us to go sailing around the bay."

Julie shot her a look of disbelief. "In November?"

"That's what I said, but he insisted it'll give us privacy, and since all the Holiday Boys will be there, they won't have to worry about fans interrupting the evening."

Julie gave a slow nod. "I guess that makes sense. We'll have to warn everyone to dress super warm. But that wasn't what I was asking about. Has anything new developed between you two?"

Meg chewed on her lip before blurting, "We kissed."

Her best friend's eyes widened. "Oh? Do tell."

"It was nothing." Meg waved her hand in front of her as though to swipe her words away. "We were scouting places for the party, and Dolores Rossi offered to introduce Tyler to Isabella."

"And what, you were staking your claim?" Julie asked, her tone filled with an amusement that Meg didn't appreciate.

"We're supposed to be fake dating. How would it look if I didn't say or do anything and let my would-be boyfriend get set up with Izzy…the girl I used to babysit? Besides, she's too young for Tyler."

"Is a thirteen-year difference considered too young these days?"

"Yes," Meg said waspishly.

Julie was quiet for a moment. "You can like him, you know. It's okay."

"I don't. Can we change the subject?"

Julie gave her an appraising look before she said, "Sure."

Thankfully, Jessica returned right then. "Meg, I'm ready for you."

Meg jumped to her feet and followed her to the dressing room. She tried on a few dresses that matched Julie's in length.

"Julie thought this one would be a nice color on you. It's also a similar style to what Kyleigh and Julie's sister will be wearing." Jessica held up a lace gown in a dark burgundy color.

It would certainly highlight the honey streaks in her hair and not drain her complexion. She remembered the dress

Clarice had insisted on for Julie. Bright orange to clash with Julie's lush red hair. The witch wanted Julie to look awful. Clarice's daughter was supposed to be in Meg's wedding, and she intended to make her daughter the prettiest girl in the ceremony. Even prettier than the bride.

"I think this is the one," Jessica said, standing back to run a professional eye over Meg. "It flatters your figure so nicely."

It was a little tighter around Meg's waist than she liked, but it didn't emphasize her stomach rolls at all. She went out to show Julie, who clasped her hands together in excitement.

"That's it. That's the one."

Meg stood on the pedestal and eyed herself critically. She couldn't find any fault in the dress. She...actually looked nice in it. She wondered what Tyler would think when he saw her. Would he kiss her again?

She could almost feel his mouth against hers, firm and thrilling in a way she never expected from him. She wished he wasn't in New York right now so she could experience those lips one more time. Maybe even— She immediately stopped that thought in its tracks.

Nodding at Julie, she said, "Looks like you've got yourself a maid of honor."

"Yay!" Julie shrieked with a clap of her hands.

After Meg changed back into her clothes, they walked to Julie's store.

Julie looked preoccupied as she stepped inside the shop.

"What's up?" Meg asked, hoping that Julie wasn't about to bring up Tyler again.

"Hmm?" she replied as she went behind the store counter and booted up her computer.

"You look like you have something on your mind. If it's about Tyler—"

"No, that's not it, though I'm happy to talk about that some more if you want."

"No, I'm really good with not revisiting that particular topic today, thanks." Julie gave her a knowing look, but Meg changed the subject. "Are you nervous about the wedding? Cause everything seems to be running smoothly as far as I can tell, even with the ridiculously short timeframe you two are operating under."

"No, that's not it either." Julie opened her mouth to speak a couple of times, but no words came out. She looked like she was getting upset about something.

Meg stilled. "Are you having second thoughts? Did he say something that upset you?"

"Of course not. I—"

"If you're having second thoughts, my car is right down the road. We'll get the hell out of Holiday Bay until the up-roar dies down. It might take a while—this town is awful about that kind of thing, but—"

"Meg!" Julie interrupted before she could get worked up with wild ideas about hunting Jake down for any imaginary hurt he caused her best friend. "It's...it's about the honeymoon."

Meg frowned. She walked over to the counter and rested an elbow against it. "Are you worried that you two won't have anything to do? You're going to Jamaica. You get to lie on a private beach at that house Jake rented and drink margaritas all day. You'll have an amazing time."

"That's not it. It's..." Julie look flustered before she blurted, "I told Jake I want to have sex with him."

That made Meg pause. The amazing thing about Jake was that he accepted Julie the way she was. With her being asexual, sex was never going to be a part of their relationship. Jake knew that going in, and he loved Julie unconditionally. It was one of the reasons Meg liked him so much. It wasn't easy for ace people to connect with others, especially heterosexual people who valued physical intimacy.

"Why do you want to have sex?" she asked. "I mean, I know sexuality can be fluid and you've always identified as graysexual, but you've never expressed sexual desire toward him."

"That hasn't really changed, but I..." Julie's cheeks heated. "I want a baby. And I don't want to go to a fertility doctor and possibly have it leaked to the news. I want us to have a baby like most people do." She crossed her arms defensively. "Besides, lots of asexuals have sex solely for procreation."

"That's fair," Meg said. "So what did Jake say when you told him?"

"He didn't say anything. He paled and then said he needed to go down to his workshop. When I went to check on him later, he was hitting a piece of wood with a hammer like it had wronged him."

Meg laughed despite the seriousness of the conversation. "Look at it from his perspective. You've always had very clear boundaries when it comes to sex, and now you told him that you want it. I'm assuming you also told him you wanted sex purely to get pregnant."

"Um, maybe?"

Meg patted Julie's reddened cheek. "Sweet summer child. If you want to get into your husband's pants, seduce the man."

Julie scoffed. "I'm not exactly an expert in seduction."

"It honestly won't take much effort. I'm confident that if you just wink at him, he'll give you anything you want.

But remember that sex is something very natural and special to him. Don't make him feel like a stud brought to the farm. Make this about you creating a baby together, not you on a mission to get pregnant. Do you know what I mean?"

Julie looked mortified by the whole conversation but nodded.

"Good, and then when you get back from your honeymoon, I want all the juicy details."

She whacked Meg lightly on the arm. "You're terrible."

"That's why you love me."

Meg pulled into her brother's driveway almost a week later. Her phone pinged as she put the car in Park, and she reached for it. A pleasant smile popped on her mouth when she saw she had another text from Tyler.

When he told her he had to go to New York, he originally thought he'd only be gone for two weeks at most, but he was under negotiations with some big-shot singer to cowrite her new album, and it was taking longer than he expected. Three long weeks to be exact.

That didn't stop him from calling or texting her every day. Sometimes they'd talk about the pre-wedding party—things that usually led to a lot of back and forth about what they would do once they got on the yacht. Other times it was random stuff about their day.

His stories fascinated her. He'd tell her how he was going to produce one of the biggest singers in the world's next album soon. How he'd run into one of Paul's ex-hookups—some A-list celebrity—who chewed him out for Paul's behavior because she didn't have access to the man himself. How he'd met an elderly couple who turned out to be retired actors who were huge during Hollywood's Golden Age.

Her stories, in comparison, must have bored him to tears.

The most exciting thing she could tell him was about a fight that broke out between Willie Burton and Scott Lyle on Main Street the other day because Scott found out Willie had gotten his sister pregnant and then refused to marry her. It was quite the scandal for Holiday Bay but also *so* small town.

Tyler never seemed bored with her stories though. He actually seemed interested in everything she had to say, but their conversations reminded Meg again of how far Tyler had gone since leaving Holiday Bay. To her surprise, she was proud of him, if not a little envious of his life. He was so out of her reach, she would never be enough for him.

She never was.

When she let herself dwell on it too much, she thought back to the comments people made about her when Sarah posted that picture of them at Wine & Stuff. Her stomach would knot as she pictured him spending his time in New York, sleeping with his choice of women. Maybe even that singer he was in "negotiations" with.

Not that it was any of her business if he did. She had to remind herself more than once since he left that their relationship wasn't real. He was doing her a favor to help her through a crappy time in her life. Was he a surprisingly amazing kisser? Yes. But she couldn't let herself think about that. No matter how much she found herself doing so anyway.

As she sat in the car, reading his latest text, her insides filled with excited anticipation.

Everything is all set for the yacht this weekend. I'll be coming into town that morning, but if you want to meet up before then, let me know where.

She typed a quick Will do, before sending Julie and Jake a message that everything was a go for the weekend. Julie responded with an excited Eeeep!!!

Putting her phone in her purse, Meg got out of the car. She walked up to her brother's two-story colonial home and knocked on the door. She was nervous to see him, not sure what Stephen wanted to talk to her about. Her mother had gotten her hopes up that maybe he would relent and let her help out at the campground.

Her sister-in-law answered the door. Kimmy was like her husband, tall and lean. Stephen and Meg had inherited opposite genes from their parents. While he had taken after their dad in stature, Meg was small like her mom. Though her mom was petite compared to Meg, probably due to her not eating away her misery like her daughter did.

Kimmy was pretty, with dark hair and freckles across the bridge of her nose that would always keep her features youthful. Despite Meg wanting to hate her for having a place at the campground that she never would, it was hard to hate Kimmy, because she was a bundle of joy.

"Meg!" Kimmy wrapped her up in a big hug. "It's been way too long, girlie. We miss you."

"Me too," Meg said, though that wasn't exactly true and it made her feel guilty for thinking that way. She shouldn't have let her anger toward her dad sour her relationship with her brother and sister-in-law so much.

"Steve's out back," Kimmy explained. "He's barbequing plant-based hamburgers in your honor."

Meg swallowed down the emotion that caused. "I appreciate it. Thanks."

She guided her to the back of the house, where Meg could see her brother on the outside patio, poking at the burgers on the grill.

"Go on outside," Kimmy encouraged. "I know Steve has been looking forward to seeing you."

"Are you sure you don't need help?" Meg asked as she watched Kimmy return to the kitchen island where she was in the middle of preparing a salad.

She waved her off, and Meg made her way outside.

"Hey, jerk," she said, using the nickname for him that she'd been using since it was obvious he was going to inherit the campground. For a long time, she meant it cruelly. Now it came out affectionately.

Stephen turned away from the grill and smiled when he saw her. "Trouble! How the hell have you been?"

"Good," Meg said as he came over and hugged her. She sniffed the air and inhaled something smoky. "Um, I think the burgers are burning."

"Crap!" Stephen shouted before racing back to the grill. He flipped them over in time to save them from being inedible.

"Still can't grill worth a damn," she teased.

"Hey! I'm the grill king. I just don't know how to cook these stupid fake burgers. When are you going to eat meat again?"

She gave him an indignant look. "I'll eat meat when you get a soul."

Stephen laughed before wrapping an arm around her shoulder. He drew her over to the patio table and chairs and they sat down.

"You look good, Meg," her brother said. "Better."

Like everyone else in town, Stephen knew how his baby sister fell apart after she and Lucas broke up. He'd tried to reach out to her back then, but she'd rebuffed her, happier to stay holed up in her apartment, unwilling to face the world.

"Thanks. I am doing better," she said.

"Would that have anything to do with Tyler Evans?" Stephen grinned widely. "Rumor has it that you two were spotted making out at Wine & Stuff."

Meg's face flamed. "Oh...you know how town gossip is. Everyone wants to make a mountain out of a molehill. You can say hi to someone, and suddenly people think the two of you had sex on Main Street. Tyler and I are working on a project for Jake and Julie."

She wasn't going to tell Stephen what that project was. Jake and Julie were still doing their best to keep their wedding a secret. Only a few people knew about it at this point. The guests who were invited didn't even know what the event was for, only that Jake was hosting a party at his house. Meg trusted her brother, but when it came to secrets and Julie, she was a steel trap.

Stephen gave her knowing look anyway. "Would that project have anything to do with the big rock Julie's been wearing on her engagement finger?"

Meg kept her face straight but didn't answer. For trying to be so discreet, Julie probably shouldn't have worn her engagement ring so proudly around town. She was surprised the news hasn't leaked already to the media, but Jake had become a master over the years at staying out of the press.

When Meg continued to sit in silence, her brother changed the subject. "Well, whatever the reason is it's nice to hear that you and Tyler haven't killed each other yet. If this project had happened when you were kids, I'd probably be watching a crime story about you two by now."

"Funny," Meg responded flatly.

Stephen stood up to take the burgers off the grill. It was getting too cold to sit outside, so they went indoors. They headed to the kitchen where Kimmy was setting the table.

They continued to make small talk as they ate. After they finished, her brother cleaned the kitchen so Meg and Kimmy could catch up. He came into the living room and handed Meg a cup of coffee before he sat in an armchair opposite her. She glanced at Stephen, then over to Kimmy, who sat on the couch, not missing the distance between them.

Her stomach dropped. "You didn't ask me over here to tell me you're getting divorced, are you?"

Her breathing became shallower, and she had to force air into her lungs.

Please no. Not another divorce in the family.

"No, of course not," Stephen said. "Why would you think that?"

"You two are the most touchy-feely couple I've ever met. You're always all over each other. But you chose to sit there and not next to your wife."

Kimmy grinned. "Everything is fine between us. I just can't stand the smell of coffee these days."

"Why? Did you have a bad experience?" Meg asked. Her sister-in-law was a coffee connoisseur. She was the easiest to shop for at Christmas. Just buy her a bag of some weirdly named coffee, and she was as happy as a clam.

"No, my senses are a little more sensitive these days," she said before patting her stomach.

"But…" Meg's eyes widened. "Are you pregnant?"

Kimmy glowed. "About eight weeks."

Meg shrieked. Carefully putting her mug on the table, she ran over to Kimmy and hugged her.

"Congratulations," she said before going to her brother and hugging him too. "I'm going to be the best aunt—you wait and see. I'll spoil them so much. I'm going to be the one they go to when their parents totally don't understand them."

Stephen chuckled as Meg settled back in her chair. "I'm glad I can count on you to corrupt my future child, but that's not the only thing we wanted to talk to you about."

She stilled as the anxious feeling returned. "Okay."

"We want to expand Archer Campground, really make us more competitive with KOA," Stephen said. "We've been in talks to buy property near Mackinaw City. It's closer to Kimmy's family, and they're going to help when the baby comes so we can launch the new site."

Meg frowned. "But that's over two hours away. How are you going to run both locations?"

Kimmy and Stephen exchanged glances before he said, "We were actually hoping you'd take over the Holiday Bay location."

Meg went rigid. "What?"

"You have a degree in business administration, and thanks to your current job, you know how to hire the staff you need."

"But—what does Dad have to say about this?" Meg asked.

Stephen shifted in his seat. "It's an ongoing discussion, but I basically told him that Kimmy and I are moving and he could either bring you on or run the campground without me."

Meg's eyes teared up. "I… I don't know what to say."

"I hope you'll say yes." Some of the excitement left Stephen's eyes and weariness took over. "It won't be easy. You'll have a lot to learn, thanks to Dad making sure you had little involvement in how we do things. The truth is, Meg, I never wanted the full responsibility of the campground. If I'd had my way, I would have gone into architecture, but Dad made it clear from an early age that the campground was going to be my responsibility. And I just accepted it. But now that Kimmy is pregnant, it got me really thinking. Especially about how I don't want to plan my kid's life for them like Dad did ours. I want them to do what they want to do. If we stay here, I think Dad will put the same pressure on them as he did us."

"Unless you have a girl," Meg mumbled.

"There is that," he acknowledged. "But I don't want her to feel undervalued like you did. I know I didn't help with that, and I'm sorry."

Meg teared up. She looked away. "It's fine."

"It's not, but I hope this makes up for it a little bit." Stephen looked regretful before he looked at Kimmy, his face suddenly determined. "It's better if we have space now— to grow our family the way we want, so that there's little opportunity for regret."

Meg nodded slowly. "If I did accept, what would my title be? How much control would I have?"

"We can figure that out. I'd need to stay on as CEO for now, since everything is legally in my name at this point, but how does president of Archer Campgrounds, Inc. sound to you?"

Meg froze for a second as she comprehended what her brother just said. When she did, her lips tweaked up before widening into a huge grin.

"I guess you have a new president, boss."

Meg drove home after spending the rest of her evening with her brother and sister-in-law. It felt good to hang out with them without feeling her normal frustration and resentment. They'd discussed the future of the campgrounds in more detail as well as their excitement over Kimmy's pregnancy.

But as she parked her car, she became lost in thought. Her brother had just handed her everything she'd ever wanted. She was going to have a say in the family business. She'd be able to run the Holiday Bay location as she'd always dreamed. Things were finally starting to go right for her.

It seemed too good to be true.

She pulled out her phone and sent a text to Tyler as she entered her building.

You'll never believe what just happened to me.

She could see the three moving dots on her phone, letting her know he was in the process of replying. It touched her that he was always so quick to respond to her, despite how busy she knew he was. It was as though he put her before everything else he had going on. And that made her feel a certain way—special.

As she climbed the stairs to her apartment, she heard the sound of a shoe scuffing outside her door.

Her head jerked up. She half expected to see Tyler.

The air punched out of her lungs when she saw who it actually was.

The one person on earth she had no desire to see again.

Lucas Beaumont.

Chapter Thirteen

Meg hadn't seen Lucas since the night he'd ended their engagement. He looked just like she remembered. Tall and lean. Ridiculously good-looking with his blond hair and blue eyes. He was a stereotypical all-American boy. When he smiled, she knew dimples would pop out onto his cheeks. She'd traced them enough with her fingers over the years.

But as he stood before her, she had to acknowledge he didn't look good. His characteristically styled hair looked unkempt, as though he'd run his fingers through it numerous times as he'd waited for her to come home. Dark shadows stood out under his eyes. His skin was pale.

"Meg," he croaked, as though he hadn't used his voice in a long time.

"What are you doing here, Lucas?" she asked stiffly. "According to your mom, you should be off exploring the world with your incredibly attractive new girlfriend."

He laughed, but there was no joy to the sound. In fact, there was something off about him. As she further assessed him, she came to the startling realization that Lucas was drunk. In all the years they'd dated, she'd never seen Lucas drink more than two glasses of wine, but as they stood there, it was obvious he'd had more than that. She stepped even closer to him and could smell the alcohol on his breath.

"You're drunk," Meg accused. "You show up here after a year and a half of radio silence, and you're hammered?"

"Couldn't get ahold of you," he mumbled as he stared at her with reddened eyes. "I tried calling and calling, but you won't talk to me."

Meg gave him an indignant look as she reached for the keys in her coat pocket. "Can you blame me?"

"Look." Lucas swayed on his feet. "Can I come in for a minute? I have things to say, but I don't want to do it in the hallway."

Meg debated for a second, but old feelings began to surface. Not desire. He'd managed to kill that in her. But concern. They'd been together for so long. This was the first man she'd ever had sex with. Hell, the only man she'd ever been with. Aside from their romantic relationship, they'd been friends. In some ways, he'd been her best friend. They'd lie in bed for hours, just talking. And that might have been what hurt more than anything after they'd broken up. She not only lost her fiancé, but she'd also lost one of her closest people. That messed with one's head.

Against her better judgment, she said, "Fine. You can come in for a minute, and then I want you to leave."

He followed closely behind as Meg entered her apartment. She kicked off her shoes in the hallway and made her way to the kitchen to make Lucas a strong cup of coffee. He walked over to the cabinet where she stored her glasses and filled one with tap water. A lump formed in her throat as he continued to move through her apartment with remembered familiarity.

When she brought him a mug a few minutes later, he was sitting in his favorite green chair, closest to the slider door leading to her outdoor deck. It always gave a beautiful view of the bay during the day, but it was currently nighttime, and the only thing she could see was Lucas's reflection in the glass.

His head leaned against the chair's headrest; his eyes were closed. He looked completely worn out. She could only stare at him, her heart breaking all over again.

Why did you hurt me, Lucas? Why?

"Here," she said, and his eyelids flew open. He reached for the coffee and sipped at it while she took a seat opposite him on her beige couch.

"So," she said slowly. "What brings you back to Holiday Bay after disappearing for a year and a half?"

He let out a deep sigh as though releasing the weight of the world in that one breath. He took another huge gulp of his drink, wincing at the stinging heat.

"I…missed you," Lucas muttered into his cup.

Fury pummeled through Meg. She jumped to her feet and began to pace around the room. The atmosphere became tight, making it difficult to breathe.

"You *missed* me?" she screeched. "You missed me."

"I know I have no right to be in your life. I—"

"You're damned right you don't!" Meg gripped her stomach as her breathing became more challenging to suck in. "You dumped me, remember? You broke up with me because you decided your mom's feelings were more important than your fiancée's."

Lucas frowned as though he didn't know what she was talking about. She wasn't sure if it was the liquor clouding his memory or he genuinely didn't remember the biggest moment of her life.

He said in a tone serious and sober, despite his state, "I didn't break up with you because of my mom."

"Really? Because I distinctly remember you telling me that you couldn't take the fighting between your mom and me anymore, and you wanted out. After being together for *years*. How could you just end things like that?"

"I'm sorry," Lucas whispered, tears turning his eyes glassy. "I didn't want to hurt you, Meg. I'd sooner cut off my arm than do that to you."

Meg turned tiredly away from him and walked over to the slider. She stared at the nothingness in front of her.

"What are you really doing here, Lucas?" she muttered.

"I told you... I missed you. You're my only friend. The only person I can talk to."

She whipped around to face him. "And that's why you're here? You wanted to have good ole talk with your friend, Meg?"

Lucas winced. "No. I told you. I—I have things I want to say to you. I owe you an explanation."

Meg crossed her arms over her chest and said nothing.

He folded his hands together, staring at them like they would answer all of life's mysteries. "It kills me that I hurt you. I can't eat or sleep knowing that I did that to you. I have enough connections in this town still to know that you haven't had an easy time since I left."

"And that's why you left me behind to deal with the fall-out by myself. Because you were so freaking concerned about me?"

Lucas held out his hands in surrender. "You're right. I acted like a coward. I shouldn't have left like I did, but..."

He didn't say anything, so she sat back on the couch and waited.

"I needed to leave town for a while. I needed a break."

"Clearly," she snapped.

Lucas got up from the chair and stumbled his way over to the whitewashed fireplace. He stared into the unlit fire grate. "Meg, you have no idea—none at all—what it's like to grow up as a Beaumont in this town. The pressure my parents put on me since I was born. 'Walk this way, Lucas. Talk this way, Lucas. Act this way, Lucas. Look the freaking part, Lucas.' I lived in a glass house all the time with people sticking their damned noses against it, watching my every move," he said. "I couldn't act like a normal teenager, because if I did, it'd get back to my parents. You think my mom was tough on you? You have no idea what I went through. By the time I became an adult, a part of me was broken. The only good thing I had was you."

He turned to face her again. She could only stare stonily back.

A weary smile formed on his lips. "I'm saying all this wrong, even after I practiced it over and over again in my head. I thought I wanted to marry you. We'd talked about it enough over the years. We both seemed like we were in a place in life where it was time. We'd have two kids and a dog and live the dream, right? But my mom wouldn't get off your back. You became the new me. Never good enough for Clarice Beaumont. Never happy or satisfied. And I realized I couldn't do it anymore. I couldn't keep letting you get exposed to her poison. So I ended things." He sighed again, the fight leaving his body, his expression turning to misery once more. "I thought I was protecting you from her. All I did was damage us both."

Meg barely heard anything after… "You *thought* you wanted to marry me? Didn't you actually want to marry me?"

Lucas's mouth opened and closed several times.

Her hand shot to her mouth. Bile rose in her throat, and she swallowed it down with a grimace.

"Lucas," she said slowly. "Were you ever in love with me?"

"Of course I love you."

She couldn't see past the tears that were now blinding her. Everything was starting to crystallize in her head.

"That's not what I asked," she whispered. "Were you ever *in* love with me?"

Lucas's face turned ashen. "I… I thought I was."

"Oh god," she said when he didn't say anything more. She jumped up and started wandering around the room again. "How could you? How could you lead me on for *years* when you weren't even in love with me?"

"I tried." Lucas's voice was broken. "I really thought I could love you like you deserved."

Meg didn't know if she wanted to scream or sob. "Was this all some kind of messed up game to you? How could you do that to me? I thought you cared. I thought—"

"I do." Lucas ran to her, grabbing her arms in his hands. "You're my best friend. The past year and a half has been miserable without you."

Meg shoved him away. "How can you look me in the face and say you missed me? My whole life has been a lie, thanks to you. You say you care about me? You don't even know the meaning of the word."

Lucas looked like he was going to be sick to his stomach. "Meg, I'm sorry."

"I don't understand how you could do it." She wiped at her tears angrily. "I don't understand how you could treat me like that. Make it make sense, Lucas."

His voice was so low when he spoke, she strained to hear him. "I—I'm gay."

The words didn't register. "What?"

He repeated it, louder this time. "I'm gay."

Meg couldn't move. Couldn't breathe. She stumbled over to the fireplace and gripped the mantle so hard, her knuckles turned white.

"Meg…" His voice was an aching whisper. "Please say something."

She opened her mouth to speak, but no words came out. She was in over her head again, suffocating. Meg tried to get air in, but her throat felt like it was closing up.

Lucas came over to her and gently put his hands on her shoulders. She shrugged them off.

"Please," he begged. "Please. I'm sorry."

"Leave," she uttered.

"Meg, I need—"

"Leave!" she screamed.

"You're my best friend," Lucas repeated hoarsely. "I can't lose you. Not again."

She squeezed her eyes shut so hard they hurt. "Someday, you and I will talk about this because, honestly, I can accept the fact that you're gay." There'd been enough signs over the years—the numerous conversations about waiting to get married, their lacking sex lives. "But what I'm struggling with here is the fact that you lied to me. For *years*. I can't… I can't even look at you right now. And I need you to leave."

Lucas sucked in a wet sob behind her, but he finally did as she asked, closing the door quietly behind him. Meg looked into the mirror that hung above the fireplace. Her face looked sickly white, her features stunned. Swiveling around, she grabbed the fertility goddess off the hallway table that'd she'd bought Lucas as a joke—turned out the joke was really on her—and flung it hard against the mirror. It shattered with a crashing satisfaction.

The feeling didn't last long. Struggling into the bathroom, she scrubbed her face until it hurt. She refused to cry anymore. Her mind was racing in too many directions to give into something as useless as tears. She felt jittery. On edge.

Swiftly changing into her pajamas, she went back into the living room and cleaned up the glass as best she could. Her cell phone rang in the distance. She ignored it.

After she was through cleaning, she shut off all the lights in the apartment, and crawled into bed. But as she lay there, her inability to breathe grew worse. She tried over and over to get air into her lungs, but the harder she tried, the more impossible it became.

Throwing back the blankets, she sat up sharply. The new angle made breathing even worse. Meg started to panic. She wanted to scream. She got up and started her nervous pacing, trying to alleviate the burst of energy that hit her as her anxiety continued to spike.

Meg felt like she was losing her mind. She didn't know which direction to go, both physically and mentally. One wrong move and she'd be under water again, and this time she might not resurface.

She wanted to call someone. Beg them to help her. But what could they do? The local therapist didn't know the meaning of the word *confidential*, and no matter how infuriated she was with Lucas, she couldn't risk his secret getting out.

She blindly reached for her phone. She wanted to call Julie. Julie might know what to do. She usually did. But when Meg saw how late it was, she paused. She didn't want to wake her up.

Her shaking hands scrolled over the names on her phone. The last text she had was from Tyler. Maybe he could help her. But what could he do for her? He was in New York. Besides, what could she say to him?

Hey, my life is a dumpster fire. My parents are divorc-

ing, I'm about to start my dream job and...what if I screw it up? What if my dad is right and I'm not good enough for it. Oh yeah, and my ex-fiancé made my whole life a lie. I'm never good enough for anything or anyone. And I feel so overwhelmed...like a huge wave is crashing over my head and I can't resurface, no matter how hard I kick. Isn't that so sexy and attractive? Clearly, I'm someone you'll want to kiss again.

Yeah, no. Meg couldn't talk to anyone. She swung her legs over the side of the bed. Clutching her stomach, she started rocking back and forth.

I need help. I need help. I need help.

But there was nowhere to turn. Meg grabbed her pillow and went back into the living room. Picking up the TV remote, she lay down on the couch. She twisted around and pulled the green blanket she normally kept on the back of the couch and covered herself with it.

Turning the TV on, Meg turned the volume all the way up. The loud sound began to block the noise in her head, and she finally fell into a troubled sleep.

Chapter Fourteen

Tyler's leg bounced up and down as he checked his phone for the umpteenth time in the past four days. The flight had been smooth so far, but he was restless. He couldn't stop worrying about Meg.

Being away from her over the past few weeks had been harder than he expected. He missed her, but at least they'd been able to communicate via text and the occasional call. Tyler was doing his best to keep things super casual between them so he didn't scare her off. Despite the recent advancement in his attempts to woo her—and he cursed Jake all over again for getting that stupid word stuck in his head—he wasn't one hundred percent sure Meg didn't still view him as her childhood archrival. But he'd taken the advice from the guys in the band seriously and was continuing with Operation Enemies to Something More.

He'd flirted with Meg, found every reason under the sun to touch her. They'd kissed—and holy hell, were those kisses amazing, considering they were pretty PG up to this point. It was as if Meg's mouth had specifically been created for his. He never wanted to stop kissing her, to taste her tongue with his as he'd done so many years ago. To do more than kiss her. He ached to have her underneath him, to explore every inch of her tantalizing body. He'd taken more than his fair share of ice-cold showers in the time they'd been separated. If she only knew how much he wanted her...

But they weren't there yet, and he didn't want to scare her off. So Tyler made sure to reach out to her every single day he was gone, in hopes that she would think about him as often as he thought of her. And his plan to slowly woo her seemed to be working.

Whether she was consciously aware of it or not, Meg had started to find reasons to touch him too, when they were together. He thought back to that moment on the platform at the adventure park where she'd clung to him after stepping off the bridge. Or how she'd placed her head against his chest when they were on the porch swing.

Texting with her over the past few weeks had given him something to look forward to. Meg would fill him in on her day, and he got to know her all over again. He knew she considered her job simply a paycheck, but he could tell Meg took pride in doing it well. That was obvious when she told him about a man who came into her office, down on his luck after being laid off from his job of twenty years. She was not only able to help get him new employment, but his employer recently promoted him to manager.

Another favorite story she told was when she experimented with a recipe her grandma used to make and her entire kitchen smelled like feet for a week afterward. Every story she provided gave him a glimpse into Meg's life, allowing him to rediscover her. And the more he learned, the more charmed he was.

It wasn't just her body that he wanted. Tyler wanted all of her. He loved her wicked sense of humor and the way she challenged him. He loved how smart and sassy she was. He loved getting a text from her in the morning and hearing her voice on the phone right before he went bed. He loved…a lot.

But something had happened a few days ago. She'd texted him, seeming to indicate that something exciting had happened. And then, radio silence for the rest of the night until the following morning when he messaged her, asking her what happened. She'd responded, I'll tell you next time I see you.

Ever since, he'd received zero communication from her. His texts had gone unanswered. He'd tried calling her a couple of times, but the calls went straight to voicemail. It was awful. He'd gone back, read and reread their messages to make sure he hadn't said or done anything that could have upset her, but he couldn't find anything.

He hated being completely cut off from her.

"Mr. Evans," the flight attendant said. Her eyes ran over his face in a way that let him know she was interested. He didn't acknowledge it. The only person on his mind was Meg. She looked disappointed but continued, "We'll be landing soon. Please make sure to fasten your seat belt."

"Thanks," he replied before grabbing his belt and doing just that.

As the plane touched down, he put on his baseball hat in hopes of keeping a low profile. As much as he loved and appreciated his fans, every instinct in his body screamed at him to get to Meg. He walked through the airport toward the baggage-claim area, his steps swift. He paused when he saw his mother waiting for him.

"Hey, sweets," she said, giving him a brief hug. "Good flight?"

"Yeah, it was fine," he responded before grabbing his bag. "Thanks for coming to get me. I wasn't expecting it. I could have rented a car."

"And miss spending time with my favorite child? Not on your life."

Despite his worry, he smiled at that. "I'm your only child."

She waved that away as they stepped outside the airport. Tyler shuddered when the cold Michigan air hit his skin.

"It's a lot colder than the last time I was here," he grumbled, wishing he'd remembered to grab his winter jacket.

His mom looked up at the sky. "I expect we'll get snow soon. Though the forecast predicts it'll get warm this weekend."

"Thank God," he muttered. When his mom looked at him questioningly, he said, "Meg will go for my throat if we all get sick for Jake and Julie's big party next weekend."

Once they settled in the car and left Traverse City to head to Holiday Bay, Tyler asked, "Speaking of, I don't suppose you've seen Meg lately?"

His mom glanced his way. "Not recently."

"Hmm." Tyler's shoulders slumped. He stared out the window despairingly, watching the trees go by.

"Trouble in paradise?" his mom prodded.

"No, things are fine. She's just been a little absent lately."

"Knowing Meg, she's probably up to her elbows helping Julie with the wedding, what with it being next weekend and everything."

"Yeah, that's probably it," he said before his eyes narrowed. "Wait, how did you know about the wedding? It's supposed to be top secret."

"Oh, honey, this is Holiday Bay. There's no better telephone line in the world than what the Bay has to offer."

"Great, that's all we need. A bunch of paparazzi to ruin things."

"Have a little faith in this town. People here are protective of their own. That includes you boys."

As they pulled into Holiday Bay's town limits, his mom asked, "How's the song writing going? Any better?"

"Yeah, I feel like things are back on track," he said.

His mind flicked to the carry-on bag in the trunk where he'd stored his journal full of lyrics. When he wasn't texting Meg while he was away or in some meeting, he'd been writing. Some of the songs were mediocre, others were good. And almost all of them revolved around Meg.

He wondered what she'd think if she knew she was his muse. She'd probably be mortified and put herself down in that way he hated. She was beautiful. Why couldn't she see that?

He pulled his phone out of his pocket and sent her a quick text. Hey, I'm back in town. Do you want to meet up before the party and make sure we have everything covered?

He hoped she'd say yes so he could figure out what was going on with her. It only took a few minutes for her to answer. Sorry—I can't. Too busy at the moment. I'll see you at the marina tonight.

Tyler sighed his disappointment but tried to get in a better mood. At least she'd responded this time. And in a few hours, he'd be hanging out with his closest friends for the bachelor party. Then—whether she liked it or not—Tyler would get to spend the rest of the evening with Meg.

Once they arrived at his parents' house, Tyler went up to his childhood bedroom and pulled out the clothes he wanted to wear to the bachelor party. Taking a quick shower, he got dressed, pulling the navy blue cashmere sweater over his head and smoothing out any wrinkles.

When he finished getting ready, he repacked his carry-on with the essentials he needed for staying overnight on the yacht. Once he had everything ready, he headed downstairs to where his mother and father were sitting in the living room, watching a James Bond movie.

"Sweets, you look so nice," his mom said when she saw him.

"Thanks." He glanced around the familiar room, taking in the overstuffed furniture and honey-mustard walls. His phone buzzed with a text, letting him know the limo arrived. Putting his cell back in his pants, he said, "You know, maybe I'll start looking for a house in the area."

Both his parents perked up at that.

"You're moving back to the Bay?" his dad asked.

Tyler shrugged. "Jake's living here full-time. And since I've been coming back here more often than not lately, it might be nice if I had my own place."

His mom winked at him. "Hmm, Jake's lived here awhile now, and you never mentioned moving back before. Does this by chance have anything to do with Meg?"

"No!" Tyler replied instantly. His parents burst out laughing. Freaking married couples. "Anyway... I should get going."

"Give Jake our love," his mom said as he was leaving.

"Make sure to give Meg your love while you're at it," his dad added.

"Good night," Tyler said, shutting the door firmly on their lingering snickers.

Tyler's skin was buzzing as he took another sip of bourbon. The club he'd arranged for the bachelor party to meet in had outdone themselves. The music blared loudly through the speakers surrounding the dance floor. On a normal Saturday night, the place was a hot spot for Traverse

City twentysomethings who came to dance, but Tyler had rented out the entire place so that their party could have privacy. That hadn't stopped the venue from playing music that compared to a New York club scene.

"To Jake," Paul toasted.

"To Jake," the party drunkenly shouted back, and they slammed another shot of whatever they were drinking.

In attendance were all of the Holiday Boys, with the exception of Zan. They were all disappointed to learn that he couldn't make it, but his wife was still feeling under the weather, so they understood. Zan assured Jake that he'd be there for the wedding. A few other people Jake had gotten reacquainted with since moving back to the bay were there, including Meg's brother, Stephen, much to Tyler's surprise. The man had walked up to Tyler earlier, given him a firm handshake and told him to treat Meg well or else.

Tyler grabbed a mozzarella stick off one of the plates in front of him and munched on it, hoping it would soak up some of the alcohol he'd already consumed. James sat next to him, downing tequila shots like he was going for some kind of Guinness World Record. Tyler frowned at him. He'd known James since they were kids, and the man rarely drank, let alone sucked down shots like his life depended on it.

"What's up with you?" he asked.

"Nothing," James said, his voice already slurring over his words. He finished off another shot and waved for the waitress to bring him more.

Tyler's frown deepened. "Maybe you should slow down."

"Maybe you should piss off."

His eyebrows shot up. Though James had suffered the worst when Holiday Boys were originally together, due to music executives forcing him to hide his sexuality, he'd always retained his temper. He was clearly having a bad night.

Tyler held up his hands in surrender. "Sorry. But know that I'm here if you want to talk."

He turned away from James to focus on Paul, who'd started dancing and singing to "Girls Just Want to Have Fun" on the dance floor. He was probably one of the few people still sober in attendance, given that he, like James, typically abstained from alcohol. He found his fun in other ways. Mainly with women.

"Mason left me," James muttered.

Tyler's head whipped back to him. "*What?*"

"Yeah." James ran a hand through his dark hair as though it irritated him. "He said he wanted to return to California to pursue his dream of acting."

Tyler wrapped his arm around his friend's shoulder. "I'm sorry. I know how much you loved him."

"You know what the real kicker is?" James asked. When Tyler shook his head, he said, "I found out Mason's been cheating on me with the director of our rehab show. When I confronted him about the affair, he didn't deny it. He said that Pierre could help make him a star and that he'd given up too much to be with me. And here I thought he'd agreed to move to Michigan because he loved me."

The waitress dropped off another shot of tequila, and he drank it down in one gulp. He slammed the empty glass on the table and told the waitress, "Keep them coming."

The waitress looked at James in concern, so he pulled out his wallet and handed her a one-hundred-dollar bill.

She practically ripped it out of his hand before she said, "I'll be right back with another for you, sir."

After she left, Tyler asked, "What are you going to do?"

James looked at his glass with bloodshot brown eyes. "What can I do? One thing I always loved about Mason is that he's stubborn. He won't change his mind." His eyes drifted to his ring finger where his shiny gold wedding band still remained. "I'm not going to do the show. I can't deal with it right now, especially if Pierre is still directing."

Tyler put a comforting hand on his friend's shoulder. "I'm really sorry, James."

"I don't know how to tell Paul. My show was his baby as much as it was mine. He did so much to get it off the ground, and now I'm going to walk away from everything he did for me."

Tyler glanced over at Paul, who was still dancing. "He'll understand."

James grabbed his empty glass, turning the crystal back and forth so that it shimmered in the light above.

"Maybe I'll move back to the Bay," he said. "I think I need a change of scene."

Tyler gave him a solemn smile. "That might not be a bad idea. Your parents and siblings are still in the area. You could spend more time with them."

"Yeah." James gave him a tired twist of his mouth. "Do me a favor? Keep this between us for now. Jake's never liked Mason, and I really don't want to hear him saying *I told you so*."

"You know he would never do that, but yeah, I'll keep this between us. You tell people about this when you're ready."

"Thanks, man," James said before going back to stare at his glass.

Giving James another pat on the back, Tyler left him to his drink. He joined Jake where he was sitting on the side of the dance floor, watching Paul make an fool out of himself with an amused smile on his face.

Tyler sat down, eying Jake's glass. "What are you drinking?"

"Ice water," he replied.

"You party animal."

Jake shrugged. "I don't want to get too drunk, so I'm pacing myself. Julie and I started having a serious conversation earlier, and I want to finish it."

Tyler frowned. "Should I be worried? You're not going to call of the wedding or anything, are you?"

"Hell no. I've been waiting for Julie for what feels like my whole life. I'm not about to let her go now."

Tyler gave a slight nod but didn't say anything. If Jake wanted to talk about whatever was on his plate, he could when he was ready.

Which was apparently now.

"Julie wants to have a baby. We've been going back and forth about it for weeks now."

Tyler stared at him in puzzlement. "Is that a bad thing? You think Dylan would have an issue with it?"

"I think Dylan would be thrilled to have a baby brother or sister. He's already an amazing brother to Charlotte," Jake said, mentioning his ex-wife's daughter that she'd had with her new husband.

"Then what's the problem?"

"Julie wants to conceive a baby the old-fashioned way."

That made Tyler's forehead wrinkle. "Oh."

"Yeah, oh." Jake glared at his water as though he wished he did actually have something stronger.

"So…" Tyler said slowly. "You should be happy about that, right? You get to have sex with your wife. You didn't think you'd have that."

"But what if it changes the dynamic between us? Julie's not into sex, and I respect that, but I am. Very much. What if I scare her with…"

"How much you want her?" Tyler said when Jake didn't

continue. He gave a stilted nod. Tyler gave him a reassur-ing smile. "Look, you love her. You won't do anything to hurt or scare her. And if Julie is telling you she wants to have sex with you, then she's clearly okay with it. She's an adult woman who knows her own mind. Respect that."

"But what if this opens a Pandora's box in me and I want sex with her all the time?"

"Do you feel desire for her now?"

"Of course I do. You've seen Julie. She's a very desir-able woman."

"But you don't act on it, right?"

"No," Jake said.

"Why not?"

Jake gave him an annoyed look. "I'm not a pig. I love her and respect her. I'll take her any way I can."

"Exactly," Tyler said. "You've gone this long without sex. You two will be fine. And who knows, maybe she'll want more kids down the road."

The side of Jake's mouth ticked up. "Maybe."

"Did I hear something about sex?" Paul asked as he sauntered over to the table and sat down. "Speaking of, I have a wedding gift for you."

Jake and Tyler exchanged worried looks as Paul waved at a waiter, who brought over a large wrapped box with a huge red bow on it.

Jake cautiously opened it as James, their friend, Trevor, and Stephen joined them. He lifted the lid carefully, looked inside and instantly shut it.

"Why are we friends again?" Jake glowered at Paul.

"You love me and you know it," he replied, his expres-sion angelic.

"What'd he get you?" James asked.

When Jake didn't say anything, Paul said proudly, "A

box of sex toys to keep Jake warm at night. In fact, there's one in there with a rubber butt and realistic vag—"

"And on that note, who's up for shots?" Tyler asked, grinning at Jake's grateful look.

Jake pushed the box aside. "I changed my mind. Let's drink."

When it was time to leave to meet up with the bachelorette party, the men walked outside into the cold November air. Tyler felt his senses come back online despite the amount of alcohol he'd consumed. Their party scooted into the stretch limo that waited to take them back to Holiday Bay. Tyler shivered and looked at the night sky before he got into the car. They were supposed to have an unusually warm evening tonight, but—and maybe it was the alcohol speaking—it smelled like snow was in the air.

He got into the limo and sat next to Trevor. He was huge in the music industry and had produced the Holiday Boys's last single. It was his yacht they were spending the night on.

"Hey, Trevor?" Tyler said.

"What's up, my friend?" Trevor replied, leaning on Paul to keep himself upright.

"How does your yacht do in snow?"

"As smoothly as a virgin on prom night."

"What?" James and Tyler asked at the same time, but Trevor was now in a deep conversation with an equally inebriated Stephen.

It took less than an hour to get to the marina in Holiday Bay where the yacht was waiting for them. They could see the women already on board. When they saw the men get out of the limo, a collective cheer went through the ladies. Stephen's wife, Kimmy, pulled up in her car, and Stephen said his goodbyes, stating he had to get up early in the morning for work.

Jake raced up the ramp leading to the yacht's bow where Julie was. He picked her up and spun her in circles until she burst into giggles. He showed zero signs of the alcohol they'd consumed.

"Show off," Tyler grumbled as he tried to put one foot in front of the other, following Paul. He had a terrible feeling he would have the hangover of the century the next morning.

His mood lightened when he saw Meg standing off to the side. She wore a thick green cable sweater over a long black skirt that fell to her ankles. Her golden brown hair was piled into loose curls on top of her head. She looked absolutely beautiful.

Paul stumbled to a stop when he walked onto the bow of the ship, causing Tyler to almost bump into him. He stared at a gorgeous blonde across the deck.

"K-Kyleigh?" he asked.

The woman looked self-conscious as she shoved her hands into her coat pockets. "Hello, Paul. It's been a long time."

"Yeah, it has. How've you been?"

"Great," Kyleigh said before looking around. "Well, I don't know about anyone else, but I'm ready to get out of this cold."

She walked inside without speaking to Paul any further. He stared after her like he'd seen a ghost.

"How do you know Kyleigh?" Tyler asked. Although he and she had graduated together, Paul and Zan had gone to school in the next town over. As far as Tyler knew, Paul didn't have any ties to Holiday Bay other than the band.

"We met at a performing arts camp one summer. She was my high school girlfriend." Paul looked at the door Kyleigh had just disappeared inside.

Tyler looked at him in surprise. Paul had a well-earned reputation as a womanizer. He was a do them and leave them kind of guy. He did his best to never get emotionally involved with any woman he slept with. So it somewhat surprised Tyler to see him shook up over seeing a woman he dated years ago.

"Paul, do you have a second?" James said as he stumbled his way over to them.

"Sure," he replied, finally pulling his attention away from where Kyleigh was last seen.

The two went to the opposite side of the ship for some privacy. Tyler stared after them in concern, knowing what James was about to drop on their friend. He could tell when James shared the news about quitting the show by the way Paul stiffened. He started whispering quickly, his hands flying wildly in the air. James muttered something else, and Paul stopped speaking. Tyler had never seen him look so serious in his life. He leaned over and gave him a hard hug. The sight eased Tyler's worry for his friends.

He made his way over to where Meg stood, talking to an older woman that Tyler didn't know.

"Hi," he said as he joined them. He thought about copying Jake, picking Meg up and spinning her, but he feared he might upchuck all that bourbon he'd drunk.

"Hi yourself," she returned, and for a moment he forgot that he had cause to worry about her. She looked just like his Meg, upbeat and perky. But as he took a closer look at her, he could see from the deck lights shining on her face that her eyelids were slightly puffy as though she'd cried recently, and no amount of makeup could cover the circles under her eye.

"Tyler, do you know Jessica?" Meg said, introducing him to the other woman. "She owns the Bridal Barn in town."

"Nice to meet you," he said politely, shaking the woman's hand.

"You too," she replied. She looked between the two of them and a smile formed on her face. "If you'll excuse me, I think I'll go inside where it's a little warmer."

Once she was gone, Tyler turned his full attention back on the woman who'd preoccupied his every waking moment over the past three weeks.

"Meg." He put his hand on her chin, lifting it so she had no choice but to look at him. "What happened? What's wrong?"

"Nothing's wrong." She pulled her face away and started walking past him. "Our two best friends are getting married next week. Let's celebrate."

She walked indoors, where there was a line of champagne glasses and shots waiting for them. Tyler groaned at the sight of them, but he followed Meg's lead…just like he always did these days.

He grabbed two glasses and sauntered back over to her. "For you, milady."

She snorted, despite whatever bad mood she was in. "Why, thank you, sir." She peered at him closer. "How much have you had to drink so far tonight?"

Tyler's forehead furrowed as he tried to think seriously on her question. He couldn't answer her, because he'd lost track. "You want me to answer that truthfully?"

"I'm not sure if I could answer truthfully myself at this point," Meg said, before taking a huge gulp of her drink.

Red flags waved in front of Tyler's intoxicated gaze that something was off, but before he could ask her again what was wrong, she yelled out, "A toast!"

"A toast!" the crowd of party gatherers responded.

And thus started a night of endless toasts. They drank to

the happy couple. They drank to Trevor for loaning them his yacht. They drank to James for finally mastering a complicated piece of choreography during their last practice.

It went on for hours. And even throughout the festivities, Tyler was hyperaware of Meg. As the night continued, he grew more concerned. She drank like she was on a mission, not because she was trying to enjoy herself.

They'd pulled it off. The party was perfect, and Jake and Julie were clearly enjoying themselves, given that they were now toasting Julie's childhood dog, Mr. Snuffles. But Meg didn't look relieved that'd they done a good job.

She looked miserable. She plastered on a fake smile when anyone glanced her way, but the shine she had these days—which still wasn't even close to the energy she had when they were kids—seemed to be absent.

A couple hours later, the party was well and truly over. James was the first to give in. He grabbed a bottle of scotch and wobbled to somewhere deep inside the ship where the bedrooms were. The guests of honor left shortly after, with Jake and Julie waltzing down the hall to their room, laughing as they went. Jessica soon followed.

"Hey," Meg said, coming up to where he sat next to Paul on a large leather couch in the spacious sitting area. Paul had been uncharacteristically quiet all night, but it wasn't surprising given the news that James was pulling out of their show. But that didn't seem to be his only distraction. He hadn't stopped staring at Kyleigh all night. At some point, he'd switched from drinking soda water to doing shots. A lot of them. After that, he got his hands on a full gin bottle, which he kept gulping from until it was practically empty.

Meg continued, "I'm going to step outside for some fresh air."

"You want me to go with you?" Tyler asked. They hadn't really had a lot of opportunity to talk all evening.

She shook her head politely. "I'll only be a minute."

Once she was gone from the room, Tyler's energy seemed to go with her. There was no party for him without Meg there.

Standing up with a stretch, he glanced over at Paul. "You good?"

"Hmm," his friend replied.

Paul continued to stare at Kyleigh, who didn't exactly ignore him, but she hadn't gone out of her way to speak with him again either. She acted like he was an old acquaintance that she had nothing more to say anything to, whereas Paul looked like he wanted to have a full discussion with her.

Kyleigh sat in a velvet chair on the opposite side of the room, discussing the pros and cons of owning a business with Trevor. It didn't matter that Trevor owned a multi-million-dollar studio that world-famous artists came to Michigan just to record in or that Kyleigh owned a small arts-and-crafts store in Holiday Bay. The way they talked, they were like two peas in a pod. If Trevor wasn't gay and happily married to his husband, Tyler wondered what Paul's reaction would have been. When he wasn't looking at Kyleigh, he was glaring at Trevor for hogging her. Tyler had never seen him act this way about a woman before. He would have been fascinated by it if he wasn't so drunk himself.

Paul took another swig from the bottle he was clutching. He soon slumped over, passing out on the couch. Tyler grabbed the bottle before it could spill. He checked on Paul through blurry eyes to make sure he was fine.

"Is he okay?"

Tyler turned to see Kyleigh next to him.

Trevor stood behind them, looking exasperated at Paul. "If he pukes, you're paying for the entire yacht to get cleaned. I'm talking the whole yacht, Evans."

"Yeah, yeah," Tyler replied.

Trevor shook his head, muttering to himself about drunken idiots as he headed toward his room.

Kyleigh continued to look at Paul with concern. Tyler wondered again what the situation was between the two. For as indifferent as she'd acted toward Paul all night, she appeared to care when he wasn't watching her.

"He's fine," Tyler assured her. He turned Paul on his side in case he got sick in the middle of the night.

When he turned back, Kyleigh was still there.

He felt the need to cast Paul in a better light. "He doesn't usually drink like this."

A single light eyebrow shot up on Kyleigh's face. "Isn't he the party boy of your group?"

"When we were kids, sure. We all did stupid things back then." Leaving Meg without a word after graduating had been on the top of Tyler's list. He continued, "Paul doesn't typically drink though. He's too focused on his business."

"Right?" Kyleigh said cynically. "Marrying off strangers."

"It's the number one show in reality TV," he defended.

"That's Paul for you." Her features turned soft as though a better memory of him popped in her head. "He never did know how to fail."

With that she left, Tyler staring after her in confusion. His fuzzy mind didn't concentrate on her for long. She wasn't the woman who'd been consuming his every thought all night.

Meg hadn't returned to the room, so he assumed she'd gone to bed while he was dealing with Paul. Tyler couldn't help but feel disappointed. He really wanted to spend a quiet moment with her, just the two of them.

As he headed for his own room, he glanced out the large window overlooking the stern. He stumbled to a stop. Meg stood at the front of the ship, her head tilted skyward. Tyler switched directions and stepped outside to join her.

"Meg, what are you still doing out here?" he asked. His speech sounded slurred to his own ears. He was going to pay for it in the morning, he just knew it. The cold air enveloped his skin, and he shivered. "It's freezing."

Meg pointed to the sky. "It's snowing."

Tyler looked up. The movement almost made him fall over. He grabbed onto the rail to keep himself upright.

It was indeed snowing. Tiny white flakes hurled down from above, getting larger the faster they fell. He stared at them, entranced by the sight as they swirled in the light emanating from the yacht.

"Oh hell," he said as he remembered something. "I thought it was supposed to be warmer this weekend."

"You spend too much time in California," she said. "You've forgotten how Michigan works."

"Do you want me to grab a jacket for you or something?" Tyler asked. "Oh wait…here."

He started to reach for the hem of his sweater, but as he tried to pull it over his head, it got stuck.

Meg laughed. "What are you doing?"

"Trying to be chivalrous," he said, his voice muffled by the fabric. "I was going to give you my sweater."

He felt her hands on his arms before she yanked his pullover back over his chest.

"I'd rather have you not suffer from hypothermia than be chivalrous," she said. She turned her attention back to the snow.

When she didn't say anything else, Tyler looked her way. She looked so sad in that moment, his stomach clenched.

"Meg…" he whispered. "What is it? You've been quiet all night."

She lifted a shoulder but didn't say anything. It bothered him, even in his intoxicated state, that she wouldn't tell him what was troubling her. If she would tell him, he could at least do his best to fix whatever it was. He'd do anything for her if she'd let him.

"You know you can tell me anything?" He grinned, drunk and stupid. "Chances are I won't remember it in the morning anyway."

"You're so drunk, Evans." She giggled at that. The sound was high pitched and loud in the quietness of the bay, but it was real, and Tyler found himself relaxing at the sound.

"So are you." He pointed a finger in her face until she went cross-eyed. He wanted to kiss her so badly. Instead, he said, "Come on, tell me what's up."

Meg let out a long, deep breath. "My brother is turning over control of Archer Campground to me."

"That's great news, right?" Tyler said. "It's what you've always wanted."

"Yeah," she murmured.

He didn't miss her lack of enthusiasm. He tried to rev up some excitement. "You should have said something earlier when we were doing our toasts. We could have toasted to you. Do you want to do one now?"

Meg covered her mouth as though the idea made her sick. "No, I don't need any more to drink—thanks."

Tyler returned his grip to the railing of the yacht, enjoying the feel of the cold metal under his hands, despite the chilly night.

"So what's Stephen going to do?" he asked, trying to focus on the conversation.

"He and his wife are moving to Mackinaw City. They're going to open a second location. They want to start a chain. He'll be CEO, and they're making me president."

He stared at her profile, expecting to see something—anything—other than the glimpse of despair on her face. "You don't seem too happy about it."

"I am."

He clasped his hand on Meg's shoulder, turning her slightly so he could get a better look at her. "What's really going on? You should be celebrating. Instead, you're acting like you're attending a funeral."

She let out a sigh that seemed to hurt her chest. "I recently found out some news that I'm struggling with. And before you ask, no, I can't tell you. It's something very private—a secret that's not mine to share."

"Okay, fair enough." He leaned an elbow on the railing of the stern. "But it's obviously something that's affected you."

She looked out toward the darkness of the water. "For so long, I had my life planned out to the finest detail. I thought I'd be married by now, maybe have some kids. But here I am. Alone. I wasted so much of my life on an impossibility."

Tyler's forehead scrunched as he tried to comprehend what she was telling him. "You can still get married, Meg. You're not dead. You can live your life, get married, have kids. All of it."

Her face turned sad. "Pretty soon, I won't even have my best friend. She'll be a unit with Jake. She'll have her own life, little babies to love. She won't have time for her pathetic single friend. She's moving on, just like everyone else does. Everyone but me."

"Meg, you know that's not true," Tyler said. "Julie loves you, and from what I know of her, she's loyal to a fault. She'd never abandon you. Will things change once she and Jake get married? Sure. But she would never in a million years cut you out of her life."

Meg wiped at her face. "Logically, I know that. I'm just being dumb right now."

He looked at her worriedly, but he teasingly said, "It's the alcohol."

"Sure, the alcohol." Meg held out a hand and caught a snowflake, watching it melt in her palm. "You know what I wish?"

"Hmm?"

"I wish I could marry someone right now. I don't want to have to go through the whole song and dance of finding someone new and dating them. It takes too long. And with my luck, I'll probably end up with someone who'll date me for years, like Lucas, and then dump me." Her shoulders dropped. Tyler opened his mouth to protest—to tell her he'd never do that to her—when she murmured so quietly, he strained to hear her. "Why can't I just get married? It could even be fake. I want the experience of saying the vows once in my life, in case it doesn't happen for real, you know?"

Tyler started to feel dizzy, but that may have been because the waves were getting choppier due to the wind that was now accompanying the snow. Or…it could have been the alcohol.

He shook his head to clear it. "Okay, let's get married."

Meg gave him a sharp look. "Ha, ha. Very funny."

"I'm serious. Let's get fake married tonight."

Meg rolled her eyes at him. "I wasn't actually serious."

"I am. We can ask the captain right now to marry us."

"What? Why?"

"Because you want to, and I want to kiss you again."

Meg's mouth dropped at that. "I...what?"

"I want to kiss you. It's all that's been on my mind since the last time we did it."

"Oh." She tugged a strand of hair behind her ear that had come loose from the wind. "You can kiss me right now. You don't have to fake marry me."

Tyler put a hand over his heart. "What kind of man do you think I am? Do you think I'm easy or something?"

Meg hid her mouth behind her hand, but he could still hear her drunk giggle.

"You know what I think?" He took a step closer to her.

The mirth left her face. She turned her head up as though she expected him to kiss her, despite what he said.

"What?" she murmured, her eyes drifting to his mouth.

"I think you want to kiss me again too."

"Pffft." Meg jutted her chin down as though that would ever prevent him from kissing her. "You wish."

"I do wish. Very much. But I won't kiss you again until you make a decent man out of me. We get fake married, or no more lip-locking."

"Lip-locking?" she responded with a sarcastic lift of her eyebrow.

Tyler's grin turned absolutely wicked. "Come on, Meg. I dare you to fake marry me."

Meg's eyes narrowed. "Okay, Tyler Evans. I accept your fake proposal."

Tyler offered his hand to Meg, and she took it. Together, they headed toward the yacht's entrance to find the captain, their drunken laughter echoing in the snow as they went.

Chapter Fifteen

Meg came to with a pounding headache. Her stomach churned with acid and leftover alcohol. She was fairly confident she was about to die.

Her eyes opened slowly before instantly shutting as bright light filtered through the blinds of the room. She groaned, rubbing at her face with her left hand as she tried to get her bearings. Something scratched her cheek. Using what little willpower she could muster, she forced her eyes open to see what grazed her skin.

Wrapped around her ring finger was a bread twist tie. When had she put that on? Her mind tried to flash back to the night before, but her head pounded angrily in protest, rejecting her attempt at forming a coherent thought.

Something shifted beside her in the bed, and she froze. Turning carefully to look over her shoulder, she saw a figure next to her on the mattress, nothing but a dark tuft of hair sticking out from the burrow the person had made inside of the comforter. Meg cautiously lifted the section of sheets that covered her own body and glanced down. To her instant relief, she saw that she still wore her bra and panties.

Being as careful as possible, Meg eased out of the bed and glanced frantically around for her clothes. She found her skirt and sweater on the floor and drew them on before she looked around the room again.

Where *was* she?

With a shaking hand, she reached for the comforter and gingerly pulled it away from the man's head. Tyler groaned in response as light hit his face. He batted away her hand with his left one, and she stilled.

Tyler wore a matching twist tie on his finger.

Meg grabbed her head, forcing herself to think about the night before through the pain of her hangover. The bachelorette party started at Wine & Stuff. Just because the Holiday Boys weren't able to go there, that hadn't meant the girls couldn't. They'd spent the evening drinking God-awful wine while hanging out with Holiday Bay's Holiday Boys Fan Club. They'd been excited beyond belief that Julie and Meg—two women actually dating Holiday Boys— were in attendance. They'd bought the party a round of shots. From there, the bachelorettes hit a dive bar and then another. Dirty Bar Hopping was what she and Julie called it back in college.

They eventually met up with the guys on the yacht. Did more shots. Meg was feeling pretty low after a three-day panic attack, thanks to Lucas's reveal. She'd drank even more.

It had dawned on her while toasting Julie that her life was going nowhere. Julie was moving on. Tyler had moved on a long time ago. Meg was the only one stuck in place, had been for years.

Her forehead scrunched. Had she mentioned that to someone last night?

She remembered going out to stern of the ship, enjoying the feel of the icy snow cooling her heated cheeks.

Tyler joined her. He'd dared her to fake marry him so they could kiss again.

And since she'd never been able to resist his stupid dares, they'd gone to the captain and asked him to fake marry them.

Meg's racing heart slowed when she realized that was all it was. A fake marriage. It wasn't like they actually got married. Her relief lasted all of 0.3 seconds before her eyes drifted over to the side table where a crisp marriage certificate sat.

Snatching it up, she read it with disbelieving eyes. And then she read it again.

Per what the words were telling her, Tyler and Meg got married at 2:03 a.m.

But…that couldn't be legit, could it?

Meg's breath became shallower and she pushed air toward her diaphragm. The muscles there tightened until they hurt. The movement didn't agree with her, and she ran into adjoining bathroom in time to empty the contents of her acidy stomach.

"What the hell?" Tyler grumbled from the bed, his voice groggy.

Meg didn't respond, merely continuing to dry heave into the toilet.

She heard footsteps as Tyler stumbled toward her. He grabbed a washcloth from the counter and wet it before placing it on the back of Meg's neck as she continued to be sick.

When she was finally done, she stood on unsteady feet. The washcloth plopped to the ground. Not looking at Tyler, she washed her mouth out with the complimentary bottle of mouthwash available on the counter.

After she was finished, she turned to Tyler, venom on her face. "You unbelievable jerk!"

"What?" He had the nerve to look shocked. "What'd I do?"

Meg marched into the other room and picked up the marriage certificate where she'd dropped it on the floor. She slammed it into Tyler's chest.

"Does this explain anything to you?"

Tyler frowned at her before he glanced down at the paper. Lines formed on his face. "But...that wasn't real."

Even though alcohol was making her overly emotional and irrational, Meg felt a little hurt at his reaction. He was staring at the paper like he was in a nightmare.

"There's got to be a reasonable explanation for this," Tyler said.

It dawned on Meg in that moment that Tyler was in nothing but his boxer briefs. Her gaze was eye level with his sculpted pecs. She couldn't have this conversation with all that on display.

She grabbed his jeans off the floor and threw them at him. "Can you get dressed?"

Tyler put the certificate on the bed before stepping into his pants.

Meg averted her eyes. Her head continued to throb, and she pushed the heel of her palm against her scalp. "Why did we even get out of our clothes in the first place? Did we—"

"No." Tyler ran a weary hand over his face. "I think we were complaining it was too hot in the room. Unless I dreamt that."

Meg's mind revealed a flash from the night before. Leaving the captain after getting married and sneaking down the hall so as to not wake the others. Laughing moronically like schoolchildren who'd gotten away with doing something naughty. Entering a room. Meg saying she was too hot. Taking off her sweater. Tyler looking at her like—

"How could this happen?" Meg snapped.

Tyler pulled on his shirt. "We don't even know *what* happened. There has to be a reasonable explanation for this. I'm sure it's not real. No one in their right mind would legitimately marry us when we were that drunk."

Meg's racing anxiety eased slightly. He was right. No one would have actually married them. There was no way they could have given legal consent.

"Come on," Tyler said after he finished getting dressed. He grabbed the certificate, meticulously folded it and put it in his back pocket. "Let's go talk to the captain, and we'll get this all straightened out."

Meg hurried into the bathroom and grabbed a fresh washcloth. Wiping at her face, she tidied her appearance as best as she could. Her hair was still in an updo, half of it coming out of the hairband, so she pulled it loose and redid it as a ponytail. She wished they'd slept in the room she had chosen the day before. Her bag was in there with her overnight items. At least she could have put on a fresh change of clothes. She didn't even know what room they'd ended up in.

Going out into the hallway, Tyler and Meg scurried to the bridge where the captain was. He sat behind the wheel with his skipper. They were drinking coffee and looking like they didn't have a care in the world.

"Well," the captain said jollily when he saw them. "How are my happy newlyweds doing this morning?"

"Aren't you two up a little early for a honeymoon?" the skipper sniggered.

Meg wanted to punch him.

"Look," Tyler said calmly. Too calmly. He was acting as

though there wasn't anything substantial going on, while Meg felt like she was being shoved under water again. "We found this when we woke up." Tyler pulled the marriage certificate out of his pocket. "Can you explain what this is?"

The captain looked at him like he was an idiot. "Your marriage certificate?"

"But we didn't get married," Meg said. She clutched at her stomach as she put pressure on her diaphragm.

"You don't remember getting married?" the skipper asked. He burst out laughing. "Classic."

The captain let out a weary sigh, as though this situation happened to him all the time. "I can assure you that you are, in fact, married."

"How could you marry us when we were obviously drunk!" Meg yelled.

The captain lifted a shoulder. "You could say your vows just fine. I did ask you both multiple times if you were sure you wanted to go through with it, and you both said yes. In fact, you were adamant about it."

Tyler pinched the bridge of his nose. "Okay, but we're not technically married until you turn the paperwork into the county clerk's office, right?"

"That's correct. So I had my second skipper deliver it to the clerk's house in Clarington this morning with a big tip included if they processed it right away. Per your request." He smiled at them both as though they should be grateful he did such a great job. When Meg and Tyler glared at him, the captain held up his hands defensively. "You made me promise I would take care of it. Again, you both insisted on it. And because I am a man of my word, I sent him out as soon as we docked."

Tyler and Meg turned in unison to look out the window, confirming that they were indeed back at the marina and

not in some horrible nightmare. The air in Meg's lungs
felt like cement. She couldn't get fresh breath in, no matter how hard she tried.

"Meg?" Tyler grabbed her cheeks in his large hands.
"Hey, look at me."

"Is there anything I can do?" the captain asked as he eyed
Meg in concern. His voice sounding muffled to her ears.

"I think you've done enough," Tyler said, though he
sounded more perplexed than angry.

He grabbed Meg's hand and dragged her back to the
room they'd exited earlier. As soon as he closed the door
behind them, Meg dropped his hand and started to pace.

Can't breathe, can't breathe, can't breathe.

She felt like she was standing over the edge of a great
precipice. One more step and she'd be gone.

"Meg." Tyler's voice came from a great distance. "Meg,
hey."

He was suddenly in front of her, stopping her from her
frantic pacing. He held a glass of water out for her. She
stared at it like it was poison. The idea of taking even a sip
made her airway tighten and her anxiety climb ten notches.

Water meant suffocation.

She pushed the glass away, the contents spilling all over
the floor.

"I—I…" Meg tried to get the apology out, but she couldn't.

Was this what it felt like to lose your mind?

Tyler put the now empty glass on one of the tables next to
the bed. He walked back to Meg and clutched her shoulders.

"Meg, I need you to breathe for me."

Meg realized in that moment that she'd stopped breathing. She shook her head and tried to get away, but Tyler
wouldn't let her go, anchoring her in place.

"We'll do it in counts together, okay? Breathe in, two,

three, four. Hold, two, three, four, and out, two, three, four. Don't focus on your breath—focus on me, all right? Breathe in, two, three, four…"

Meg stared into his eyes of painted colors and did as he asked. They continued to do this until Meg's panic started to subside.

When she felt a little more in control—though the jittery feeling didn't leave—she pulled back from Tyler. This time he let her go. She walked over to the bed and collapsed on the soft mattress, her legs too weak to support her anymore. He sat beside her, though he gave her plenty of space.

"How do you know how to calm a panic attack?" she asked, not meeting Tyler's eyes.

He ran a hand through his hair. "James used to get really bad anxiety attacks before we'd go on stage. Jake and I learned different methods to help him."

Meg gave a short nod before her shoulders sank. How had she gotten herself into this situation? She and Tyler were all wrong for each other. He had his fantastic life away from Holiday Bay. She was as small town as they came, not even good enough for the mayor's son. Just ask anyone in town. It didn't matter that Lucas was gay.

She wasn't good enough for her dad. She wasn't good enough for the Beaumonts. If Holiday Bay crucified her for Lucas dumping her, how would the rest of the world react when people found out she drunk-married one of the planet's most eligible bachelors?

Just the idea of it made her want to throw up again.

"This is such a mess," she whispered. "What are we going to do?"

Tyler tried to put on a brave face despite how shaken he felt. Not only from the morning's events, but from seeing

Meg—his strong, beautiful, brave Meg—so upset and vulnerable. He wanted to hold her close and tell her everything would be okay. But she looked so fragile, he worried that if he did, she'd break apart in his arms.

He clasped his hands together in his lap, his right thumb going over the twist tie on his ring finger as he tried to think. His brain felt liked it was dipped in bourbon. He had trouble focusing on anything other than a strong desire to go back to sleep.

Forcing himself to concentrate, he said, "Here's what we're not going to do. We're not going to run off and get an annulment."

Meg gave him a scathing look. "You can't be serious."

"Hear me out. Jake and Julie are getting married next weekend. We'll keep this quiet for now. The last thing they need is anything stealing attention from their big day. If we try to do something right now, we risk the chance of the news leaking. Once they're married, we'll figure it out. I'll reach out to my lawyer and see what we can do to get this quietly annulled. But we don't do anything until our best friends are married. Agreed?"

Meg wiped her sweaty palms on her skirt. "Agreed."

She stood up and started for the door.

Tyler jumped to his feet and instantly regretted as his whole body protested. "Where are you going?"

He didn't want her to leave. Not when things were so unsettled between them.

"I'm going to find my room so I can grab my stuff and get the hell off this yacht."

"Meg, wait."

She paused but didn't look at him.

"How long have you been dealing with panic attacks?" he asked.

She continued to keep her back to him. Her shoulders stiffened but she merely shrugged off his question.

When her hand was on the door handle, Tyler quietly said, "A therapist might be able to help you with those. There's no shame in seeing one, you know."

Meg whirled around then, her eyes blazing. "I don't care what a piece of paper says. You're not actually my husband. And my mental health is none of your business!"

She ripped the twist tie off her finger and threw it on the floor. Opening the door, she peeked her head out. When she saw that the coast was clear, she left without another word.

Tyler got off the bed with limbs that felt like rubber. Going over to Meg's discarded twist tie, he picked it up. He held it between his thumb and index finger, staring at it. Despite the mess they were both in—not to mention what Meg had just said—something ached at the site of the crumpled ring.

He knew she didn't want the marriage. And despite his deepening feelings for her, he didn't want her with him against her will.

He couldn't deny that he was falling for her. She'd not only grown into a beautiful woman, she had so much spirit. It was addicting to be around. Sure, she tried to hide it. But it was there, just under the surface. The Meg who challenged him and made him laugh. The one he'd thought about so many times over the years.

What he needed was time. Time to date her for real. To make her see that they could be good together. And then they could get married under circumstances they both wanted.

Grabbing his wallet from where he'd thrown it on the side table the night before, Tyler opened it and carefully put Meg's twist tie inside.

Chapter Sixteen

Jake and Julie's wedding arrived on a perfect November day. The leaves were in the midst of their fall splendor. The air was bright and clear. Excitement was in the air.

Meg felt dead inside.

Whenever she thought about Julie's wedding over the past week, hysterical laughter would surface on her lips.

Because Julie's wedding was a stark reminder that Meg was now a married woman herself.

And no one knew it except Meg, Tyler and the crew of the yacht.

Meg had dreamt of her wedding day since she was a little girl. She always pictured it being like the one she'd planned with Lucas. It was supposed to be something special…memorable.

The reality was something entirely different.

Julie's wedding party occupied the upstairs floor of Jake's mansion, while the men got ready in the deluxe basement. Kyleigh sat in a lounge chair, buckling her heels on. Julie's sister, Veronica, hogged the long, gold-framed mirror as she examined herself in her bridesmaid dress.

"I wish you would have picked out a more flattering color. This red doesn't go with my hair at all," she complained. Like Julie, Veronica was a natural redhead, though her hair was a shade darker than Julie's electric-red hair.

"I did ask you to come into town when we picked out the dresses," Julie gently reminded her.

"You're not the only one who's busy," Veronica snapped before she turned to Kyleigh and began to tell the story about her daughter's emergency veneers.

Meg had wanted on more than one occasion to call Veronica and chew her out for how she abandoned Julie, making her sister take on the responsibility of their mother, emotionally, physically and financially by herself. Veronica always used the excuse that she was either too far away or too busy with her own life to be able to help. It didn't matter that before Jake entered her life, Julie had run herself ragged trying to live her own life, while also being the primary caretaker of their mother. That alone was sometimes a full-time job, even with her mom staying in assisted living.

For the sake of Julie's wedding day, Meg held her tongue and didn't tell Veronica to shove it, as she deserved.

"You look absolutely gorgeous," Meg told her best friend as she zipped Julie's dress up for her.

The lace dress Julie picked out fit her like a dream. Her long, stunning hair was pulled into a low chignon. A large magnolia flower held it in place. Meg got a little misty-eyed looking at her.

She hugged Julie tight. "Jake's not going to know what hit him."

"Speaking of," Kyleigh said getting up from the lounge chair. "We should get downstairs so you can get married."

"Can I get a minute with Meg first?" Julie asked.

Kyleigh nodded and left the room. Veronica continued to look at herself, patting her chin-length bob, before she followed Kyleigh.

Before she left, she turned back to her sister. "You know. It's not too late for Kyleigh and me to switch groomsmen. I could walk down the aisle with James, and she can walk with Jake's son…"

"For the last time," Julie said, a little shorter this time. "After the ceremony is over, you're walking back down the aisle with Dylan, Kyleigh is walking with James."

Veronica looked annoyed. "I don't see what the big deal is. James and I *did* used to date, you know."

"And now you're married and he's gay. Let it go, Veronica," Meg said. Would Veronica ever stop being a narcissist? She always made everything about herself. Apparently, even her sister's wedding day.

Veronica stomped out of the exit, shutting the door firmly behind her.

"I swear, she never changes," Meg muttered. "What did you want to talk about? Maybe sabotaging your sister in front of your guests? If you don't know what to do, don't worry. I've had years to plot her public humiliation. Let me give you a list."

Julie laughed lightly. "I'll keep that in mind, but that's not what I wanted to speak to you about."

Meg inspected her best friend, not missing the contentment on her face. She was the picture-perfect bride.

"What's up?"

"Jake agreed to try for a baby."

Meg whooped as she hugged her again. "You are going to be the best mom. You already are the best stepmom to Dylan."

Julie smiled, a faint blush on her cheeks. "Well, he said we could try. We both agreed we need boundaries. He doesn't want to make me uncomfortable, and I don't want him to feel bad or like he's taking advantage of me.

If it's too much for either of us, we'll find a discreet fertility doctor."

Meg gave her a watery smile. She was so happy for her friend, but there was a tiny part inside of her that ached. She wished in that moment that she could unload on her friend, tell her everything that had happened in the past few weeks. Especially regarding Tyler.

As though sensing something was off, Julie eyed her in concern. "Hey, are you okay?"

She couldn't do it. Julie didn't need to worry about her right now. Meg would tell her everything after. Maybe someday they'd even laugh about it, drinking Long Island ice teas on Jake and Julie's patio while their future kids ran around the yard playing.

Meg swallowed. "Yeah, everything is perfect. I'm so happy for you, Jules."

Kyleigh poked her head in the room. "Julie, if you're not planning on standing your man up, we need to get downstairs."

Julie grabbed her bouquet of magnolias off the guest bed. She looked at her two closest friends and smiled so brightly it lit the room. "I'm ready."

The bridal party made their way to the atrium where the wedding was to take place. Dylan stood at the entrance, pulling on the tight tie around his neck. He looked so sweet and nervous, Meg wanted to walk over and fluff the teen's hair.

"Dylan, you look very handsome," Julie said, kissing her soon-to-be stepson on the cheek.

Dylan looked embarrassed at the attention. "Thanks, Julie."

He offered her his arm, and she took it. Meg peeked around the corner and into the large glass atrium.

It looked absolutely beautiful. Normally, plants filled the room, but those had temporarily been replaced with magnolia trees strategically placed throughout the area. Each tree had a string of white lights wrapped around it, which sparkled and cast the atrium in warmth. Julie had told Meg that Jake planned on planting the trees around the property after the wedding so they'd always have reminders of their special day—the romantic sap.

Meg recognized Jake's mother and sister sitting on the right side of the room, though she hadn't seen them in years. Neither had been back to Holiday Bay due to some bad behavior relating to Jake's father and the vicious rumor mill that followed his actions. Julie had wanted his sister to be a bridesmaid, but she'd politely refused, not wanting to be in town any longer than she needed to be.

Meg felt a lump in her throat when she saw Julie's mom sitting in a wheelchair up in the front with a nurse. She knew Jake must have arranged that her mom could be there for Julie, even if she didn't know who Julie was at this point. Meg's own mom was there, sitting beside Jake's mother. It made sense that they were both invited, considering how much time Jake and Julie spent at Tyler's and Meg's homes growing up.

Meg watched as Veronica made her way down the aisle, followed by Kyleigh. It was her turn next.

Hugging Julie one more time and giving Dylan an encouraging nod, she turned and slowly made her way down the aisle. She smiled at friends she saw. She grinned at Jake, whose eyes were firmly on the archway as he waited for his bride to make an appearance. She took in the magnolias placed throughout the room, making it smell like sweet heaven. The only person Meg didn't look at was the best man.

Her husband.

Tyler.

The two hadn't spoken to each other since their own nuptials the week before. It wasn't for a lack of trying on Tyler's part. He'd called her several times and sent her a few texts, but she hadn't answered. She needed space to process what had happened.

Her anxiety had been out of control since the moment she'd woken up married. She'd barely slept all week. When she finally did, she had dreams of being chased by Tyler's fans screaming at her that she wasn't good enough for him. Clarice always led the pack, reminding her that she wasn't good enough for *anything*.

During the hours Meg needed to be awake, she could barely focus, her mind racing in too many different directions. Her diaphragm ached all week due to her constantly putting pressure on that area. She'd take in huge gulps of air, but her lungs never seemed to fill to capacity, no matter how hard she tried. And then she would obsessively think about breathing, which would then stop her from doing it even more. It was a vicious cycle that she didn't know how to break.

She just wanted it all to stop. The noise in her head. Her obsession with her diaphragm and breathing. But since she didn't know how to stop it, she did what she did best. She compartmentalized it, ignoring her problems as best she could.

And that included Tyler.

She'd shown up late for the dress rehearsal the night before, so they didn't have time to speak to each other. As soon as they wrapped for the evening, she'd latched onto Julie's side, not giving Tyler a chance to say more than a few words to her. She could see the frustration in his eyes, but she didn't know what to do or how to handle the situation. She supposed she could act like a freaking adult and just talk to the man. But whenever she opened her mouth to say something, that drowning feeling overtook her, making her feel like she was suffocating again.

Meg joined the wedding party at the front. The violinist Jake and Julie hired began to play Canon in D. The crowd stood up as Julie and Dylan started walking down the aisle. It was only then that Meg made the mistake of looking over at the groomsmen. Her eyes immediately met Tyler's, who she'd felt staring at her as soon as she had entered the room. She couldn't look away from him even as Julie met Jake at the makeshift arched altar wrapped in magnolias. Dylan hugged his dad before joining the other groomsmen. Nothing interrupted the intense stare-off between the maid of honor and best man. It was only when Julie handed Meg her bouquet that Meg finally looked away.

The vows were exchanged. They were sweet and beautiful, just like the couple getting married. More than one person in the audience dabbed their eyes when they were pronounced husband and wife by the officiant. A cheer went through the crowd as Jake and Julie kissed. Exchanging exuberant smiles, they ran back down the aisle.

Tyler walked over to Meg and offered his arm as though daring her to not take it in front of everyone. Straightening her shoulders, she latched onto it as they followed the bride and groom.

A photographer guided the wedding party outside for pictures. Meg plastered a frozen smile on her face when the photographer told her to look into Tyler's eyes. He looked annoyed for a moment at her unnatural grimace before a sly smile appeared on his face. She grew instantly wary. She knew that smile well. It meant he was up to something.

Before she could guess his intentions, he poked her side,

right on her ticklish spot. She barked out a laugh, and the camera snapped.

"Perfect!" the photographer said. "You two make such a cute couple."

The humor instantly left Meg. She turned to walk away from Tyler. He grabbed her hand before she could get too far.

"When are you going to stop treating me like an infectious disease?" he hissed.

"I don't know what you're talking about," she said defensively.

"I never knew you to be a coward, Meg," he said.

Anger lit inside her.

"How dare you call me a coward!" she hissed lowly, so that the others wouldn't overhear. "I find myself unexpectedly and unwantedly married. How am I supposed to react?"

Tyler's face was carefully composed as he said, "You're not the only person in this situation. You could work with me instead of treating me like your enemy."

A man dressed in a chef's uniform came outside. "Dinner is served."

Not giving Tyler another chance to speak to her, Meg moved to Kyleigh's side. They walked inside to the home's ballroom—because of course, Jake owned a house that had one. White tables and chairs had been set up on one side of the room. A DJ was getting the sound system set up on the other side.

Meg just had to get through the night, and then everything would go back to normal. Jake and Julie would be off on their honeymoon, and Tyler and Meg could quietly annul their mistake of a marriage.

She just had to get through the night.

Chapter Seventeen

Tyler wanted to punch something. He was beyond frustrated, and he didn't know what to do about it. He wasn't sure how to get Meg to acknowledge him, let alone speak to him.

Yeah, the marriage was a mistake. He wouldn't lie to himself and say he didn't want Meg. But he didn't want her *this way*, with her choice taken away. He wanted to date her, make love to her, marry her in a place of her choosing. Not marry her when they were both so trashed they couldn't even remember the ceremony.

Because if there was one thing that came out of this completely awful situation, it was Tyler being forced to recognize his feelings for Meg. He knew it when she'd walked out on him the day they were on the yacht.

He was in love with her. He'd *been* in love with her for years. Not once in the past twenty years had a time gone by where he hadn't thought of her. It might not have been an everyday occurrence, but something would trigger her image in his head. A song would play on the radio that he remembered Meg blasting from her house when she was a tween. Eating strawberry shortcake, a favorite dessert of Meg's that she always had at her birthday parties his mom forced him to go to.

She never stopped being a part of his life.

And he absolutely intended to make her his wife for real. But not like this. He wanted her to want it.

The wedding party went to their table for the reception. Tyler figured Meg would have no choice but to speak with him since they were sitting right next to each other. After the servers dropped off their food, he watched as she cut her vegan steak methodically into tiny squares.

When she went to cut them into even smaller pieces, he leaned toward her and said, "I think it's already dead...not that it was ever living to begin with."

Meg gave him a dirty look before popping a piece into her mouth with her fork. She reached for her water a couple of times while she chewed but kept putting it back down.

"Do you want my water?" he asked.

"Why would I want your water?" she replied. He took it as a win that she didn't outright ignore him.

"You keep reaching for your glass. If it's dirty or something, you can have mine."

Her face softened slightly. "My glass is fine."

As though to prove it, she took a tiny sip before hastily pushing it away.

It soon became time to give the toasts. Meg went first, giving a hilarious speech about back when she'd convinced Julie to get their belly buttons pierced in college. Julie passed out when she saw the needle go into Meg, and Meg ended up taking her piercing out in solidarity.

"I'll always have your back, no matter where either of us end up in the world," Meg continued, her tone serious. Tyler frowned at her. What did that mean? Was Meg planning on moving somewhere? His heart sank at the idea. Julie was also looking at her in concern. "And now that Jake is married to you," she continued, "I have your back too, Jake."

Cheers went out. Champagne was sipped. And then it was Tyler's turn.

"I'm not much for speeches," he said. Laughter rippled over the crowd, everyone knowing that Tyler was a professional songwriter. "I write songs, but the process takes time. You have to get the right fit, but once you do...you know you have a hit on your hands. Jake and Julie, you are absolutely the right fit. Here's to you."

Everyone drank. Everyone but Meg, who looked pale. Tyler tried to think what he might have said to upset her, but she immediately started talking to Julie. When the dancing started, Tyler gave up on trying to get his wife to speak to him. He paused in the process of standing up.

His wife.

Despite the awful circumstances, he did like the sound of that, even if she didn't. He liked it very much.

Wandering through the crowd, he saw Zan sitting by himself, tapping his thumb against the table as he stared toward the direction of the bathroom.

"Hey," Tyler said as he sat down next to him. "Long time, no talk. How've you been?"

"Fine," Zan replied, but he was clearly distracted.

Tyler looked to where his friend was staring and figured he was waiting for his wife. He'd seen the couple earlier in the crowd. Mary still carried herself like a model, so she was hard to miss. Even though she would always be beautiful, Tyler noticed she looked pale and thinner than he remembered.

"How's Mary doing?" he asked gently.

"Mary is..." Zan sighed heavily. "Mary has leukemia."

Tyler's breath caught in his throat. "Oh god, I'm so sorry. What are you going to do?"

"She's going to start treatment soon, but she wanted to wait until after the wedding. You know she loves all of you guys." Zan's voice broke as he added, "She's always been our biggest fan."

Tyler clasped his shoulder. "If you need anything, anything at all, you let me know, okay? You need me to come to Maine and watch the kids or something, I'll be there."

Zan let out a watery snort. "I'd like to keep my kids safe and sound, so I'll pass on the babysitting, but thank you anyway."

"Hey, I'd be an awesome babysitter," Tyler said with a slight grin.

"Excuse me, Mr. Chen, can I take your plate?" a short woman with black hair asked Zan. Her name tag said *Isabella*. She was familiar, but Tyler couldn't place her at first.

Then he remembered. He snapped his fingers. "You work at Florentina's, right?"

She looked at him in surprise just as she picked up Zan's half-eaten plate of spaghetti. It tipped sideways in her grasp, and tomato sauce and noodles landed in Zan's lap.

Isabella looked mortified. "I—I'm so sorry."

An older man hurried over to them. "Izzy, what did you do?"

"It was my fault," Tyler quickly said. "I distracted her."

Isabella grabbed a discarded napkin from the table and tried to wipe at Zan's pants. He jerked in his chair when she got a little too close to his groin, and she jumped back, her face going beet red.

"Oh my god, I'm sorry." She looked like she wanted to disappear into the floor.

"It's fine," Zan said, taking the napkin from her and wiping at the crotch of his slacks.

"Forgive my daughter—she's all thumbs," the older man said.

Mary came over at that moment, taking in the scene.

Laugh lines appeared around her mouth, but she kept her tone straight as she asked, "Everything all right?"

Zan instantly forgot his soiled pants. He jumped to his feet, the remaining noodles falling to the ground. "Yeah, everything is fine. Are you all right?"

She smiled at Tyler before she told her husband, "Actually, I think I might go back to the hotel and lie down for a bit."

"I'll go with you," Zan said.

"No, stay and enjoy the party," Mary insisted, patting his chest.

He waved at his pants. "Not like this. Come on." He wrapped his arm around her waist before nodding at Tyler. "I'll call you later."

"Yeah, later." Tyler watched them go. Isabella's dad followed them, continuing to offer apologies. He heard a sniffle and turned to see Isabella picking up noodles off the ground.

Tyler leaned over to help. "It's seriously okay. Zan probably has about a hundred pairs of pants just like those at home."

"I'm so embarrassed," Isabella muttered. "And of course, I did that to a Holiday Boy in front of a Holiday Boy."

Tyler chuckled. "It's fine. Don't even give it a second thought."

He helped her pile the remaining noodles back on the plate. She took it from him and headed for the kitchen where the waitstaff could be seen coming and going. He hoped she didn't take it to heart. It was an accident, and had Zan been in a better frame of mind, he would have given her better reassurance. If he'd come across as upset, it certainly had nothing to do with the pasta in his lap.

God, Tyler hoped Mary would be all right. He didn't know what Zan would do without her.

A DJ began playing hits, and people started swaying around on the dance floor. Tyler joined Paul at one of the other tables. Paul, for once, didn't seem in the mood to talk. He was too busy staring at Julie's friend Kyleigh. Again.

Tyler frowned as he thought back to when he met Paul and Zan right before their senior year. He remembered Paul used to leave rehearsals to meet up with some girl, but he hadn't known it was Kyleigh.

"How come I didn't know you and Kyleigh used to date?" Tyler asked, nodding toward the woman.

"Hmm?" Paul said before he focused on Tyler's question. "Oh…we kept it quiet. I only ever told Zan. Her dad didn't approve of me. You remember that guy?"

Tyler nodded. "Sheriff Sinclair."

"Yeah." Paul grimaced as though he thought of something unpleasant. His gaze went back to Kyleigh and his expression softened. "But we didn't care. It was love at first sight."

"It didn't last though," Tyler said.

Paul ran a hand down the side of his cheek. "What can I say? I was young and stupid. As soon as we got the contract for Holiday Boys, I broke up with her. I went out in the world, determined to make a success of myself. Last I heard, she'd settled down with some boring jerk, got married and had a kid."

Tyler frowned. "I don't think she's married anymore. Julie mentioned something about how Kyleigh might be single, but she was still a better choice to walk with James down the aisle than her married sister. Not that James would take notice of either of them anyway."

"Yeah," Paul replied as his phone went off. Groaning, he answered it with a short, "What?"

Tyler watched the couples go by, his eyes drifting back to Meg every so often, who was now conversing with Kyleigh since Tyler wasn't sitting between them anymore.

The DJ announced, "Ladies and gentleman, please clear the floor for the bride and groom to do their first dance as a married couple."

Jake and Julie walked onto the dance floor. Jake twirled Julie around before bringing her close to him. He whispered something into her ear that made her laugh. Tyler felt sentimental as he watched the pair. Jake had been through so much when he was younger, from growing up in a toxic home to a horrible first marriage. His best friend deserved the world. Tyler was glad he finally found true happiness.

As the song drifted into another slow one, the DJ said, "Now let's have the maid of honor and best man join the happy couple."

Hope flamed deep in Tyler's chest as he slowly rose from his chair. He walked onto the dance floor and waited for Meg to join him. For one horrible second, he thought she wouldn't, but to his relief, Meg was soon in front of him, her burgundy dress shining under the crystal light of the chandelier above.

"I thought you were going to leave me here by myself," Tyler murmured as he put his hands on her waist and drew her close.

"I'm not that heartless," Meg said before letting out a weighted breath. "I saw what you did for Izzy."

"Hmm?"

"The waitress. I bet she's in the back berating herself for dumping spaghetti on Zan. I've known her since she was little. She's always been really sweet but sensitive. It was nice of you to help clean up the mess."

"It was the least I could do," Tyler said, pulling Meg in slightly closer and internally cheering when she didn't pull away. "It really wasn't that big of a deal."

The rest of the wedding party joined them on the dance floor. Kyleigh and James talked lightly to each other, even though James looked like he'd been drinking again recently. Maybe he hadn't stopped since the night of the bachelor party. Veronica and Dylan soon followed. Veronica looked pained, while Dylan stared at his feet, counting aloud the steps as he moved.

"Meg…" Tyler murmured, his hands roaming to her back. "Do you think you and I can call a truce for right now? I don't want what happened to ruin us—I mean—to ruin our friendship."

She stared at him, her hypnotic blue eyes glowing in the light. "Is that what we are? Friends?"

Tyler swallowed over the sudden lump in his throat. "What would you call us?"

"I—" Meg stopped speaking as she looked over Tyler's shoulder. A frown formed on her face.

Cell phones were pinging throughout the reception. Loud whispers started spreading like wildfire around the room. People stared at them, disbelief written over their faces. They weren't looking at Jake and Julie or the wedding party in general.

No, they were staring specifically at Tyler and Meg.

Meg's breathing became shallow. "What is going on?"

Tyler let go of Meg to grab his cell phone out of his pants. Before he could even pull up anything, Jake and Julie ran over to them. Julie looked upset, while Jake looked at Tyler with a cocked grin.

"Well, well, well, you son of a…" he said.

"What's going on?" Meg repeated, her voice tense.

"Meg, how come you didn't tell me?" Julie said, hurt drawn all over her face.

"Tell you what?"

Julie grabbed Jake's phone out of his hand and showed it to them. On the screen was a gossip site, and right on top of the page was a picture of Tyler and Meg. They were exchanging their twist tie rings. Meg had a piece of paper towel on her head, which he assumed was supposed to be a veil.

Tyler Evans Secretly Marries Former Neighbor, the article screamed.

Oh. Crap.

Chapter Eighteen

"Meg, why didn't you say anything?" Julie walked around the formal dining room, the skirt of her wedding dress swaying with each step.

They'd moved to the room to get out of the sight of prying eyes since Meg and Tyler were now officially the hot topic of the wedding.

Meg stood in the corner of the room, looking like she was going to throw up. "We didn't want to take away any attention from your big day."

"But this happened last weekend," Julie said. "You couldn't say anything leading up to that?"

"What did you want me to say, Julie?" she snapped. "Guess what? Tyler and I got super drunk at your pre-wedding party and eloped without realizing it was real. Yeah, that's something I want to tell people."

"Ouch," Jake whispered to Tyler, who was trying not to take Meg's dismissive description of their wedding to heart. It wasn't like she was lying. But…yeah. Ouch.

"We were trying to keep everything quiet until after you were married," Tyler explained, not looking at her. "Like Meg said, we wanted today to be about you. We were going to meet with lawyers in the next couple of weeks and see about getting an annulment. It was genuinely not something we were trying to hide or be deceitful about."

Tyler's and Meg's moms burst into the room, interrupting the tense atmosphere.

Greta ran over to Meg and hugged her. "Baby, why didn't you tell me? I'm so happy for you. Did you think we wouldn't be happy about this?"

"Sweets," Tyler's mom said. "I'd smack you for not telling your dear old mother, but I'm too happy right now. How could you not share this with us though?"

"Oh my god," Meg muttered.

His mom looked at him proudly. "Greta and I have been saying since you two were babies that you were meant to be. Haven't we?"

Greta looked like she was going to start crying all over Meg as she continued to hug her daughter. "Yes, you two are just perfect for each other. And, oh, Marie, they're going to give us the cutest grandbabies."

Tyler tuned them out, his eyes locked onto Meg. She looked like she was on the verge of a panic attack. It was funny how quickly he had gotten to know her expressions. To know every nuance of her face, letting him know when she was struggling.

"Look," he said, pulling his gaze away from her. "This is obviously a shock to everyone, including us. Would you mind giving us a moment?"

Jake grabbed his wife's hand. "We can talk to them later. We have a honeymoon to get to."

Julie blushed, and her face softened as she looked at Meg. She hurried over to her best friend and gave her a hug. "We'll talk more when I get back, okay? And I'm sorry for how I reacted to the news. I was in shock, but that doesn't excuse my behavior."

She whispered something else in Meg's ear. Meg's eyes went wide as her gaze jerked to Tyler briefly before looking away.

Before he could ask what that was about, his mom came over and gave him a tight hug, followed by Greta doing the same thing, her face emotional and happy.

When they were finally alone, Tyler stepped over to Meg and grabbed her hands. "You still with me?"

Now that no one else was in the room, Meg's panic blasted out on full display. She jerked her hands out of his hold and began to pace frantically.

"How did this get leaked?" she said.

Tyler pulled his cell out and read the text exchange he'd had with Trevor, who owned the yacht. Tyler had messaged him earlier when he and Meg had headed into the dining room with Jake and Julie.

He grimaced as he read the latest text. "Apparently, one of the crew members secretly recorded our nuptials and sold it. Trevor sends his apologies and said that the crew member was fired."

"How does that help us now?"

"Meg." Tyler stepped in front of her to stop her anxious pacing. "I know this is a shock and not what you wanted, but I need you to breathe for me, all right? Take a deep breath, two, three, four…"

He walked her through the breathing exercises until her chest no longer looked like it was struggling to get air in.

When she seemed like her anxiety attack was lessening, she sank into one of the dining room chairs wearily. "What are we going to do?"

Tyler's heart ached as he stared at the misery on her face. He turned from her to stare out of the room's gigantic windows. It was snowing outside, big flakes that were piling on the ground and lingering. He wondered how much snow his ranch had and wished more than anything he could be there right now. It was his happy place. His escape when things became too heavy.

A thought popped into his head. Pivoting on his feet, he walked over to Meg. He sat in the chair next to her.

"I have an idea," he said. "I think it would be best if we lie low for a while until another story hits the gossip sites and takes the heat off of us."

"What do you suggest?" she asked listlessly.

"I told you before about my ranch in Wyoming. It's quiet and secluded with no neighbors for miles. It'll give us time to sort through everything, without having to answer to anyone but ourselves. Plus… I'm behind on work and it's usually my go-to place to write. It'll also give you some time to decompress."

"I don't need to decompress," Meg grumbled.

Tyler was very careful to hide his smile at her petulant expression. "Okay, then it'll give you a nice place to take—what I'm assuming is—a long overdue vacation from this town and the storm that's about to hit it once this news goes national. If it hasn't already."

Meg shuddered.

"Will you be able to get time off of work?" he asked.

"It shouldn't be a problem. I haven't taken a vacation in years. We have a temp who covers for Wendy when she leaves. I'm sure she could help again if I asked. My only concern is that my mom and I were planning on going to Stephen and Kimmy's for Thanksgiving, but I'm sure they'll understand, given the circumstances."

When she still didn't say anything after several suspenseful minutes, Tyler asked, "What do you say?"

Meg lifted her chin bravely, and Tyler had to resist the temptation to lean down and kiss those perfect lips.

"When do we leave?"

Chapter Nineteen

Snow crunched under Meg's boots as she walked down the long driveway leading to Tyler's ranch. The long brick building came into view, and Meg felt herself relax even more at the sight.

It was remarkable. They'd only been at the ranch a few days, but it already felt like home to her. Tyler had been right, as much as she hated to admit it. Leaving Holiday Bay had been the best thing for both of them, even though she knew they couldn't hide forever. Per a text she'd received from Kyleigh, reporters and paparazzi had descended on Holiday Bay like flies feeding on a dead carcass. Not only had Jake and Julie's quiet ceremony made the news, but Tyler and Meg's elopement had also caused a frenzy in their small town.

And thanks to Meg's former engagement to the mayor's son, people had a field day selling whatever dirt they could on her. She had a feeling she was coming across as a train wreck of a woman who'd jumped from fiancé to husband in the blink of an eye. Or at least, that was what she assumed they were saying, since she refused to look at social media while she was at the ranch.

If only people knew the full truth about why she and Lucas ended their engagement. Not that she would ever tell anyone. She wouldn't do that to Lucas, no matter how upset she still was with him.

Though the fresh Wyoming air had given her some perspective.

Because of her relationship with him, she'd lived in the spotlight for years, having to be perfect and live up to his family's precious reputation. If she stepped one foot out of line, Clarice had been all over her, quick to criticize every second of her existence. Meg couldn't imagine how the Beaumonts would have treated Lucas if it ever came out that their golden boy was gay. They weren't exactly the most accepting people in the world. Meg wasn't excusing Lucas for using her as cover, but maybe a part of her could sympathize with his situation, given what she was currently facing herself.

As she entered the house, she stomped the snow from her boots before taking them off and placing them on the mat next to the door. After putting her thick winter jacket in the closet, she made her way to the kitchen where his housekeeper was preparing a green-bean casserole for their Thanksgiving dinner.

"Hi, Margie," Meg said.

"Hello, darlin'."

Margie was a sweet woman in her sixties who'd worked at the ranch with her husband, Hans, long before Tyler ever owned the property. She took care of the household, while Hans helped out with the rescue animals Tyler owned—which Meg hadn't even known was a thing he did. But he had three rescue horses, two pigs, three goats and multiple chickens—all who'd been destined for the slaughterhouse. When Meg learned that little fact, her heart flipped. But she refused to fall for her husband, even if he'd been secretly helping animals in a way she'd wanted to for years.

Not that she ever saw the man to get a *chance* to fall for him. Ever since they'd arrived at the ranch, he'd disappeared into his studio, working on songs day in and day out. Apparently, the writer's block he'd been dealing with had resolved itself. She wondered if she'd even see him for the Thanksgiving dinner Margie was working so hard on.

Meg grabbed a glass of juice before turning to the housekeeper. "It smells good in here. Are you sure there's nothing I can do to help?"

"Not with this." Margie gave her the same answer she'd given Meg earlier when she'd offered. "But if you could be a dear, would you mind taking that to Tyler?"

She nodded toward a plate covered in Saran wrap. "That boy never eats once he gets into one of his creative zones."

Meg drank her juice and put the dirty glass in the dishwasher. Grabbing the plate, she answered, "Sure."

She walked out of the room and headed toward Tyler's studio. She'd never been in there before, considering it was his space. Holding onto the plate with one hand, she knocked on the door with the other.

"Come in," Tyler mumbled from somewhere deep inside.

Meg entered before glancing around. On one side of the room was a recording booth. Next to it, there was a control panel. Black pleather couches filled most of the rest of the room, big enough to seat at least ten people. Tyler sat on one of them, his socked feet sprawled along the length of it. On his lap was a spiral-bound notebook, his hand swiftly making notes in it. He looked intent and so handsome in his worn jeans and dark red-and-black flannel shirt that Meg's breath caught in her chest.

Pulling herself together, she walked over to the long black table next to Tyler's couch, her steps muffled by the plush gray carpet under her feet.

"Thanks, Margie," he said, not looking up as he continued to write.

"You're welcome," Meg responded.

Tyler's eyes jerked up to her. Surprise captured his features before they softened.

"Hey," he said, closing his book with a gentle snap. He swung his legs off the couch, silently inviting her to sit next to him by patting the spot beside him.

"Hey, yourself." Once she sat down, she pushed the plate of food toward him. "Margie said you don't remember to eat when you get in your zone."

He grumbled, "Margie should mind her own business."

"She cares for you." Meg motioned toward the notebook. "She's also cooking up a storm in the kitchen for Thanksgiving. You think you'll be done in time to eat?"

He took a bite of the grilled-cheese sandwich Margie had prepared. "Yeah, I just want to get some more lyrics down."

"What's your song about?" Meg asked.

He went still, causing her to look at him suspiciously.

"Oh, this and that," he murmured.

She lifted an eyebrow. "Is that what it's called? This and that?"

"I haven't titled it yet, but I'll keep that in mind."

Meg noticed that he didn't answer her. She watched him finish off his food before she said, "Come on, tell me what it's about."

"It's nothing. Just some gibberish." He leaned back in his seat, resting his head against the back of the couch. "Sorry I haven't been around much since we got here. How are you liking Wyoming so far?"

"It's beautiful. I don't see how you can ever leave."

"Trust me, there are days when I don't want to."

They sat in silence for several moments before Meg gave

him her best glare. "Don't think I didn't notice you changed the subject."

She cocked her head, taking in the way he was acting squirrelly and evading her eyes. A thought popped into her head. "Is it about me?"

Tyler stiffened but didn't answer.

"What are you writing?" Meg said, starting to get upset. Why wouldn't he tell her? Was he writing about how he got hitched to a pain in the ass?

Tyler inspected her, taking in the distress on her face. He grabbed the book and handed it to her. She snatched it from him, ready to start yelling—or to beg him not to publicly humiliate her any more than she'd already been over the past couple years.

She paused when she took in the words before her. They were lyrics about blue eyes—her blue eyes—that haunted his dreams. Lines about how he longed to hold her against him. How the kiss they'd shared as teens had haunted him for years.

Meg's mind tried to recalibrate what she was reading.

"Is this…is this true?" she whispered.

"Which part?" he asked.

She didn't address his comments about her eyes or body. She couldn't comprehend that. "You've thought about our kiss for years?"

He didn't look away. "Yes."

"But you left. You never tried to see me again."

He took his book back, only to put it on the table in front of them, easy for her to grab if she wanted to. "Meg, you were still in high school and I just graduated. You were too young for me then. But I did come back. By the time I did, you were with Lucas."

"Would it have made a difference if I hadn't been?" She needed to know.

He lifted a shoulder. "I guess it doesn't matter now. We both moved on."

Had she though?

"I should go get ready for dinner," he said, changing the subject. He was really good at that. "God knows I could use a shower."

"Yeah, you probably should. You stink," she joked, though he didn't. He smelled like he always did. Wonderful.

He chuckled before leaving the room. She stared after him. A part of her wanted to chase after him. To demand that he give her a better answer. Would they have ended up differently if she hadn't clung so tightly to Lucas?

She couldn't deny that there had always been something between her and Tyler, whether it had been animosity or unexpected attraction.

Too many thoughts began racing through Meg's mind, overwhelming her.

Glancing at his notebook again, Meg got up, taking his empty dish with her.

Later that night, they sat at the kitchen table, eating their way through the feast that Margie made for them. It was too much food. They'd be able to survive off it for the next week.

"So have you been able to explore the ranch?" Tyler asked as he helped himself to more mashed potatoes.

"Yeah, a little. Hans showed me around the barns," Meg answered, scooping up a forkful of sweet-potato casserole.

"When the snow isn't as bad, I'll take you on a tour. There's a beautiful creek not too far from here. You've got to see it," he said, watching her every move.

She gave a half smile but didn't say anything. Something had changed between them since that moment in his studio when he admitted he'd never forgotten their kiss. Just as she never had. There was a charge in the air—something electric. Meg wasn't sure if she wanted to ignore it or not.

"And this is how you spend most of your time when you're here?" she asked. "Locked up in your studio working? Don't you ever get out and enjoy the ranch?"

He looked more relaxed than she'd ever seen him. He was well and truly home here.

"I do leave my room on occasion, yes," Tyler replied, leaning back in his chair. "I help Hans out when I can with the animals."

"What made you decide to get into rescue work?"

"You," Tyler said simply.

Meg frowned at him. "That doesn't make any sense. We've hardly seen each other over the years."

"What can I say, the chicken-napping you did when we were younger inspired me. Covering for you when you put the chickens in my parents' shed gave me my first taste of animal rescue."

"But still…"

"Meg, you've been a huge part of my life for as long as I can remember. You truly don't think your influence has rubbed off on people?"

"I guess I never really thought about it. I assumed you'd forgotten about me."

"As we established earlier, I've never forgotten about you."

Meg cleared her throat. She glanced around the farm-house-style kitchen, taking in the white cupboards and deep fireclay sink, to avoid the way Tyler was looking at her. He stared at her in a way that made her insides want to catch fire.

An idea popped into her head, providing a welcome change of subject. Apparently, his influence had rubbed off on her too. "We should go look at Christmas trees tomorrow."

Tyler gave her a baffled look. "You want to get a Christmas tree?"

"Yeah, we can make this place super cute for the holidays. You have decorations, right?"

"You plan on being here for Christmas?" Tyler asked.

"Oh…" Meg's face heated. For a second, she forgot none of this was real. She'd be back in Holiday Bay for Christmas. Her brother wanted her to start at the campground by then. She was about to have everything she ever wanted. So why did it feel like her stomach had turned to lead. "No, never mind. It was a stupid idea and—"

"Meg," Tyler interrupted.

She swirled her fork through the vegan gravy Margie made. "Yeah?"

"Since Margie and Hans live here full-time, I'm sure they'd love to see the place decorated. Margie has lights and Christmas stuff in the attic. We'll go get a tree tomorrow. And if you want, we can always come back here the week of Christmas."

For some reason, Meg wanted to cry. She said quietly, "Our marriage will be annulled by then."

Tyler didn't look at her as he stood up, carrying his plate over to the sink to rinse it off. "You're always welcome here. We'll go get that tree in the morning."

Meg fiddled with her fork, feeling suddenly depressed. She wished she'd never brought it up at all.

The annulment would be a good thing for both of them.

Did she wish more often than not that the marriage wasn't a mistake? Maybe. But it wasn't fair to trap Tyler with someone like her. She couldn't even take a sip of water without freaking out, for Pete's sake. He'd find someone perfect for him.

It really was for the...best.

Chapter Twenty

Meg was quiet the next day as Tyler drove them into Jackson Hole to go tree shopping. He wanted to kick himself for asking her to confirm her plans for Christmas because her mind immediately went to the end of their marriage.

He didn't want to get their marriage annulled. He wanted Meg. Period. Her face had lit up when she talked about decorating the ranch, and then he had to go and ruin it.

"Are you going to be warm enough?" he asked for nothing but to break the silence between them.

She gave him a disbelieving look. She currently wore her winter coat, thick gloves, a long scarf and a multicolored hat with a purple pom-pom on the top.

"I think I'm covered," she said drily as they pulled into a parking lot full of Christmas trees. She looked at them eagerly. "You know, I've never had a real tree."

"No?" he asked.

She shook her head. "Stephen was allergic to them. He had an asthma attack around one before I was born, so we always had artificial."

"Well then, you get the honor of picking out our tree," Tyler said, not even noticing that he said *our* until he saw Meg go slightly rigid.

He inwardly sighed, wondering how he was ever going

to break through the barrier Meg had placed between them. He needed to make her see that they could be really good together. He'd tried to give her space since they arrived, but maybe that had been a mistake. To use Jake's words, Tyler should have been wooing his wife since the moment he got her on the plane to Wyoming.

She got out of the ranch's pickup truck, and he followed. Her expression brightened as she walked between the rows of trees, breathing in the piney scent that surrounded them. She finally paused in front of a large blue spruce.

"This is the one," she said, her fingers running lightly over the branches.

"Great choice," said one of the workers who'd been hovering nearby. "We'll get this prepared and can take it out to your car for you."

Tyler paid for the tree and pointed out his truck to the worker. Grabbing Meg's hand, he dragged her over to a food truck that was serving hot chocolate and cinnamon doughnuts.

"It's a tradition," he said before ordering the doughnuts and drinks. "Whenever my family went out to get our tree, we'd always get hot chocolate after."

They walked over to a nearby picnic table. Tyler set their meal down on the table. He brushed snow off the seat for Meg before doing the same for himself.

"After you." He waved his hand at the bench, only sitting down after Meg did.

Meg tried not to let Tyler's little consideration go to her heart, but she felt flustered despite herself. Who knew wiping snow off a seat could be such a romantic gesture?

This isn't real, Meg kept trying to remind herself. Their marriage was going to be annulled any day now. In fact, she was surprised Tyler hadn't brought it up already. Neither of them seemed to be in a hurry to discuss the dissolution of their marriage though.

When they were finished eating, Tyler excused himself to use the bathroom before they headed back to the ranch. Meg placed her elbows on the table, taking in the atmosphere. Soft Christmas music played over the tree lot's speakers. Gentle snow began to fall and Meg watched it come down with her head in her gloved palm.

"I can't believe he married her," a woman whispered behind her.

"Wasn't Tyler dating someone famous a few months ago?" a man asked. "She was really hot."

"Yeah, that model, Jasmine Reed. I wonder why he married *her*?"

"She must have blackmailed him," the man said. They both laughed, the sound growing distant as they walked away.

Meg felt as though the snow had frozen her to her spot. Poison overtook the sweetness of the day. Anxiety began to build inside her, wiping away any earlier serenity she felt. Pressure formed around her diaphragm, and it started to hurt as she pushed air toward it. The stress of the whole situation—something she'd been able to compartmentalize so well—began to crack and seep through to the surface.

She couldn't breathe.

She. Couldn't. Breathe.

"Meg, what's wrong?" Tyler was beside her before she knew it.

"Can we go?" she asked. She tried to put on a brave face, but she wasn't sure if Tyler was buying it. "Please. I think the hot chocolate didn't agree with me."

"Sure," he said. The look in his eyes told her he didn't

believe her, but he didn't say anything as he helped her out of her seat. She let go of his hand after she was on her feet.

Meg hurried to the car, relieved to see the tree was already situated and ready to go. Tyler got in the truck after she did. She could feel his eyes on her, but she didn't look at him as he put the car in motion and they set off for the ranch.

Anxiety overwhelmed her. She wanted to scream. Her lungs refused to take in air naturally so she kept manually forcing breath in. She opened her mouth to ask Tyler to drop her off at the nearest hospital so someone could fix the mess inside her brain.

Everything seemed to overwhelm her at once. The Beaumonts, her new role at the campground, her marriage to Tyler, people's reactions to everything she did.

She felt jittery. Out of control.

. She needed help. And she didn't know where to turn to. So Meg did nothing but watch the scenery go by, taking in shallow breaths with every mile that passed.

Tyler got up from the couch in his studio and stretched. He didn't know how long he'd been in there, but it was dark outside. He was worried about Meg, which had made it difficult to get much done, but she'd stonewalled his attempts to find out what had happened while he'd left her alone at the tree lot and on the way home.

One minute she was happy and relaxed. The next it looked like someone had shot a dog in front of her. When they'd gotten back to the ranch, he'd helped her set up the Christmas tree, but she and Margie insisted on decorating it by themselves, telling him it needed a woman's touch. He retreated to his studio, feeling as though something had slipped through his fingers that he didn't even know he was holding.

It led to a very frustrating afternoon, but somehow the day had gotten away from him anyway. His stomach growled and he looked at his watch, shocked to see that it was well past 1:00 a.m. At some point, someone had brought in a plate of food for him, but it had gone cold by now. He picked it up and carried it back to the kitchen. The sound of the TV blaring somewhere in the house distracted him. He placed the plate in the sink before he followed the noise. He came to a halt when he entered the living room.

Meg and Margie had decorated the tree in white sparkling lights. Multiple ornaments in silver and white complimented the silver garland they'd found somewhere in storage. A tote rested on the floor next to the couch. Tyler could see there were a few more decorations inside that he assumed Meg had been too tired to put out. His heart thumped when he saw her on the couch, a blanket over her as she slept. He walked over to the TV to turn it off, with the intention of carrying her to bed.

"Don't," she said, startling him before he could do anything.

He swung around to look at her. "I thought you were asleep."

His forehead wrinkled as he peered at her closer. Meg looked completely frazzled. Her face was pale, her eyes wide and unfocused. She didn't seem to be breathing correctly. Peeking out from the blanket, Tyler noticed a tablet clutched in Meg's hand. He squinted to see that she had some kind of gossip site pulled up, a picture of him kissing his ex-girlfriend on full display.

"What are you doing?" he asked cautiously.

"Do you know people think I blackmailed you into marrying me?" she choked. "I can see why, when you dated models like her."

"Meg…" He took a careful step toward her, slowly taking the tablet away from her and shutting it off. "Jasmine and I dated for a few months last year. It was over before it started."

"People don't think I'm good enough for you. That I can only land someone like Tyler Evans if I have some kind of blackmail on you. I'm never good enough."

Her shallow breathing became more rapid. Tyler had never seen Meg like this, not even after she found out that they married. She looked like she wasn't even there.

"Screw what other people think, Meg." He crouched down next to her and grabbed her hand. "No one else is in this relationship. Just you and me."

She laughed bitterly. "We don't have a relationship though, do we?"

Before he could respond—deny what she was saying—the TV blared an annoying Christmas jingle.

"Meg, let me turn down the TV at least," he pleaded.

She immediately shook her head. "No! It blocks out the noise in my head."

"What noise?" Tyler asked gently.

"Everything," Meg rasped. "Every negative thing in my life. Lucas. The Beaumonts. Your fans. My parents' divorce. My father. All of it. It keeps building and building in my head until I can't hear anything else. The TV blocks it out."

Tyler nodded, though he didn't understand.

"What can I do to help?" he asked.

Meg's grip on his hand tightened. "I always feel like I'm standing on the edge of a cliff. One more step and I'll never make it back. I'll just be gone."

Tyler pulled her palm to his chest, resting it against his

steady heartbeat. "I won't let you fall. Do you hear me? I've got you, Meg."

A tear slid down her cheek. He ached to hold her. Give her reassurances that he wasn't sure he could deliver on. He didn't know what he was dealing with here.

"Meg…" he said carefully. "How long has this been going on?"

"Forever," she muttered. "I don't know. I've been dealing with anxiety for years, but it seems like since Lucas and I broke up, everything keeps piling on until I feel like I'm going to lose my mind."

With his free hand, he cupped her cheek. "Meg, I know you might not want to hear this, but there's no shame in seeing a therapist. They can help you get things sorted out in your head. I've been seeing one for years."

Meg looked at him with big eyes. "You have?"

"Yeah. It wasn't an easy transition going from being a no one to the level of fame I achieved at such a young age. A lot comes with that—the pressure to remain on top of your game, the expectation to always deliver. It can weigh someone down."

Meg's gaze continued to bore into him. "Do you think it'd really help?"

"I do," he responded firmly. "And if you don't think so, we'll look into to some other options. We'll figure it out. Together."

A tear streaked down her face, which he tenderly wiped away. "Will you help me find someone to talk to?"

"Yeah, I can do that," he assured her.

He would give her the world if she asked for it.

Chapter Twenty-One

Meg's leg bounced nervously as she sat in Tyler's home office, waiting for the psychiatrist to join her virtual appointment. Thanks to Tyler using his connections, he was able to set her up with someone the day after she revealed how much she was struggling. She'd never thought much about therapy in the past—mostly due to her bad experience when she was younger. She wasn't sure if this would even work, but she was desperate to give it a shot. She hadn't been exaggerating when she'd told Tyler she felt as though she were standing on the edge of a cliff these days. She wondered sometimes what would happen if she did jump, but a bigger part of her didn't want to know.

A woman popped up on the screen. She had gray hair held up in a high ponytail and wore a sweater with cats all over it. Written across her chest were the words *We Wish You a Meowy Christmas.*

"Meg, hello. It's so nice to meet you. My name is Dr. Wilder, but you can call me Farrah."

"Nice to meet you," Meg mumbled to be polite.

"So let me explain my process a little bit before we begin. I want you to feel free to share whatever you want. There's no pressure here. If you're not ready to explore something right now, that's fine. While we're talking, I'm going to take some notes, if that's all right with you?"

"That's fine," she said.

Farrah nodded. "Great. Why don't we start with you telling me what brings you to me today."

Meg frowned. "I… I've been struggling lately. With anxiety and panic attacks."

The doctor gave her a kind smile. "And when did this begin?"

Meg picked at the corner of Tyler's desk. "I can't remember, to be honest. I feel like I've been dealing with anxiety since I was a kid…"

With Farrah's encouragement, Meg told her everything that had been weighing on her. About her father not letting her be a part of the family business, to getting engaged to Lucas, only to find out he was gay years later. She talked about dealing with Clarice and how Meg had been treated by the town after she and Lucas broke up. She spoke about her parents' divorce. She talked about how sometimes when she drank water or stood in a steamy shower, she felt like she was about to drown. She talked about her feelings of inadequacy.

And Tyler. Tyler was brought up time and again throughout the whole conversation.

"Meg, let me ask you something," Farrah said after she typed something on her computer. "It seems like no matter what you've done or how much you've accomplished, you never feel like you're good enough. From what you're telling me about your relationship with your father, you learned at an early age that you didn't measure up to his expectations. When you look at yourself in the mirror, what do you see?"

Meg's breathing became shallower.

"Meg?" the doctor asked, her tone soft. "What do you see?"

"A mess," she whispered.

"What's a mess from your viewpoint?"

"Can you not see me? My hair looks like limp straw. I have deep wrinkles on my face, and I'm…fat."

"Is that a bad thing?"

"Have you not seen society's standards of what is considered beautiful?"

"But again, is it a bad thing to not fit society's mold of what you're supposed to be?"

"Considering how much I don't seem to fit anywhere, yeah, I think so."

Farrah gave Meg a steady, assuring look. "Tell me what you're looking to get out of therapy."

She blinked back tears that started to form in her eyes. "I want to stop holding my breath and obsessing over my breathing. It's starting to make me nauseous the more I do it, and my stomach seems to hurt all the time. I want to feel like I'm not about to lose my mind. I want to be able to drink something even when my anxiety is high without feeling like I'm drowning. I want to understand what I'm dealing with here."

Farrah leaned back in her chair. "In a nutshell, I'd diagnose you with a generalized anxiety disorder with OCD tendencies. The good news is there are things we can work on here. What I'm going to recommend is that we put you on a low-dose anti-anxiety medication to see if that helps with your feelings of being out of control and with some of your panic attacks. . I'd also like to have you speak with my colleague who specializes in exposure therapy."

"Exposure therapy?"

"Yes, it's a form of treatment to help you conquer some of these fears. You mentioned breathing is a huge trigger for you. You can start off by doing small daily sessions of meditation, for example. There are some great apps online that can also help with this."

"I can't do meditation," Meg instantly objected. "The whole thing is about breathing, breathing, breathing. Last time I tried to do it, I almost had a panic attack. It makes me think too much about breathing, and then I can't do it naturally."

"That's part of exposure therapy. Do it for short sessions initially, and then slowly start to increase your time. Once you feel you're improving, we can focus on the issue with your water intake. It won't be easy, Meg. Healing never is, but I have every confidence we can get you there. But you have to be willing to try. Are you willing?"

Meg wasn't sure about much these days, but she did know one thing. She didn't want to live her life like this anymore.

"Yes, I want to try."

A week later, Meg reached out to stroke Pepper's nose. The beautiful gray mare nuzzled Meg's pocket, looking for a hidden sugar cube. She laughed, pulling out a couple to give to her.

"You're a scoundrel, do you know that?" she murmured against the velvety nose.

As she finished helping Hans feed the horses, a sense of calmness settled over her. Aside from doing virtual therapy appointments twice a week, Farrah had put Meg on the anti-anxiety medication. She was already starting to notice a difference—not so much from the medication—Farrah said it wouldn't work that fast, but by having a professional to talk to. It felt like someone had finally thrown her a life-buoy before she could sink under again.

Though she knew she had a long way to go in terms of

her therapy, she finally felt like there was hope when she'd felt so helpless before.

And she had Tyler to thank for it.

She half expected him to treat her like a freak or like she needed be handled with kid gloves, but he treated her the same way he always did. Half sarcasm, half teasing. She was thankful for it.

But that resulted into an even bigger problem.

Meg had stupidly, unimaginably fallen in love with her husband.

She didn't know when she fell for him. Maybe it was all those years ago when they'd kissed on graduation night. Maybe she fell the night she'd married him, her subconscious telling her she needed him like she'd never needed anyone before.

All she knew was that in their time at the ranch, he had shown her a side to him that had always been there, but she'd been too stubborn to see. He was kind and caring and compassionate.

Sometimes she wondered if he had feelings for her too. There were hints, but maybe she was reading too much into them. He always found some reason to touch her, for example. She didn't remember him being overly affectionate when they were kids. The only time he touched her back then was if he tackled her in a neighborhood game of football. Her mind flashed to the night her anxiety became too much.

I won't let you fall. Do you hear me? I've got you, Meg.

Her heart melted all over again when she thought about how much he'd done for her since then. How tightly he'd held her hand that night, grounding her. He showed her in so many different ways that he cared.

But…was she reading too much into it?

After finishing up in the barn, Meg headed to the house. As she walked inside, she could hear Margie upstairs vacuuming. She wondered what Hans and Margie thought of Tyler's marriage, with him sleeping in a separate bedroom from his wife.

Meg entered the kitchen and came to a stop. Tyler was there, leaning against the counter, a mug of coffee in his hands. His eyes were closed, exhaustion written all over his face. He'd been up too late working on his songs again.

"Hi," she said lightly.

His eyes snapped open and he looked at her. His face relaxed at whatever he saw in her expression. "Hi yourself. You're looking good. Happy."

Meg laughed self-consciously as she continued over to him to get some coffee for herself. "I'm a mess, but thank you. I probably smell like horse."

He grinned at her, causing her heart to speed up. He was truly, ridiculously handsome. "Helping Hans again?"

"Yeah. I never thought I'd enjoy being around horses. They always scared me when I was little."

"I didn't know that," he said.

Meg snorted. "There's a whole vault of weaknesses I hid from you when we were kids. I would never have revealed one of my fears to my greatest nemesis. That would have been giving you too much ammunition."

She hip checked him lightly to let him know she didn't mean anything by it.

He was quiet for a moment before he said, "You know what I was thinking?"

"Hmm," she said as she poured herself a cup of coffee.

"We're supposed to head back to Holiday Bay next week."

"Yeah." She had talked to Wendy earlier in the week. Her

boss had been more than gracious to accept Meg's imme-
diate resignation. Her replacement was doing a great job,
and thanks to Meg's elopement, it wasn't like she could return to work without people stopping by all the time to ask
her about it. She had also talked to her brother about starting at the campground the first of the year instead of in a
couple of weeks as they'd originally planned. Their hope
was that the paparazzi would be gone by then so Meg could
focus on her training.

"I think we should go on a honeymoon," Tyler said.

Meg nearly tipped her coffee over but caught the mug
in time before it could spill. Placing it on the counter, she
looked at him in shock.

"What?" she squeaked.

"You and me. Go on a honeymoon. I can take you anywhere you want to go. Costa Rica, Bali. Somewhere warm
and tropical."

Meg grimaced. "No one needs to see this body in a
swimsuit."

Tyler put his cup roughly on the counter next to hers.

"I hate when you talk about yourself that way," he said
roughly. "Your body is perfect."

"Pull the other leg," Meg muttered. Great, this was going
to turn into another conversation she'd need to analyze
with Farrah.

"I'm serious," he said, looking her dead in the eye so
she could tell he wasn't joking. "It's perfect. Womanly."

Meg's face flushed. She cleared her throat. "So, um,
why a honeymoon?"

Tyler's jaw tightened before he looked away. "Do you
really want to go back to the Bay right now? My mom said
there's still a lot of press there. And Jake texted me earlier that he and Julie are staying away until Christmas. It's

a hell of a mess for Julie to be away from the shop during the holidays, but Dylan volunteered to help your mom while she's gone."

Meg's stomach twisted sickeningly at the thought of returning to a media firestorm. "I'm not really eager for that. But why do we need to go anywhere? I thought the purpose of coming here was to hide out."

Tyler stared at the floor. The frown lines around his mouth deepened. "You're right. We can stay here. Forget I said anything."

Meg swallowed as she tried to work up some nerve. If she was reading this situation wrong, she didn't know if she would be able to recover from her impending humiliation. The temptation to push air toward her diaphragm was overwhelming. Instead, she moved so that she was standing in front of Tyler. She put her arms on either side of him, caging him in. She took it as a good sign when he only looked at her in surprise instead of disgust or horror.

"Why do you want to go on a honeymoon?" she asked again.

She held her breath as he slowly reached for her ponytail, running his fingers through the strands of hair.

"Because I want to spend time with you," he confessed quietly. "Just you and me. I want to go somewhere where the only thing to focus on is each other."

"Why, Tyler?" *Please. Please don't let me be reading this wrong.* "It's not like we're really married, right?"

His fingertips traveled forward as they traced her ear before drifting down to cup the back of her neck. Sparks ignited every place he touched on her skin.

"Would it be so bad if we were?" he whispered, and a part of her wanted to do a victory dance.

"What are you talking about?" she responded, needing

to be sure before she made another mistake when it came to men. "We're totally unsuitable for each other, aren't we? You date models and movie stars. You can have anyone."

"But what if I only want you?" he murmured.

Meg didn't have time to rejoice. Tyler bent down and captured her lips in his. The sparks he'd created by his mere touch turned into an inferno as his tongue dipped into the recesses of her mouth, taunting and teasing hers.

She groaned as she leaned against him fully, wrapping her arms around his waist, needing to be closer to him. The feel of him against her was all-consuming. She wanted to lose herself in the kiss but wondered if she would lose herself even more if he stopped.

Tyler finally broke away, leaning his forehead against hers, his chest heaving as though it cost him everything to stop kissing her.

"You and I are more than suited, Meg," he said. "Give me a chance to prove to you that we are."

Meg met his eyes. She asked unsurely, "You want to?"

"More than you could know."

Her heart soared at the confession. "What did you have in mind?"

"You and I go on a date. Tonight. We don't even need to leave the ranch. We can have dinner here and treat it as a real date."

Her eyes narrowed at the determination she heard in his voice. "Are you daring me, Tyler Evans?"

He shook his head. "No. No dares. I want you to want this."

It was *all* she wanted.

"Okay," she responded, a smile brightening her face. "It's a date."

Chapter Twenty-Two

Meg nervously ran her hands over the velvet red dress she wore. She'd thrown it in her bag when she'd hurriedly packed for Wyoming, never expecting to need it, but she was glad that she had brought it. It emphasized her curves in a way that made her slightly self-conscious, but if Tyler was to be believed, he liked her body. This dress showed it off in spades, and maybe it was her pride talking, but she wanted to look good for her husband.

It was a bit surreal to her that she was about to go on a date with Tyler Evans. Tyler. Her childhood enemy. The international superstar. But as she'd told him a few weeks ago, she never saw that side of him. Not unless she decided to be masochistic and search for his name online. She'd done that the night of her severe anxiety attack, finding more than enough pictures of him and his perfect ex-girlfriend, Jasmine. She didn't need to do that again.

Leaving her honey-brown hair soft and down around her shoulders, she headed downstairs. Tyler waited for her in the living room. The Christmas tree lights were the only lights on in the room, casting it in a soft glow. A fire crackled in the fireplace. The curtains framing the large floor-to-ceiling windows on either side of the fireplace were left open, allowing a beautiful view of the snow falling outside, highlighted by the full moon as it tried to push past the clouds covering it. Soft music filled the air.

Meg would have appreciated the ambience of the room if Tyler wasn't looking so beautifully distracting. Like Meg, he'd cleaned up for their date, wearing a black button-down shirt and slacks. His hair was tastefully styled, his ever-present five-o'clock shadow neatly trimmed. He took her breath away. He turned from where he stood next to the fireplace and watched her move down the stairs.

"Wow," he whispered before walking toward her. "Meg, you look beautiful."

"So do you," she murmured before she could stop herself.

Tyler's smile caused adorable crinkles to form around his eyes. He offered her his arm. "Shall we?" he said.

She let him lead her to the kitchen. Margie had outdone herself once again, cooking up an Italian dinner of fettucine with homemade red sauce, fresh bread and herbed zucchini.

"Dinner is ready," she said. She poured them both a glass of wine. Giving Meg a wink, she left the room.

They began to eat their meal. Meg was quiet, her brain scrambling for something to say. She was nervous. She kept trying to remind herself that this was Tyler. The same guy she'd grown up with. But in so many ways he had become a stranger to her.

"You're quiet," he said, echoing her thoughts.

"I was just thinking I don't really know you anymore. Not like I used to anyway."

He lifted a brow. "Meg, I'm pretty sure you know me better than a lot of people do, but what do you have on your mind?"

She looked around the kitchen. "Have you had a lot of dates at your ranch?"

Tyler's lips twitched. Meg felt stupid. She had no reason to feel jealous or possessive of Tyler, but there it was anyway.

"No," he assured her. "I haven't brought any women here besides you. I only come here to work." He paused before asking, "What about you?"

Meg smirked. "No, I've never brought any dates here."

"Ha, ha," Tyler replied. He grabbed his glass and swirled the wine, watching it like it was the most important thing in the world. "You and Lucas. You were together for years. Do you still regret how things ended up?"

Meg's stomach sunk slightly, but remarkably, it wasn't as painful a reminder as it had been a few weeks ago.

When she continued to sit there in silence, Tyler quickly said, "Forget it. I shouldn't have said anything."

"No, it's okay. You have a right to ask." Meg smiled, though it didn't quite reach her eyes. "If you'd asked me last month how I felt about Lucas Beaumont I might have either broken down in tears or hit you."

Tyler's gaze was gentle on hers. "And now?"

Meg shrugged. "Lucas and I were never meant to be together. Even if we'd ended up married, eventually we would have divorced. Lucas did the right thing by not allowing it to go that far."

"You say that with a lot of confidence."

Meg lifted her chin. "Because it's the truth. Lucas and I should have ended our relationship years ago."

She didn't say anything else about it. Even though she was coming to realize that she trusted Tyler more than she'd ever trusted anyone else in her life, she wouldn't out Lucas. That was his business to tell people, not hers.

They finished their meal and cleaned up the kitchen so that Margie wouldn't have to. After they finished, they returned to the living room. Tyler grabbed his phone out of his pocket and pulled up a playlist. The jazz music playing over the room's speakers changed to soft rock.

He sat down, pulling Meg next to him. She curled into his side, breathing in his fresh cedar scent. Placing her head against his chest, they watched the snow fall outside in compatible silence. She honestly couldn't remember the last time she'd had a better date. Whenever she'd gone out with Lucas, she'd felt more like a performing monkey, always on display, always aware of people watching her.

"What's your dad think of you taking over the campground?" Tyler asked as a piece of wood cracked loudly in the fireplace.

Meg nuzzled in closer. "He didn't really have much of a choice. Stephen wasn't messing around when he said that Dad had to choose between either letting me take over the Holiday Bay location or lose both of us."

Tyler tightened his arm around her. "But how has he been with you?"

Meg frowned. "We haven't really talked much about it. That's nothing new. He never thought I had much use anyway. But as Farrah told me, I can't let negative people dictate my life. I need to set boundaries for myself. I've accepted that my dad has his limitations when it comes to me. I've lived with his rejection my whole life. And quite frankly, I don't need his acceptance anymore to feel validation. I've made it this far without it, and I can continue without it."

Tyler's lips brushed against her forehead. "Good for you."

"Yeah," Meg said. It still made her sad. But there was nothing she could do about the situation. All she could do was focus on herself and her own therapy.

A slow song from the 1980s came on, surrounding them with its sweet melody.

"I love this song," Meg murmured.

Tyler stood up, disrupting their cuddle. When she looked at him in confusion, he offered his hand to her.

"Will you dance with me?"

Warmth blossomed inside Meg. She nodded before placing her hand in his. He clasped his hands around her waist and pulled her full against him. They began to sway to the music.

"You are so beautiful," Tyler murmured against her hair.

She wasn't sure if she'd ever believe him, but God, did she want to.

His hands ran down the curve of her waist, settling on her round hips. She tried not to feel self-conscious.

It didn't work.

"You don't mean that," Meg whispered.

"Don't I? Then why do I dream about running my hands over every curve of your body? Of feeling your legs wrapped around me as I enter you over and over again? Why is it that I wake up every morning, hard, with your name on my lips?"

Meg's eyes jerked to his, taking in the seriousness on his face.

He took advantage of her head tilt and crushed his mouth against hers. He pulled back to whisper, "You seriously have no idea how attractive you are, do you?"

"I…" Meg started to say but couldn't speak even if she wanted to. Not when Tyler broke the seal between her lips with his tongue.

She opened her mouth to him, tasting the wine he'd drunk earlier. He bent down, putting his hands on her bottom and lifting her so that her feet hovered above the

246 THE FAKE DATING DARE

ground. She wrapped her legs around his waist, and they continued to kiss as though they'd discovered a new addiction that neither were willing to give up.

"Meg," Tyler groaned against her mouth. "I want you so much."

Meg knew that. She could feel his erection against her.

"You should know..." she said breathlessly. "I don't sleep with someone on the first date."

Tyler gave her a teasing look. "Not even your husband?"

"Good point," she murmured before tightening her legs even more firmly around him.

He took it as the signal she was giving him.

He carried her up the stairs and into his bedroom, closing the door softly behind them.

Chapter Twenty-Three

Meg woke the next day, her body humming, her skin feeling electrified. She turned carefully on the mattress and found Tyler lying next to her, his body curved toward her, his head on his pillow. He was fast asleep. Meg wanted to reach out and trace the outline of his cheek, but she also didn't want to disturb him. They'd been up late.

As quiet as possible, she pushed back the sheets and tiptoed out of bed. Meg crept toward the door and entered the hallway, closing the door lightly behind her so she wouldn't wake him. She hoped she didn't run into Margie or Hans, considering she wasn't wearing a stitch of clothing, but Meg also couldn't find it in herself to care.

Walking into her room, she went into the bathroom and grabbed her anxiety medication, taking a pill before any evil thoughts regarding the night before could enter her head and sour the memory. She glanced at herself in the mirror and couldn't help but stare.

Meg looked different. If she was being a complete sap, she would say she was even glowing.

Holy hell, did Tyler know how to make a woman's body respond. Granted, she only had Lucas to compare to, and sex with him had always been...fine. With hindsight, she knew now why things had never really clicked in that de-

THE FAKE DATING DARE

partment, but she had nothing to compare it to, so she'd just assumed that was what sex was all about. To be honest, she'd never understood what the big fuss was about.

Now she did.

She giggled as she remembered how Tyler had played her body like an instrument, making it thrum. He was truly an artist at his craft. He'd known just how to touch her... taste her, make her scream his name. She'd forgotten all about the few extra pounds around her waist, because Tyler hadn't cared. He only wanted her—couldn't seem to hide his insatiable need for her.

After brushing her teeth, Meg stepped into the shower to get ready for the day. Her fingers brushed against her neck. It felt raw from where Tyler's beard had scratched her as he'd sucked and teased her skin with his mouth.

She turned her face up to the water. She could almost feel Tyler's hands on her, his talented fingers drifting down her body, touching her right where she needed him the most, parting her, seeking...

Meg turned the water temperature down as she tried to cool her overheated skin to a simmer. She was half-tempted to turn off the shower and crawl back into bed with Tyler, ready for a repeat performance.

The glass door of the shower opened, startling her. She looked over her shoulder to see her very naked husband step inside. He leaned toward her, that stupid, teasing smirk on his face, the one she wanted to smack off his head when they were kids but now wanted to feel against her mouth.

"Good morning," he said, kissing her, his breath scented with minty toothpaste. "I wondered where you ran off to."

"I didn't run," she said distractedly, her fingers skating down the firm muscles of his abs.

He stepped closer to the shower, feeling the cold water and his expression turned cocky.

"Needed a cold shower on this freezing Wyoming morning, did we?"

Meg glowered at him, refusing to give into his overblown ego. "Cold water helps me wake up."

"Sure, Meg, whatever you say."

"And what do you think you're doing?" she asked. "Don't you have your own shower?"

"I do," Tyler replied, "but there I couldn't help you wake up even more."

Before she could ask what he meant, he sank to his knees, and Meg lost her ability to think.

Much later, they lay in her bed under the sheets, their hands entwined together.

"How is this going to work?" Meg asked.

Tyler brushed his lips against her forehead, in a gesture that was becoming familiar and comforting. "What do you mean?" he asked.

"How is this going to work between us? Holiday Boys are going on tour next year, aren't you? Not to mention, you have a very in-demand career as a songwriter. You need to be in California and New York to keep that career going, don't you?"

"Meg, I can be anywhere I need to be. There is such a thing as email, virtual meetings—"

"You know what I mean," Meg said, her grip tightening on his. "I need to be in Holiday Bay. My brother is giving me the chance to run Archer Campground the way I've dreamt since I was a kid. I don't want to give that up."

Her anxiety was trying to make a comeback, the temptation to push air toward her diaphragm overwhelming, but she didn't allow it. Instead, she focused on her breathing exercises that Tyler had showed her and Farrah and her colleague encouraged her to continue.

As though sensing she was having a moment, Tyler pulled her even tighter to him. "I would never ask you to give that up. I know it's something you've talked about wanting to do for years." He turned them so they were facing each other in bed, his hand landing on her waist, his thigh settling between hers in a deliciously distracting way. "Let's just take it one day at a time, okay? Why don't we try another date? I'll take you out to Jackson Hole tonight for dinner. We can walk around town and take in the Christmas lights after. What do you say?"

An unsettled feeling swamped her, but she nodded. "Okay."

"Hmm, that didn't sound too confident," Tyler murmured. He moved his thigh upward, rubbing where she was most sensitive.

Meg sucked in a breath. As her body arched in response, she forgot what she was worried about in the first place.

Meg and Tyler left the restaurant later that evening, holding hands as they made their way toward the center of town. It had been a quiet, uneventful evening. People had either not noticed or cared that Tyler was sitting within their vicinity. It had helped that he wore black-rimmed glasses that made him look like Clark Kent.

"For eye strain," he'd explained with a sheepish smile. "Part of the joys of getting older."

They'd been able to talk about everything and nothing all at once. It was one of the best evenings Meg could remember having in a long time.

So, of course, she should have expected it to go to hell.

Flashes lit the dark evening as paparazzi swarmed them.

"Meg, how does it feel to land America's most eligible bachelor?" one yelled.

"Tyler, did she coerce you into getting married?" another shouted.

"Any plans to sue the crew for allowing you to get married when it was clear you were both drunk?" a kinder one asked.

"Tyler, why her? She's not exactly your type. You dated Jasmine Reed, right? Her body is smoking."

Meg flinched. Tyler took a step toward the smarmy man as though he was going to punch him. He might have if Meg hadn't been holding his hand in a death grip.

"No comment," he yelled, pulling Meg closer to him. Instead of heading into town like they'd planned, he steered her toward his truck. Pulling her coat's hood over her head, he did his best to shield her from the cameras. Helping her into the car, he got behind the steering wheel and roared the truck to life.

They were five miles down the road before Tyler pulled over. He grabbed her chin and turned her head until she had no choice but to look at him. "Don't listen to them, Meg. They'll say whatever garbage they can to get a reaction out of someone."

"I know," she said, her tone careful as she tried to focus on her measured breaths, counting each one as best as she could. The panicky anxiety was doing its best to pull her under like a riptide. She needed to do anything she could to tread water and not sink.

"Meg…" he said cautiously.

"Tyler, please. Can we just get back to the ranch?"

He stared at her for a few more seconds before sighing. He let her go to put the truck back in gear. They drove to the ranch in uncomfortable silence, so different from their carefree mood driving into town.

Once he parked in front of the house, Meg hurried inside. She walked into the living room, staring blankly at the empty fireplace. Tyler came up behind her, wrapping his arms around her and pulling her back against his chest. He put his head on her shoulder and took a deep breath as though the scent of her perfume calmed him.

"Talk to me," he pleaded. "Tell me what's going on inside that head of yours."

She shrugged him off and took a few steps away from him. "I'm thinking that we were kidding ourselves."

His eyes went wide. "What are you talking about?"

"Tyler…" Her voice broke, and she cleared her throat before she continued. "Have you even seen what people are saying about us? Have you looked at the headlines since we eloped?"

"I don't care what anyone says about us," he told her. "It's just you and me. That's all I care about."

"But I do care," she whispered, looking away from him. "What we experienced tonight is just a taste of the hateful rhetoric that people are saying when it comes to me and you. Saying that I tricked you into marriage. Comparing me to all the women you dated before me. I… I can't do it. Not right now."

She finally met his gaze and wished she hadn't. His face was pale, his eyes bleak and pain-filled.

"No," he finally said. "I'm not listening to this. Meg, you're a fighter. You've been a fighter since we were kids. Where's that Meg? That Meg doesn't give up."

She lifted her head. "That Meg grew up and became a realist a long time ago. Our marriage was a mistake."

"It wasn't a mistake!" Tyler shouted, surprising them both. He took a deep breath to control himself before he said, "If it was a mistake, then why have I thought about you almost nonstop since I kissed you on my graduation night? How come I've missed you so much that I couldn't settle down with anyone else, even after hearing you had gotten yourself engaged to some idiot who would never understand you like I do?"

"Tyler..." Meg wanted to cry. "I need you to hear me right now. I...*can't* do this right now. My mental health is hanging on by a thread, and to live like this with people thinking I somehow tricked you into marrying me because, God forbid, you're actually attracted to me—"

"I *am* attracted to you." Tyler took several quick steps toward her. He took her hands and held them to his chest. "Didn't last night and this morning prove that to you? I want you. Only you. And not just for the sex—which is incredible—I want *you*. All of you. I want to argue with you in the morning and go to bed with you in the evening. I want to grow old with you, having you test me the entire time. Don't throw this away. Don't throw *us* away. I need you, Meg."

Meg opened her mouth to say yes. To give into what he was saying. But she couldn't. Because she couldn't breathe. She was underwater again, unable to surface. She was standing on the edge of that cliff, her foot dangling in the air. The sound of the paparazzi's taunts echoed in her ears. She closed her eyes and could see the cruel words of the online trolls, telling her she wasn't good enough to be with Tyler Evans.

She was never good enough.

Unable to look at him anymore, she pulled her hands away.

Turning on her heel, she headed toward the stairs, tears blinding her.

"I'm sorry. I can't."

Chapter Twenty-Four

Tyler lay on the couch in his studio, staring listlessly at the ceiling.

Meg had left him a month ago, and ever since then, he'd spent his time either blissfully drunk or pacing around the room. It wasn't like he could do anything else.

He couldn't write anymore. His will to do any song-writing left the same moment Meg had. He couldn't sleep. Food tasted like garbage. He spent his time drinking his way through his well-stocked collection of alcohol, depleting a supply that had taken years to build.

Margie tried feeding him his favorite meals, her disapproval in his behavior clear by the tsking noise she always made whenever she wandered into his studio. He debated locking the door to keep her and the rest of the world out, but he lacked the motivation to leave his couch.

So he was pretty pissed off when the door to the studio banged open with a loud crash and the lights overhead flew on, causing him to groan miserably.

"Jesus," Paul muttered to James as they stared at him.

Tyler blinked twice to make sure he wasn't imagining his bandmates. "What are you doing here?" he croaked.

"Margie called us," James explained.

"I'll fire her." Tyler reached for a new bottle sitting on the table next to his couch.

James strolled over to him and yanked it from his hand. "No, you won't. You'd be completely lost without Margie, and the ranch would go to hell if you got rid of her."

He glared at his friends, reaching for the bottle in James's hand as he pulled it further out of his reach.

"What are you two doing here? Besides making me miserable," Tyler grumbled, blinking around for another bottle to open since James was stubbornly refusing to give back his bourbon.

"We're here to ensure you don't drink yourself into a coma," James said.

"That's rich coming from you," he replied, not so kindly reminding his friend that he'd spent the past couple of months drinking his liver away after his husband left him.

"Low blow, dude," Paul muttered. "I forgot what a miserable drunk he was."

"You're right," James said, ignoring Paul. "I haven't handled the end of my marriage well. But let's keep things in perspective here. Mason left me because he cheated on me with someone he thought would help advance his floundering acting career. Meg left because she was scared. You still have a chance with her, if you'd pull your head out of your ass."

Tyler went to stand up before collapsing against the couch again. Pins and needles shot through his body. Jesus, how long had he been lying there?

"She doesn't want me," he finally said after feeling returned to his body. He buried his face in his hands, half-afraid he was about to bawl in front of his friends.

Paul scoffed. "Pretty sure anyone with eyes at Jake's reception could see you two want each other plenty. That's not the problem."

"I begged her to stay, and she still left." Tyler's voice sounded muffled behind his hands.

"Yeah," Paul said. "Because the paparazzi are vile pieces of filth who would scare anyone who's not used to it. You told us Meg hasn't had an easy time over the past couple of years, thanks to her trash fiancé—"

"Come on, you don't know what Lucas's reasoning was," James interrupted. When both his friends gave him disbelieving looks, he glared at the floor. "Ignore me."

"The point is," Paul said, "our lifestyle isn't easy. You have to give Meg some time to adjust."

"And if I give her time and she still doesn't want me?"

"You respect that," James said.

Paul rolled his eyes. "You two are helpless. Go win your wife over. Show her how much better life will be with you than without you. And if that doesn't work, then yes, you respect her decision. But don't give up before you've had the chance to fight for her. Have you even *tried* to fight for her? Or did you just give up? You've been obsessively talking about this woman since you were a teenager—"

"I have not," Tyler protested.

"Then when she got engaged, what did you do?" Paul glared at him. "Nothing! That's what you did. You never went back for her. You never tried to stop her from making the biggest mistake of her life. But now you finally— *finally*—get your chance with her, and you let her go at the tiniest obstacle. What the hell, man? I don't get you."

Tyler rubbed his face, wincing at the sharp bristles of his unkempt beard. "I don't know what to do."

Paul threw his hands into the air. "Have you not heard a single thing I said? Hasn't your entire relationship been fighting with each other since day freaking one? Go fight for your woman."

Tyler looked from one friend to the other. "I'm going to need a lot of coffee."

Margie walked into the room with a pot in one hand and a large mug in the other. "Already ready for you."

"And then shower time, my friend," Paul said. "Because, dude, you stink."

Tyler flipped him off before gratefully taking the mug from Margie's hand.

Meg glanced around the office of the campground with tired eyes. Her brother had run out to get them lunch. They'd spent most of the morning going over the books, but when their stomachs started to growl, Stephen had offered to go get some of Franki's Pasties. Once he got back, he was going to train her on a new reservation system Kimmy had implemented.

Meg stared at the numbers in front of her. She tried to focus her exhausted brain on how much staff she would need to hire over the summer season, but she was struggling. She hadn't slept well lately.

She missed Tyler. She ached for him in so many ways. She'd been tempted more times than she could count to pick up the phone and tell him she'd made a huge mistake. But whenever she started to, she thought about the comments the paparazzi made and she resisted.

She needed to focus on her mental health.

Besides, it wasn't like he called her either.

Not that she was bitter about that or anything.

Meg couldn't help but wonder for the millionth time if leaving Tyler had been the biggest mistake of her life. According to Farrah, she *had* made a mistake, though her doctor said it in much nicer tones. They discussed the situation at length in that morning's session, as they'd done for the past few weeks. She told Meg that her fear of rejection was understandable. She'd lived with rejection for years, thanks to the copious amount of daddy issues she had, which she then transferred into Lucas issues. But as Farrah gently put it, running away was no way to live either.

Apparently, Meg loved punishing herself. For feeling like she wasn't ever good enough. For not meeting people's expectations, like her dad's. First, she'd punished herself by pressuring her diaphragm until she was sick. Now her punishment was pushing Tyler away. The one amazing thing she had in her life.

Searching online for what trolls had to say about her was another thing she was working on with Farrah. To not seek out the negative.

Don't ignore it, Farrah told her just that morning. *But don't let it be all-consuming and take over your life. Because when that happens, what kind of life do you have in the first place?*

It was a hard lesson to accept, but Meg was trying.

The door to the office opened, and she looked up cautiously. When Meg returned to town, she'd hid in her apartment the first couple of weeks, worried that reporters would ambush her. Thankfully, they lost interest when some mega-singer started dating a football player and they decided to stalk them instead. That didn't mean she wasn't still paranoid that they'd remember her.

Meg froze when she saw it was her dad.

"Hi," she said nervously.

He glanced around the office, a frown on his face. "Where's your brother?"

She tried to hide her hurt. As usual, Meg wasn't the one

he wanted. "He went to go get us some food. He's training me so that I can take over the campground starting next year."

A muscle ticked in her father's jaw. "He told me."

Meg wanted him to say something about how proud he was of her. How maybe he'd made a mistake by not including her. Instead, he simply stood there.

Meg tried not to let the disappointment crush her. "Is there something else you needed?"

Her father shoved his hands into his pockets. "I was going to wait until your brother got back, but... I've decided to step down from the campground."

She could only stare at her father. "What?"

"I've come to realize lately that it's time for me to step aside."

"This campground is your whole life," Meg said before her stomach sank. "Is this because of me? Because Stephen's putting me in charge here?"

When her father continued to just stand there, Meg blurted, "Do you even love me?"

It was something she'd wondered about often.

Her dad's expression turned to bafflement. "Of course I do. Why would you ask that?"

"Because you've never taken an interest in me, never encouraged me to do anything, and the moment you found out I'm going to have a say here, you, what? Up and retire?"

Her dad's shoulders slumped. He walked over to her as though he'd aged three decades in a second. "I am leaving because of you," he said. Before she could even react to how hurt she was, he added, "I've come to realize lately how much I've wronged you, Meg."

That made her pause. "I... I don't understand."

Her father looked at her sadly. "For so long, all I could

think about was doing my father proud. We didn't have an easy relationship. He never acted like I was good enough. When he died, I promised myself that I'd finally make him proud of me. Make my mark in the world and leave behind a legacy. But instead of proving anything, I treated you like my father treated me. Not to mention, my son almost abandoned the business I created for him, and I ruined my marriage. So yes, I've decided to step down. I'm stepping out of your way, Meg. Like I should have done years ago. But don't think I don't love you. I couldn't be prouder to have such a beautiful, intelligent daughter."

Meg didn't know what to say or do. A part of her wanted to run over and hug him, but she couldn't erase years of hurt with a few words.

She asked instead, "What will you do?"

Her dad lifted a shoulder. "Probably go stay with your uncle in Arizona for a while. Or maybe I'll buy a cottage not too far down the road from here and become a hermit. I don't know yet. But I'll figure it out. In a way, this is actually freeing for all of us, isn't it?"

He didn't wait for her answer before turning and walking out of the building.

Freeing?

But what a price they'd paid.

Chapter Twenty-Five

Meg wandered down Main Street the next day and entered Julie's store.

Julie had returned from her honeymoon just the day before. Meg had stopped herself from running over to Julie's as soon as she got home. She didn't want to burden her friend with her Tyler issues right after she had a long flight, especially if Jake was around. Jake and Tyler were best friends, and Meg really didn't want him overhearing the mess that she'd made of their relationship.

"Meg, hello!"

She glanced toward the counter where her mom stood, ringing up a customer's purchase. The customer grabbed her bag and turned to leave, pausing when she saw Meg there.

"Aren't you Tyler Evans's wife?" the girl asked.

Meg didn't know what she was, to be honest. The thought of ending her marriage to Tyler tore her apart, but *was* she his wife, especially with how she'd left things between them? She decided the best course of action was to smile politely but say nothing.

The girl took her reaction as an affirmative. She squealed before saying, "Tyler was always my favorite when I was younger. I'm so glad he settled down with someone like you."

"Like me?" Meg said, her stomach aching painfully.

"Someone normal. Not some stuck-up celebrity. You two are such a cute couple, and you give hope to the rest of us." She winked at Meg before leaving.

"Will we be seeing that husband of yours anytime soon?" Meg's mom asked from behind the counter.

She sighed. "I don't know."

"*Liebchen*," Her mom walked over to her. "You can lie to many people, but you can't lie to me. You look miserable. What happened in Wyoming?"

"Nothing," Meg said. "Tyler and I are just adjusting— that's all. He's working at the ranch still, but I needed to get home so I could get things rolling with Stephen at the campground."

Her mom looked at her sadly, clearly not believing her. "You know you can talk to me."

"I know." Meg forced a false smile on her lips. "Everything's fine. I actually just stopped by to see how Julie's vacation was. Is she in yet?"

Her mom looked like she was about to say something else before she replied, "No, she was in earlier, but she was pretty jetlagged so I told her to go home. She should be back tomorrow if you need her."

Meg nodded. "I didn't need to speak with her about anything major. I'll call her later."

"Meg—"

"Gotta go, Mom."

She quickly exited the building. She wasn't ready to tell her mom the whole truth. Not when everything felt so raw. How could she explain the whole fake—turned not so fake—relationship to her? Where did she even begin?

"Meg?"

She came to an abrupt stop as a man stepped in front of

her. For one second, she worried that it was paparazzi until she recognized the person. "Lucas?"

"Hey," he said, his expression wary.

"Hi." She shifted on her feet, unsure what to say. Once upon a time, she thought she knew Lucas better than anyone on the planet. Now she realized she didn't know him at all. She was on unfamiliar ground, but what else was new.

He waved at the bench that was in front of the store next to Julie's. "You have a second?"

"Sure," she said after a moment's hesitation.

They sat down, an awkward silence settling between them.

"Look, I—" Lucas started to say.

"You—" Meg said at the same time. They smiled at each other. She nodded at him. "Go ahead."

Lucas tugged at the hem of his jacket. "I just wanted to say again how sorry I am for everything. For not being truthful with you, and for leaving you to deal with the fallout of our breakup by yourself. I know how this town can be, and I should have stuck around and helped you through it. But for what it's worth, I'm really happy that things worked out for you like they were supposed to."

She stared at him, her comprehension not working as it should. "What are you talking about?"

Lucas frowned at her. "You and Tyler. Your marriage."

As Meg continued to look at him, her vision went blurry as tears filled her eyes.

His face became alarmed. "Meg, what is it?"

She swiped at the tears that started down her cheeks, but they wouldn't stop.

Lucas wrapped an arm around her, bringing her to him. "For what it's worth, I still think of you as one of my closest friends. I know I don't deserve you, but if you need to talk, I'll listen."

She buried her face against his shirt and sobbed harder.

"Shh," Lucas said. "You'll be okay. It's fine."

"It's not," Meg muttered into his shirt.

He kissed the top of her head, and the gesture was so reminiscent of what Tyler would do, it only made her cry harder.

"Meg, stop," Lucas said more firmly. "You're going to make yourself sick. Come on, talk to me."

"I left Tyler," she muttered against his coat.

"What?"

Sniffing, she pulled away and wiped at her face again. "I left him."

"Why would you do that?"

"It wasn't real. None of it," Meg confessed before spilling the whole story to her ex-fiancé. "So it was fake," she said when she finally finished. "All of it. It seems to be what I specialize in—relationships that aren't real."

Lucas winced before his face turned stern. "I'm calling bull."

Meg frowned at him. "What?"

"I'm calling BS. I saw the video of your wedding. Anyone with eyes can see that you two are crazy about each other. Tyler's a songwriter, not an actor. You can tell that he worships you."

As Meg stared at Lucas, something dawned on her. When she was with him, she changed so much about herself to fit into his world. No matter what she did, it had never been good enough. Tyler's world was so much vaster, yet he's only ever encouraged her to be herself. He'd accepted her, flaws and all. Everything that she'd tried to repress for the Beaumonts were the things that Tyler tried to bring out in her. She was enough for him.

Hope blossomed in her heart. It hit her that maybe her instincts weren't so off. Perhaps Tyler cared for her more than she realized. Maybe he even loved her like she loved him. And if he didn't, if he wasn't there yet, maybe he was close.

Meg leaned toward Lucas and kissed his cheek. "Thanks, Lucas."

"You're welcome." She went to stand up, but he put his hand on her arm to stop her. "Are we friends again? I know I don't have a right to ask, but I miss you, Meg. I really miss you."

Meg swallowed hard before answering. "I'm still super pissed at you. But…we can take it one day at a time, okay? Maybe we can go for some pasties next week or something."

His handsome face lit up. "I'd really like that. Did…did you ever tell Tyler the truth about me?"

She shook her head. "That's not my secret to tell."

Lucas smiled sadly at her. "You can tell him, you know. It might help clear the air between you."

With a pat on his shoulder, Meg said, "Thanks, Lucas. Now, if you'll excuse me. I need to go."

He raised his eyebrows, mirth lighting his eyes. "Going anywhere in particular?"

She smiled for the first time in weeks. "Yes. I'm going to go get my husband."

Meg ran up the stairs to her apartment, her mind on what she needed to do to get back to Wyoming. She worried that she wouldn't be able to get a flight. Tomorrow was New Year's Eve and she was sure the airlines were already booked, but she had to try. Worst-case scenario, she'd drive to Wyoming. It would take a lot of caffeine and driving her junky car in snowy conditions, but a woman had to do what she had to do.

She came to a stop when she saw a man sitting next to her door. Her hand flew to her pocket to grab her pepper spray when she realized who it was.

"Tyler?" she whispered.

His head jerked up, and she sucked in a breath. Tyler was the most handsome man she'd ever met, but she had to admit he didn't look great.

"What the hell have you been up to this past month?" she asked, taking in his red-rimmed eyes and slimmer face.

"Drinking," he responded. He stood up from the floor, bones cracking as he stretched.

"Why?" she asked, not sure how to interpret his mood.

"Why have I been drinking?" he repeated. "How about because my wife left me?"

Meg didn't say anything as she unlocked the door and walked into her apartment. Tyler followed quickly behind, almost as though he was afraid she'd shut him out.

"I saw your face the morning we discovered we were married," Meg said as she turned to face him. "You looked horrified."

"I wasn't horrified. I was shocked when I saw the certificate," Tyler responded. "That's not how I wanted to marry you. I wanted to give you a storybook wedding."

She stilled. "You wanted to marry me? Even then?"

"Meg." He walked over to her. "I've wanted to be with you since my graduation night, but it wasn't the right time for us. I tried my best to move on, but I never stopped thinking about you. I still don't know if you're hung up on Beaumont—"

"I'm not hung up on him. I care for him deeply. But I'm not in love with him anymore."

"What if he decides he wants you back?" Tyler whispered.

"He won't," Meg assured him. "And even if he did—

which he doesn't—I wouldn't want him back regardless. Because like I said, I don't love him. Not like that anyway."

"But—"

"Lucas is gay."

Tyler's head cocked as he comprehended what she said. "Oh. That's why…"

"Yeah," Meg replied. "He couldn't keep lying to me or himself, so he ended things. I didn't know that until he came to see me a few weeks ago and he confessed everything. It didn't help with my anxiety, but I appreciated the truth regardless. It explained why things never really clicked with us."

"Clicked, how?" Tyler asked, though a slight smile appeared on his lips that she wanted to kiss off.

Meg folded her arms over her chest. "Now I know the difference between sex and making love to a god. Happy?"

He laughed softly before he carefully pulled her to him. "So…"

"So," she responded.

Tyler closed his eyes and put his forehead wearily against hers. "Meg, I know my life is unconventional, and I know you have a lot of things on your plate that you're working through. If you really can't deal with my baggage, I'll let you go. But if you'll give me the chance, I think I can prove to you that no matter what, it's you and me, taking on the world together. Just like we always have. I love you, Meg. I've been in love with you for years. Give me a chance to prove that our lives together will be worth it. Please."

Meg covered his mouth with hers, pouring all her love into that kiss. It was unguarded, leaving them both breathing hard when they finally parted.

"You don't have to prove anything to me, Tyler," she whispered. "I love you too."

His shoulders relaxed at her words. He reached into his pocket.

Meg's breath caught as he pulled out an engagement-ring box.

"I know it's not a twist tie, but I tried to find something similar." He kneeled in front of her and opened the box. A large circular diamond attached to a band of twisted white gold sat nestled inside. "Will you marry me, Meg?"

Her eyes misted. "We're already married."

"We'll get married the right way."

Meg covered his lips with her hand. "I don't need to get married again. I just need you."

His voice was muffled against her palm as he asked, "Does that mean you'll…"

"I mean, it's no twist tie," she joked, pulling her hand away.

"Meg…" Tyler growled, though the earlier shadows on his face were gone.

"Yes, I'll stay your wife."

Tyler took the ring out of the box and gently placed it on her ring finger. He kissed it before standing, then wrapped her in a hug, lifting her off her feet so that their mouths could meet again.

"I love you," Tyler murmured against her lips.

"Love you," Meg replied, wrapping her legs around his waist. "I love you so much."

New Year's Day dawned bright and early. But that was always the way things were in Wyoming. Tyler's rescue rooster, Hercules, never failed to holler as soon as he sensed the sun was near, his loud call cackling across the property.

Meg groaned as she snuggled closer into her husband.

He kissed her head as his fingers traced sensuous circles

on her naked hip. Tyler had offered to take her anywhere in the world for their honeymoon, but Meg had wanted to return to the ranch, enjoying the solitude it offered.

"Good morning," Tyler said. He moved so that he could nuzzle her neck, his morning beard scratching her skin in a way that he knew drove her crazy.

"Good morning," she replied, her hand dragging through his hair.

He bent and kissed one of her exposed breasts before leaning back on his pillow, his hold never leaving her. "So, I was thinking…"

"Was it that you should finish what you were just getting started?" Meg asked, craving her husband like she always did. She wondered if that would ever go away—the constant hunger for him.

"Oh, don't you worry about that, Mrs. Evans. We have the whole week to never leave this bed."

"We'll have to leave sometime to eat," she reminded him.

"No need. I'll just have Margie leave it at our door."

Meg laughed. Tyler was always good at finding a way around things. That was usually how he got away with so much when they were kids, while she ended up grounded.

"I was thinking," he continued, "that once we get back to Holiday Bay, we should go house hunting."

Meg was in the middle of shifting closer to him when she paused. "Really?"

"Yeah, I mean, we can stay in your apartment if you want—"

"Who said I'm inviting you to move in with me?" she scoffed.

He pinched her side lightly. "Sorry, babe. You accepted the ring. You're stuck with me."

Meg sighed dramatically. "I guess there are worse things in life."

"Hardy har," Tyler replied. "Back on subject."

"Sorry." She leaned over to kiss his pec, sucking on the skin until he shuddered.

"Stop distracting me, woman."

"Sorry," she repeated, not meaning it in the least.

"Anyway, I thought we could go house hunting when we get back. I know you'll be busy taking over the campground, and Holiday Boys are preparing for that tour next year—though I guess that's going to depend on what's happening with Zan and Mary now—but we could go look at houses in the evenings or whenever works best for you. Jake told me a house not too far from him and Julie just went on the market."

Meg paused in her attempts to seduce her husband. "Yeah?"

"Yeah." Tyler rolled her on her back so that he could settle between her legs. "What do you say, wife?" he asked as his seeking fingers drifted between her thighs. "Do you want to get a place with me where we can grow old together and live happily ever after?"

She gasped when he touched her where her body ached for him the most.

"Come on, Meg," he teased into her ear, his voice thick with need for her. "I dare you."

And of course, Meg said yes.

Tyler's dares were irresistible.

* * * * *

Get up to 4 Free Books!

**We'll send you 2 free books from each series you try
PLUS a free Mystery Gift.**

Both the **Harlequin® Special Edition** and **Harlequin® Heartwarming™** series feature compelling novels filled with stories of love and strength where the bonds of friendship, family and community unite.

YES! Please send me 2 FREE novels from the Harlequin Special Edition or Harlequin Heartwarming series and my FREE Gift (gift is worth about $10 retail). After receiving them, if I don't wish to receive any more books, I can return the shipping statement marked "cancel." If I don't cancel, I will receive 6 brand-new Harlequin Special Edition books every month and be billed just $6.39 each in the U.S. or $7.19 each in Canada, or 4 brand-new Harlequin Heartwarming Larger-Print books every month and be billed just $7.19 each in the U.S. or $7.99 each in Canada, a savings of 20% off the cover price. It's quite a bargain! Shipping and handling is just 50¢ per book in the U.S. and $1.25 per book in Canada.* I understand that accepting the 2 free books and gift places me under no obligation to buy anything. I can always return a shipment and cancel at any time by calling the number below. The free books and gift are mine to keep no matter what I decide.

Choose one: ☐ **Harlequin
Special Edition**
(235/335 BPA G36Y)

☐ **Harlequin
Heartwarming
Larger-Print**
(161/361 BPA G36Y)

☐ **Or Try Both!**
(235/335 & 161/361 BPA G36Z)

Name (please print)

Address   Apt. #

City   State/Province   Zip/Postal Code

Email: Please check this box ☐ if you would like to receive newsletters and promotional emails from Harlequin Enterprises ULC and its affiliates. You can unsubscribe anytime.

Mail to the **Harlequin Reader Service:**
IN U.S.A.: P.O. Box 1341, Buffalo, NY 14240-8531
IN CANADA: P.O. Box 603, Fort Erie, Ontario L2A 5X3

Want to explore our other series or interested in ebooks? Visit **www.ReaderService.com** or call 1-800-873-8635.

*Terms and prices subject to change without notice. Prices do not include sales taxes, which will be charged (if applicable) based on your state or country of residence. Canadian residents will be charged applicable taxes. Offer not valid in Quebec. This offer is limited to one order per household. Books received may not be as shown. Not valid for current subscribers to the Harlequin Special Edition or Harlequin Heartwarming series. All orders subject to approval. Credit or debit balances in a customer's account(s) may be offset by any other outstanding balance owed by or to the customer. Please allow 4 to 6 weeks for delivery. Offer available while quantities last.

Your Privacy—Your information is being collected by Harlequin Enterprises ULC, operating as Harlequin Reader Service. For a complete summary of the information we collect, how we use this information and to whom it is disclosed, please visit our privacy notice located at https://corporate.harlequin.com/privacy-notice. Notice to California Residents – Under California law, you have specific rights to control and access your data. For more information on these rights and how to exercise them, visit https://corporate.harlequin.com/california-privacy. For additional information for residents of other U.S. states that provide their residents with certain rights with respect to personal data, visit https://corporate.harlequin.com/other-state-residents-privacy-rights/.

HSEHW25